Some fragrance stirred his brain, like a wisp of fog reaching out to him,

cooling and calming, to bathe away the feverish night horrors. Daniel raised an eyelid and realized it was Nancy's hair, the clean-washed scent of her snuggled against his chest. She must have slept beside him to keep him from thrashing in the night, for her arms enfolded him still. She was awake, watching Trueblood build up the fire, waiting for him to wake up, as well.

He felt a strange reluctance to do so, to break the spell of her caring. Sleep was all he wanted so long as she was beside him, yet he greedily kept himself awake so as not to lose one moment of her nearness. He shut his eyes gently and concentrated on feeling the pressure of her hands, the feathering of her hair against his cheek….

Dear Reader,

Talented author Laurel Ames crosses the ocean to a young America for the setting of her newest book, *Nancy Whiskey*, the story of a daring British nurse and an American spy who discover love and adventure on a journey across the wilds of Pennsylvania, despite incredible hardships. Don't miss this delightful tale from an author whom *Affaire de Coeur* describes as "...excitingly original...."

In *Quicksilver's Catch* by *USA Today* bestselling author Mary McBride, a runaway heiress throws herself at the mercy of a tough-as-nails bounty hunter who is determined to make as much money as he can from their association, if she doesn't drive him to drink first. And Margaret Moore's *The Rogue's Return* is the next installment in her MOST UNSUITABLE... series set in Victorian England. In this story, from one of our most popular authors, a devil-may-care nobleman finds redemption in the arms of a respectable woman.

Our fourth title for the month is *Outlaw Wife* by Ana Seymour, a bittersweet Western about the daughter of a notorious outlaw who loses her heart to the rancher who saves her from jail.

Whatever your tastes in reading, we hope you enjoy all of our books, available wherever Harlequin Historicals are sold.

Sincerely,

Tracy Farrell
Senior Editor

Please address questions and book requests to:
Harlequin Reader Service
U.S.: 3010 Walden Ave., P.O. Box 1325, Buffalo, NY 14269
Canadian: P.O. Box 609, Fort Erie, Ont. L2A 5X3

Laurel
Ames

Nancy
Whiskey

Harlequin Books

TORONTO • NEW YORK • LONDON
AMSTERDAM • PARIS • SYDNEY • HAMBURG
STOCKHOLM • ATHENS • TOKYO • MILAN
MADRID • WARSAW • BUDAPEST • AUCKLAND

ISBN 0-373-28978-2

NANCY WHISKEY

Copyright © 1997 by Barbara J. Miller

Books by Laurel Ames

Harlequin Historicals

Teller of Tales #163
Castaway #197
Homeplace #226
Playing To Win #280
Besieged #289
Tempted #338
Nancy Whiskey #378

LAUREL AMES

Although Laurel Ames likes to write stories set in the early nineteenth century, she writes from personal experience. She and her husband live on a farm, complete with five horses, a log springhouse, carriage house and a smokehouse made of bricks kilned on the farm. Of her characters, Laurel says, "With the exception of the horses, my characters, both male and female, good and evil, all are me and no one else."

For reenactors everywhere,
who keep history and its lessons alive.

Prologue

Summer, 1793

"Nancy! You are back, finally, though I almost wish you had not come home," Aunt Jane said, wringing her hands. "We might then have been able to put him off, even hide you from him."

"Who? Reverend Bently?" Nancy asked distractedly as she set down her basket of medicines in the hall and undid the ties of her cloak.

"What? No, of course not. *Your father has come.*"

"But how is that possible?" Nancy asked, her blue eyes alight with excitement. "I thought he was dead."

"He is sitting in the library drinking a whiskey and demanding to see you."

"I must go to him, then." She tucked her long blond hair behind her ears and smoothed her work gown.

"But he means to take you away with him."

"To the army?" She looked expectantly at her diminutive aunt.

"Nancy, he means to carry you to America," Jane said tearfully.

Nancy rushed into the library, torn between excitement and fear. The man she encountered was not what she had expected. He was old, for one thing, his face red-veined from a life of hard drinking, and at the moment, also suffused with anger.

"Ah, Nancy dearie," he said, changing his scowl to a smile as he rose to embrace her. "Ye've the look o' yer dear mother. I would have known ye anywhere."

She looked to her uncle for confirmation that this was her father, and he nodded sadly.

"I do not understand," she said, stepping back. "You are going to America? But there is no war in America."

"No, but there's land, Nancy, and opportunity fer an adventuresome man. I've left the army and I've a bit o' money by me now. 'Tis my one chance fer a life. Ye mean ta say ye will nay come with me?" the Irishman pleaded in his lilting voice.

Nancy hesitated, all eyes upon her. Oddly, she thought not of her papa, whom she had never known, nor of her aunt and uncle who had raised her, but of the somber Reverend Bently, whose imminent marriage proposal she could now escape. She pictured him fuming at her departure. "Yes...I will come."

"Wot did I tell ye? She's a plucky lass, fer all ye've cosseted her like one o' yer own. I'm not unmindful o' that, and I thank ye heartily, but she's my dotter when all's said and done, and I've a right ta have her by me in me last years."

As this impassioned speech put an end to all argument, even from Nancy's now-tearful aunt, Nancy fled upstairs to pack her trunks and fend off the questions of her younger cousins about her coming journey.

Chapter One

It was night, and Daniel Tallent was hanging over the heaving side of the *Little Sarah,* feeling rather unwell, when he noticed Nancy Riley come through the companionway door onto the rain-slicked deck. Though she was bundled in a cloak, he knew her, for she was the only woman on board the merchant ship. He was about to call a warning to her when she made her way to the opposite rail by the expedient of having the ship lurch and throw her there. He shouted to her, but the wind beat the words back at him. So he waited for the ship to wallow again before crabbing his way across the deck to grab her.

"Let go of me!" Nancy shouted, slapping him. "What do you think you are doing?"

"Why in God's name have you come out in a squall like this?" Daniel demanded, keeping his tenacious hold on her arm. "You could be swept overboard."

"I wanted some air," she shouted over the roar of the wind.

"Air? Air? Are you mad? This isn't Hyde Park, where you can take the air when you please. Now come below."

She opened her mouth to answer him, but was silenced by a cold wave that drenched them both and left her gasping.

"The next time she rolls to port make a run for the hatch," he ordered.

Nancy nodded, but the ship pitched them so violently toward the rail it knocked the wind out of them, and it was all they could do to hang on. A huge man loomed over Nancy then, put an arm around her waist and whisked her across the deck to the companionway, thrusting open the door and holding it against the wind as Nancy made her way down the stairs. Trueblood turned to look for Daniel, but his brother collided with him and they more or less tumbled down the companionway in a heap, carrying Nancy to the bottom.

"In here," Trueblood ordered. Giving her no time to protest, he pushed Nancy into a cabin and onto a cot. Daniel crawled back up the steps to secure the door, then followed them in and fumbled with a light.

"Well, Daniel," Trueblood drawled in a deep voice, "are you going to light the lamp or not?"

"I am trying, but are you sure it is a good idea? If we break it, we could roast alive in here."

"I am too wet to catch fire," Nancy offered, ringing water out of her cloak, then looking apologetically at the puddle it made on the floor as the lamp cast a glow over her slim form. She noticed Daniel staring blatantly at the thin gown that clung to her, so she pulled the dripping cloak shut again.

Then she stared with fascination at Trueblood's large form crouched in the small cabin. They had been sitting at table together for weeks, but he looked immense in the small sleeping cabin the Tallent brothers shared. Also, his straight black hair, loosed from its normal neat queue, gave him a more sinister appearance. Trueblood must have sensed he was looming, for he sat on the other cot, and Daniel slid down onto the floor.

Daniel looked more appealing than usual for being completely drenched. His shorter hair clung to his brow in wet strands or curled against his neck, and those thick eyelashes set off the blue of his eyes in a heart-stopping way. He was not a small man by any means, but he was dwarfed by Trueblood. Anyone else might have thought Trueblood the older, but Nancy knew the lines of care around Daniel's eyes placed him at least a decade beyond her three and twenty years.

"Well, Daniel, did you get rid of what was disagreeing with you?" Trueblood asked with his usual condescension.

"No, for you are still here."

"I meant the salt pork."

"No, it is still lying in my stomach like a cold lump."

"I was being very foolish. You saved my life," Nancy said to both of them.

"I have had a lot of practice," Trueblood said, stealing the compliment as he glanced at his brother.

"I would have managed it, eventually," Daniel said defensively. "And whatever made you go up on deck in weather like this?"

"The same thing that drove you there," she replied. "My cabin seems to be full of vile odors, I suppose from the bilgewater being stirred up. It was almost too much for me. And Papa's cabin is worse, for he has been sick since the storm began."

"Are you sure it is not the rum rather than the weather?" Daniel asked as he stripped off his soaked coat in the confined space, revealing his hard-muscled frame through the wet cloth of his shirt.

"No..." Nancy faltered, trying to regain control of herself. "That's rather forward of you."

"Forgive my brother, child," Trueblood said gently. "He was raised in the colonies and never had any pretensions to manners. Whereas I went to Oxford."

"They are not colonies anymore, but a country, as you well know," Daniel countered.

"Of course, Daniel. At least they pretend to be a country. But with all the petty bickering and backbiting, not a country I hold out a great deal of hope for."

"Why did you fight beside me then?"

"Hush, Daniel. I suppose we are not very alike for brothers, even half brothers."

"Ah, but you argue like brothers, so appearances make no matter. And it was not the rum, for Papa can, in the ordinary way, drink like a fish with no ill effects." Nancy shivered a little, then clamped her pale lips shut so that the men would not notice. "I must go back to my cabin now or I will catch my death of cold."

"Let me escort you across the hall," Trueblood said as he stood up to offer his arm, almost stepping on Daniel, who scrambled up and inhaled to let them past him. Her cabin was no more than two steps away, but Nancy took his arm anyway, with a nod gracious enough to match Trueblood's manners. Somehow his playacting stole away the horror of almost having been washed overboard. But she had not been swept into the cold sea, so she decided not to dwell on it.

"Well, Daniel, not a very propitious encounter," Trueblood said on his return to the cabin, his dark eyes twinkling in amusement.

"And Miss Nancy Riley is as much of an enigma as ever," Daniel answered as he stripped off the rest of his wet clothes and managed to dry himself, though the tossing ship thrust him from bed to wall a dozen times. He was wondering how Nancy could possibly manage and wished he could help her.

"Does everything have to be a mystery to you?"

"She is far too genteel a lady to be traveling with a rough soldier. I cannot believe he is her father. Have you seen the way she blushes sometimes at meals at the language he uses?" Daniel pulled on dry breeches and a shirt, leaving his damp hair tousled.

"That has nothing to say to anything. Any woman might blush who must dine with half-a-dozen men, and Sergeant Riley is not the only one who forgets to guard his tongue. That trader Dupree sneaks in some very rude comments in his French, and they make her blush more than anything her father says.''

"I must know her story or I cannot be easy in my mind about her.''

"What are you thinking?" Trueblood whispered with a twinkle in his eyes. "That she is a spy, like you?"

"Of course not. I only want to make sure she travels with the man willingly, and I do not know how to broach the subject." Daniel stripped the wet blanket off the bed and stretched out upon the narrow mattress.

"Simply ask her. Riley does not hang about her neck. When he is not off playing cards with that Canadian, Dupree, he is so drunk he pays no attention to her."

"Yes, Riley is as thick as thieves with Dupree."

"Who else has he to talk to with you ignoring him and me looking down my nose at him?"

"And Dupree, taking ship with us at the last moment like that," Daniel whispered. "I think he may be on to me."

"Well, Daniel," Trueblood said in a quiet voice, "why did you stay in Washington's employ if you are to be forever looking over your shoulder?"

"You did not think performing secret services such a bad life those last years of the Revolution."

"It paid well, and someone had to keep you from getting shot or hanged."

"You did not care about the money any more than I did. I still don't care about it. We make plenty on trade alone."

"Why do you do it then, little brother?" Trueblood asked.

"What else do I have? You can go back to Champfreys. Your mother wants you home. She said so in her last letter."

"As I recall, she begged you to come home as well."

"Not until Father admits he was wrong, and he will never do that."

"The war has been over a long time. If Father was a

Loyalist then, he is not now. You do not have to keep playing the rebel all your life.''

"That is not why I bolted," Daniel almost shouted.

"Why then?"

"I cannot tell you."

"Secrets even from me, Daniel?"

"Do not ask, Trueblood," Daniel begged in anguish as he closed his eyes. "It was not true, what he accused me of. That is all I can say."

"I believe you, little brother. But it has been sixteen years, half your life, since you left. Most likely he has forgotten what he said to drive you away."

"Ah, but I have not."

"So you remain in service, Captain Tallent, un-uniformed, unappreciated and a prey to every suspicion that flits across your mind."

"What will become of Nancy if Riley gambles away all his money before we reach Philadelphia?" Daniel had put his arms behind his head and was now staring intently at the bulkhead, his blue eyes troubled.

"Daniel, you can take on the affairs of a whole country if you want, but you cannot save every orphan and stray dog in it."

"I know. She just seems so particularly defenseless."

"I have a suggestion."

"I know, mind my own business." He rolled onto his side and buried his head in the pillow.

"Why don't you just ask her about her circumstances?"

"At which point she will accuse me of being forward again. You would love that. You seem to take more than a passing interest in her yourself."

"Good manners should never be mistaken for self-interest. I really am not trying to cut you out with her."

"But you always seem to be there to leap into the breach when I have made a misstep."

"If we are speaking of the Loyalist lady, she was using you, Daniel."

"Her loyalty to the rebellion was never in question."

"Precisely. Her interest in you had only to do with flag and country."

"That's not the way I remember it," Daniel said as he drifted toward sleep. When his breathing became regular, Trueblood threw a blanket over him and got out a book to read in the uncertain light from the lamp.

Daniel was at the rail the next morning, feeling rather better since he had foregone breakfast. The rock and creak of the ship was restful, the rush of water against the *Sarah*'s side benign in contrast to the previous night. When Nancy came on deck she pointedly ignored him, and he looked away, remembering the slap. But one of his furtive glances in her direction caught her looking at him, and she smiled, so he made his way over to her.

"How is your father?" Daniel asked.

"Better, now that the weather is fair and the wind is causing no more than a gentle roll to the ship."

"I am not much of a sailor myself."

"I love it," she said, taking a deep breath and smiling. "I never thought I would set foot outside of Somerset."

"You don't seem as though—I mean, you seem so gently bred. I would almost take you for..."

"For a lady?" Nancy asked in amusement.

"I did not mean anything by it, but there is such a contrast between you and your father."

"Not unlike the disparity between you and Trueblood."

"I had that coming."

"If I am not prying, why 'Trueblood'?"

"His mother named him. He carries the blood of the great Oneida, Shenandoah, in his veins."

"Shenandoah." Nancy pronounced it wistfully. "What a musical name."

"A legendary Indian chief who brought corn to the starving troops at Valley Forge. Though Trueblood and I are only half brothers and 'not much alike,' we are very close.

Now, if I am not prying, why is there such a difference between you and your father?"

"I was raised by my aunt and uncle. I never saw my father until last month, when he came for me. It is strange. I have waited for him all my life, waited for him to come and take me away to wars in strange lands. I have taught myself everything I imagined a soldier's daughter should know. But now that it is really happening, I find I cannot quite believe it."

"And the strange land he is taking you to is America. What does he mean to do there?"

"He speaks of buying an inn."

"He may do well for himself then."

"If he does not drink all the profits."

"Where does he mean to settle?"

"Pittsburgh."

"I lead pack trains to Pittsburgh," Daniel said eagerly, his eyes alight. "Perhaps we can travel together. If you need temporary lodgings in Philadelphia, I am well known at Cook's Hotel there. Until you decide what you mean to do, it is as good a place to stay as any."

"I should be glad for your advice. I did not mean to sound so angry last night. I did not know how much danger I was in."

"It doesn't matter. I have been slapped before."

"Indeed? With good reason?"

"How am I to answer that?"

"Carefully. I am quite sure Trueblood would be able to turn this conversation to his advantage. I have scarcely ever seen so much social adroitness packed into one person, albeit a large one."

Daniel gaped at her and then smiled appreciatively. "You have his measure, then."

"I do not mean to offend you. Your brother has been most kind to me, besides helping to save my life. But I always find myself wondering what is going on behind those dark eyes."

"A great deal, I assure you."

"If I were a hostess, I would always invite Trueblood, for I would know I could depend on him to handle any social disaster that might arise, or at least, dispose of it skillfully."

"But you would not invite me," Daniel concluded, his eyebrows furrowed delectably.

"Oh, yes, I would, for one always needs a brooding, mysterious man about."

"To create the sort of social disasters Trueblood is adept at handling."

"You make an admirable pair. I am sure the English ladies adored you."

"We were invited everywhere, but then Trueblood has many friends in England. Do you entertain much in Somerset?"

"My aunt does. She could have turned me into a nanny for the children, but she raised me almost like a daughter."

"Rather terrible of your father to tear you away." Daniel tried to sound regretful.

"I assure you he came just in the nick of time," Nancy replied with an impish smile.

"What?" asked Daniel, who had been watching for the dimple that lurked at the left corner of her mouth.

"I lived in momentary dread of Reverend Bently making an offer for my hand. Both Aunt and Uncle seemed to think I would make an admirable wife for a man of the cloth, seeing as I have a bent for nursing."

"And like a dutiful and grateful niece, you would have accepted him."

"Oh, I don't know. If I could not have thought of a way out of it. But it does seem so often, when I am in the most desperate straits, that a solution will pop into my head from nowhere."

"Desperate straits?"

"He nearly proposed to me one Sunday, but I fainted."

"But how do you know then—"

"I didn't really faint, of course, but only pretended so I would not have to accept or refuse."

"That bad, is he?"

"I have no particular aversion to Oliver Bently. He is rather more than twice my age, but he is not ugly by any means. There is only this, that having regarded him as my spiritual leader, I could not imagine myself crawling into bed with him."

Daniel broke into laughter, and Nancy admired the way his blue eyes lit when the corners crinkled.

"It is nearly time for the midday meal, if I am counting the bells aright," she said of the muffled clanging. "Would you be kind enough to lead me in, sir?"

"I would be honored, Miss Riley." Daniel took her arm with great ceremony.

"What do you suppose is the correct protocol for a stairway that is little more than ladder? Shall I go first so as not to expose my ankles?"

"No, I must go first. In case you should fall, I will catch you."

"We will try it your way. I am sure when I query Trueblood he will say the opposite of whatever you have done."

"Undoubtedly, Miss Riley."

They were expecting to see land within the hour, and Nancy had been hugging the rail to get the first possible glimpse, her golden hair licked about by the wind. She was not used to being idle, so the whole trip had been in the nature of a tour for her, though the hardships of being confined with little privacy, frequently tossed about a small cabin and fed on boiled peas and salted meat would not have seemed a treat to many young women.

"Trueblood," Daniel shouted from the deck to his brother perched in the rigging, "do you see anything?"

Trueblood turned from his scrutiny of the horizon. "A ship," he called down through cupped hands, risking a fall from the ratlines, where he clung by his legs.

"What flag?" the captain called, handing a telescope to a seaman and sending him climbing the lines to the top of the mainmast.

"I cannot make it out," Trueblood shouted.

Even before the answer came the captain began giving orders, and sailors scurried aloft to let out more sail, while others began to load the deck guns. They had only two six-pounders and a bow chaser, besides the stern guns, none of them much use if they were being pursued by a warship.

"French, sir," the seaman called down.

"Damn!" the captain said, and he turned to Daniel. "I'll have to ask you to take Miss Riley below. We won't give up without a fight."

"No, I won't go," she protested, pulling away from Daniel's grasp and going back to the rail.

He came to stand beside her, watching the frigate overtake them with alarming speed and wondering what inducement he could offer to get Nancy below hatches. "We are very much in the way here. If we hinder these seamen in their work, we may face capture."

As the captain sent crewmen hurrying to load the carronades in the stern, Daniel pulled Nancy across the deck. The enemy ship loomed larger and a warning shot passed across the bow of the *Little Sarah* but the captain ignored it.

"Daniel, why are they firing on us?"

"This is a British ship."

"But we are in American waters."

"A moot point if they capture us. Now, stop struggling and come below where it is a little safer."

The second shot passed over the deck and caught a luckless sailor. Nancy gaped as blood spattered in all directions and his headless trunk fell to the deck. She could not even insist that she should stay to render aid. The man was obviously beyond help.

Daniel followed her down the companionway ladder. "Stay low, lower than the bed," he warned her as he thrust her into her cabin and pulled a crate against the outside of her door. Ignoring her shouting and pounding, he joined Trueblood on deck to help reload and aim one of the carronades, freeing the gun crew to climb aloft and help let out more sail. The privateer had their range already. Its next volley of shots could sink them. But the *Little Sarah* had turned tail and headed south. The back of the ship presented a smaller target, of course, but a more vulnerable one. And they were heading away from Delaware Bay. Both men knew that a heavily laden merchant had little chance of escaping a fast warship.

"Try for the rigging!" Trueblood shouted above the roar of fire from the other ship.

"That is all we can hope for, to hurt their steering. We cannot do any real damage."

Daniel held the gun steady and shouted now for Trueblood to touch the piece of smoldering hemp to the fuse.

The small shot carried away a few lines and put a hole in one sail. Meanwhile the privateer's bow chasers splintered the mounting of the *Sarah*'s rudder. The brothers looked at each other hopelessly as the ship started to drift.

A cannonball through the mizzenmast sent splinters into a half-dozen screaming men and brought the whole twisted load of sail and lines down on top of the Tallents.

"Ouch," Daniel yelped, as Trueblood freed him from the tangle. "Damn, a splinter in my leg."

Trueblood tied his handkerchief tightly above the wound on his brother's thigh and said, "Do not—"

Before he could finish the warning, Daniel had pulled the object out. His leg bled furiously then, but he scrambled to his feet.

The frigate had come up on their side and now laid a shot into the hull near the waterline. Only this convinced the captain to have the signal for surrender run up. They would have had to retrim and lay the ship over to get a patch on the hole or they would not have been able to pump fast enough to keep the vessel from sinking. There was no way for the battle to continue.

"You brothers and the Canadian are safe enough," the captain said to the Tallents, "but what is to become of Riley and his daughter I do not know."

"We shall think of something," Daniel said as he hopped toward the companionway door, his only thought now of rescuing Nancy. Trueblood helped him down the ladder.

Nancy was still pounding and pushing against her door. "Daniel, let me out! I had rather drown in the open sea than be shut up down here like a rat!"

They ignored her. "Give me that packet you are carrying, Daniel."

"Right. We shall have to weight it and toss it over."

"If you can take care of Miss Riley, I'll go over the side with it. The thing is sealed with wax, is it not?"

"Yes, but you cannot possibly stay concealed."

"Of course I can. We are not more than a few hours from port."

"No, I will do it."

"Daniel!" Nancy threatened when she heard them talking. "If you do not let me out this instant, I shall make you sorry."

They pulled the crate away and freed Nancy. Her father lay asleep on his bunk when they opened the door to check, but Dupree was not below decks.

"Daniel, you are bleeding," she said, her anger dissipated now that she saw he was hurt. She pulled a roll of lint out of her inner pocket and forced her hands to stop shaking. What was the point of panic now, when she had something to do? She knelt to run the bandage around his leg over his beeches. There would be time to clean the wound later. For now she must get the bleeding stopped.

"It is nothing," he said, wincing at the strength with which she tightened the dressing and tied it off. It occurred to Daniel that probably only Nancy carried an entire medical kit in the pocket tied around her waist under her skirts.

"Nancy, dear, can you speak French?" Trueblood asked.

"Yes, of course. I thought it might be useful." She finished her work and rose to support Daniel under one arm. Now that she did not feel so helpless, her confidence was flowing back. Besides, if they were really sinking, Trueblood and Daniel would not be standing here calmly arguing over a packet.

"No decision then, Daniel. If Nancy can speak French, you do not need me," Trueblood concluded, then went to fetch an oilskin packet from their cabin.

"It is my packet. It should be my swim," Daniel argued, trying to wrest the object away from his brother, who was already thrusting it inside his shirt. They all lurched as the ship shuddered and reeled.

Nancy turned a beseeching look on Daniel and he hugged her to him.

"No time. We are being boarded. Do not attempt to wrestle me for it, little brother. You will never win in your present condition. You take care of Nancy."

"Where is he going?" Nancy demanded as Trueblood slipped into the captain's cabin.

"Out the window and over the side," Daniel answered.

"But we are not even in sight of land."

"He will not try to swim for it. He will just cling to the ship until we are close to shore. With this damage they will make for Philadelphia immediately."

"What if he cannot fit out the window?"

"I had not thought of that. Trueblood will manage something." A crash and the sound of splintering glass came reassuringly from the cabin. "Nancy, listen to me. We do not know what will happen to you, since you are English. I want you to tell them you are my indentured servant. The worst that can befall your father is to be taken as a prisoner of war."

"What? But he has left the army."

"He still wears the uniform, and your papers say you are English, not Irish."

"And why would an indentured servant speak French?" she demanded, loosening herself from his grasp as many feet thumped on the deck and orders were issued above their heads in that foreign tongue.

"I am trying to protect you, and it is the best I can think of," said Daniel as he tried to keep his balance.

"It is a stupid plan, Daniel. I can think of something better than that. Now get out of my way. I may be needed up there to bind wounds or to translate." She pushed him away, causing him to hop and collide with the wall.

"If I had a ring," he called after her desperately, "I would say you are my wife."

She turned with a startled expression on her face.

"Well, you act the part of a shrewish wife to perfection."

Then she smiled at him, not desperate or frightened anymore, but with the impish grin that almost convinced him she was now enjoying herself. The last he saw of her was her shapely ankles, until he crawled up the ladder to find her negotiating the terms of their surrender with a rather handsome French captain.

With a sail patching her bow hole, and a cobbled-together rudder, the *Little Sarah* made port with the English crew below hatches and a prize crew from the *Embuscade* in charge. Nancy, Daniel and the wounded were allowed to remain on deck, since they seemed harmless enough, and Nancy, apparently, had asked the French privateer if they could. The captain of the pilot boat that guided them up the Delaware seemed to ignore her shouted recriminations against the French ship that followed them. Nancy was preparing a withering testimony against their captors, for she had, with Daniel's aid, been bandaging some ghastly wounds, and she now recalled the beheaded seaman.

"What is going on, Daniel?" she asked of the commotion at the docks. "Why would they be cheering a French pirate?"

"The American public is rather fickle, and the new French ambassador, Genet, has taken the city by storm, or so I hear."

"But this is disgusting."

"It would be politic not to say so."

She looked belligerently at him, but the worry in his eyes assured her compliance, for he did look so appealing when he was hard-pressed.

"Daniel," she whispered. "What about Trueblood? The French pirate knew he was on board, for he asked specifically where he was."

"What did you tell him?"

"That he was taken over the side by the cannon fire."

"Did he believe you?"

"I think so."

"I saw him swim to an American cutter an hour ago, while we were being guided up the channel."

"That's a relief."

"Now, if we can just get safe on shore."

The British crew, including their wounded, were ferried to the docks in a lighter and given their freedom. Daniel refused to go with them. On the quay the English captain had a one-sided discussion with the French privateer, pointing to Nancy, where she stood at the rail with Daniel. Two French seamen tried to part Daniel from her, and he resisted, until Nancy cast a stream of oaths at them that set them back on their heels. The French captain grinned and motioned his men away. He had himself rowed back to the prize and boarded it, and now took Nancy's hand in such an obvious offer of protection that it took both seamen to restrain Daniel from attacking him.

Nancy did not cringe, but answered him quite volubly, causing a crease to appear between his brows. A snapped order brought seamen scurrying with the Rileys' trunks and those from the Tallents' cabin. Nancy's baggage was pulled open and her store of herbs and salves discovered. Another rapid interchange in French ensued as she knelt to repack her precious medicines.

To Daniel's utter surprise, the baggage was all piled into the lighter and Nancy was helped down into the boat. He was left to hand himself down into the tippy vessel as best he could. He had to shove over onto the seat by Nancy to make way for her father, who still looked blearily drunk and scarcely aware of what was going on.

"Whatever did you say to him?" Daniel demanded as they were rowed to the quay.

"I'll tell you later," Nancy said, stroking his cheek with one small hand and looking at him fondly. This was done so much for the Frenchman's benefit that the effect was quite spoiled for Daniel. He struggled onto the dock and pulled Nancy up beside him.

Trueblood was there in different clothes, to help her father up and unload their belongings. He looked rather surprised to see them released so expeditiously.

"You are rather damp, Trueblood," Nancy chided. "You may catch cold over this."

"I do not think so," he said with a wink to Daniel.

"All safe then?" Daniel asked.

Trueblood nodded.

"Let us go home then," Daniel said with a sigh of relief. "By the by, just what did you say to that fellow that got us dumped on the dock, bag and baggage?"

"Porter, here!" Trueblood commanded to a cartman, who came to load their effects, including Sergeant Riley.

"I don't think I will tell you."

"Whatever it was, it fairly shocked the captain."

"Probably because he did not realize you have a mistress in keeping."

"But I have not— By all that is holy, you never told him you were my mistress."

Trueblood chuckled at Daniel's discomfort.

"I will thank you to lower your voice so as not to make it common knowledge," Nancy warned, her small chin coming up in mock resentment.

"That does not account for his eyes bulging in that way, or for him thrusting us and ours from the ship as though we were a couple of lepers."

"No, that was when I told him I needed my herbs for my cure."

"But—but you are not ill," Daniel sputtered.

"Oh yes I am, with the pox."

"What?" Daniel staggered into Trueblood.

"Not really, but I thought it would hasten our departure. Daniel, do not gape so. For you do not yet know."

Trueblood was by now losing a valiant struggle to contain his guffaws.

"I have shocked you," Nancy surmised.

"Of course you have shocked me," Daniel shouted. "A girl of your tender years should not know anything about such matters."

"Forgive Daniel," Trueblood gasped. "He has a habit of underestimating women."

"How is he unique in that respect?"

"Touché," Trueblood countered. "I wish you would take Nancy home, Daniel, before you say something indiscreet. I will see to the baggage."

"Something indiscreet?" Daniel shouted.

"Also, the very sight of your aghast face is going to send me into a fit of the giggles and the game will be up."

"And you thought *my* plan was stupid," Daniel grumbled in an outraged undertone as they followed the cart with the sleeping Riley away from the hubbub of the dock. "What if that officer had been a victim of the same disease himself? He might have kept you on board to care for him."

"I had not considered that," countered Nancy, taking his arm and compressing her lips in thought. "But then I could

have given him some really vile medicine and still he
would have wanted rid of me.''

"Is there no end to your invention?''

"I have always prepared myself for any disaster. During
a battle one must have bandages ready at hand. I would
assume one must sleep dressed ready to travel. I have
drilled, you see, to be able to wake up and flee or fight at
a moment's notice. I know I was not much use in the beginning, but it was my first battle, Daniel. Did I account
myself so very ill?''

He softened at the hopefulness in her young face. "I
suppose not. Another woman might have swooned.''

"That would have been singularly useless, for then the
pirate might have carried me to the captain's cabin.
Though, of course, I would fit through the window once
Trueblood broke it, so I suppose I could have gotten away
no matter what.''

"And if he had tied you?''

"I carry a knife in my stocking.''

"Is there nothing that would daunt you?'' Daniel asked
sternly.

"But Daniel! This was an adventure! I have been preparing for such things all my life. Think how gratifying it
is to realize it has not all been in vain, that I can take
effective action in an emergency.''

"You enjoyed all this?''

"No, not that man dying, of course, but the rest of it
was not so bad. And I feel sure you would have enjoyed
it, too, if your leg had not been aching.''

"My leg is fine. It was having you to care for that worried me,'' he blustered.

"Well, now you see there was no need.''

"I grant that you slid though this situation on sheer gall
and luck, but you have no idea what awaits you next.''

"Yes, isn't it exciting?''

Daniel groaned.

Chapter Two

Cook's Hotel was a formidable brick house half-a-dozen blocks from Water Street, with a pair of ornate hitching posts by the front door and a fenced garden in the rear. Mrs. Cook was able to offer Nancy and her father one small room, though Nancy doubted they would have been admitted at all if not for Trueblood vouching for them and then helping her father up the stairs, over Mrs. Cook's suspicious questions about his indisposition.

"Miss Riley may have Trueblood's room for her use, and Trueblood can share with me," Daniel told Mrs. Cook, taking that buxom lady aback with these high-handed orders.

"Why do you offer Trueblood's room?" Nancy asked, before Mrs. Cook could protest.

"Because Daniel knows there are any number of disgusting saddle packs in his room," Trueblood said, as he came down the stairs. "Also, mine has an excellent view of the river and a number of volumes on plants I hope you will avail yourself of."

"But I cannot put you out. It looks to me as though this is your home."

"I assure you, the invitation was on my lips as well, and it would have been a more gracious one than what Daniel ripped out with. But he was always one to rush headlong, unheedful of giving offense."

"You make it difficult for me to refuse," Nancy said ruefully, looking from one brother to the other, then to her bemused hostess.

"Do not, I beg you." Trueblood bowed and kissed her hand, winning a satisfied smile from Mrs. Cook and a glare from Daniel.

"I suppose it will only be for a few days, until Papa decides what he means to do."

"Well, now that's all settled," Mrs. Cook interrupted, to keep Daniel from replying. "How about a nice cup of tea in the parlor before dinner?"

"Let me help you," Nancy offered, wanting to make sure she had an entrée to the kitchen.

"That's very kind of you, but I have got two girls to help me, empty-headed though they may be," Mrs. Cook said as she shepherded Nancy out. "I shall be glad of some female company at table rather than rough seamen or worse." She cast a disparaging look at Daniel as they exited, and Nancy's chuckle was lost in the bowels of the house.

Trueblood helped the limping Daniel up the stairs.

"Nancy said that French privateer pointedly asked where you were," Daniel whispered. Once Trueblood had pulled the door shut behind them Daniel dropped down onto the bed.

"I caught a glimpse of Dupree on the French ship," Trueblood answered, searching Daniel's bureau and finally discovering a worn shirt, which he quickly reduced to bandages. "He did not seem best pleased to see me. But the privateer captain gave me a salute, the sort of gesture one reserves for a worthy opponent." Trueblood demonstrated to Daniel.

"So I was right about Dupree."

"Possibly, or Dupree may have been making new friends. He is, after all, French-Canadian."

"Don't be so gullible, Trueblood."

"Just a counterweight to your suspicious nature, Daniel. The packet is in your trunk. Do you want me to take it round for you?"

"No need. It is no more than a few minutes walk." Daniel got up with a grunt.

"Suit yourself, but you do look a sight."

"I'll change first."

"A fresh bandage would not come amiss, either."

"Oh, very well, but be quick about it."

"Where is Daniel?" Mrs. Cook demanded when she came into the sitting room with the tea tray.

"He had an appointment," Trueblood said, and received a skeptical look from Nancy, who was following her hostess with a plate of cakes.

"And on that leg," Mrs. Cook scolded as she poured each of them a cup of tea.

"So long as no splinter remains in the wound, it were better it had some exercise to keep from stiffening up," Nancy replied as she seated herself and looked contentedly around at the polished cherry furniture and cozy chairs. She was wearing a crisp white apron to hide the blood spatters on her gown. "Fancy having an appointment across all those miles of ocean and to arrive within an hour of the time." She glanced at Trueblood over her teacup.

"All business, is our Daniel," Trueblood countered before he gulped his tea and reached for the cake.

"Ah, yes, you are traders. How could I have forgotten?"

"We run pack trains of dry goods overland to Pittsburgh and bring back whiskey or furs."

"Oh, I see, the main part of your business is not with England then. Is it worth it?"

Trueblood passed over her first remark to answer, "Not according to Daniel, but I find so much to interest me in the way of plants I would enjoy the trip even if we made nothing."

"We were discussing herbs on the ship," Nancy confided to Mrs. Cook. "But I had thought Trueblood's interest entirely culinary."

"Trueblood knows a great deal about healing herbs, as well," Mrs. Cook said with a nod of approval.

"I have brought some dried ones from home—fennel, mint, tansy and the like. Also some seed. But I know nothing about what I might find growing here."

"European herbs were introduced so long ago only my people know which ones are native," Trueblood said proudly. "That is why I have been cataloging them and describing their uses. I have been told I can draw, so I have illustrated a volume to be published in London."

"Oh, so that was why you were in England," Nancy said, as though this were a matter of great concern to her.

"Yes, that was it." Trueblood downed another cake.

"You should see his drawings." Mrs. Cook beamed as she refilled Trueblood's cup.

"We have many plants in common now, of course," Trueblood continued. "Comfrey, foxglove, mint, yarrow..."

"Is there a place to come by a supply of Peruvian bark and some rhubarb, as well? I have not much with me."

"I can get you a supply of Peruvian bark at the apothecary's shop," Trueblood volunteered.

"I have rhubarb in my garden, dear," Mrs. Cook replied.

"Are you indeed practiced enough in the healing arts to use such things?" Trueblood enquired.

"Oh yes. You see, I have always thought my father would take me off to war with him, so I have studied all manner of fevers and know how to treat wounds. But in Somerset, most of the time I was called on to attend birthings. I must say, I like that better than illnesses, for usually the outcome is good even if the woman has had a difficult time."

"It does not frighten you, being unmarried and all?" Mrs. Cook asked in a confidential tone.

"It did at first, but the people there are poor. If they had any money they would spend it on food, not on an apothecary. They never blame me if someone does not recover. They know I have done my best."

"So you have lost...patients?" Trueblood asked, staring at her with those penetrating dark eyes.

"Three. Two mothers to fever and one baby, but he was short-term. I doubt anyone could have saved him," Nancy said sadly.

"We have seen nothing like the yellow fever that has seized upon the city this summer," Mrs. Cook offered.

"Describe the symptoms to me," Nancy prompted as she took a sip of tea. "I have heard of it and had thought it no more than another sort of ague."

"Violent fever and delirium, and the poor sufferer turns all yellow. That's why they call it the yellow fever."

"Jaundice? That is not consistent with the ague."

Trueblood had been about to pick up another cake when Mrs. Cook continued, "The worst part comes when they start to vomit up the black blood, pints of it...."

"Internal ruptures, then. How many survive?" Nancy asked between bites of cake.

Trueblood decided against the cake and merely stirred his tea.

"Depends how hard they are taken with it. I know many who have survived."

"I should like to talk to them. Do you suppose an application of leeches—"

Trueblood dropped his spoon into his saucer with a clatter. "Excuse me, I just remembered a pressing errand." He exited the room and closed the door softly behind him.

"You know, I do not believe he was feeling quite well," Nancy confided to Mrs. Cook.

"Possibly the sea voyage. Or it may take him a few days to adjust to our climate again."

"Hmm," Nancy said, thinking of Trueblood's exertions of the past hours and why a discussion of illness would bother him. She could only think he did not like to mix such things with his food, which he plainly enjoyed. She would remember that. She wondered if Daniel had to play second best to Trueblood everywhere; Mrs. Cook clearly held the younger brother in more esteem. Nancy supposed so, since Daniel took the slights with resignation rather than resentment, almost as though it did not matter, in the face of more important issues. And what could be so important? That packet surely was not just commercial papers. Daniel was an extremely complex man and Trueblood was merely a part of his disguise, a distraction for anyone who might suspect he was up to something. She let her mind wander pleasantly over all the things she imagined Daniel might be up to.

Daniel had been admitted to a prosperous-looking house on York Street, then let into the library by a retainer who knew him on sight. As the room was empty, Daniel seated himself, then stood with a groan and proceeded to pace the room. Trueblood had bandaged his leg tightly again, but the wound looked to have broken open from the walking, for there was a growing bloodstain on his clean breeches. He was just applying another handkerchief to this when a middle-aged man entered the room and came to shake his hand.

"Daniel, good to see you. Why the devil are you limping?"

"Hello, Norton. Our ship was captured by a French privateer. I took a splinter."

"God's death. That was close. Is your brother all right?"

"Fine. Yourself?" Daniel sat with a grunt, as Norton motioned him to a chair.

"I had the yellow fever last month," Norton said as he poured them each a brandy from the decanter on his desk. He handed a crystal goblet to Daniel. "Not a bad case by all accounts, but it nearly did me in. Tell me what is going forward in England." Norton pulled his desk chair around to face Daniel.

"Little of interest to us, and except for a certain street in London, little climate for inciting rebellion on the American frontier."

"You are assuming Britain has some control over the situation. They can no more control Canada at this great distance than they could control us. Witness Dorchester's inflammatory speech to the Indians."

"The English are as surprised by the antics of the Governor General of Canada as we are." Daniel took a swallow of brandy. "They might not be unhappy if he did manage to incite the tribes to harass us. They will even turn a blind eye to the encroachment of Canadian forts on American soil, but will not, I think, go so far as to declare war."

"Not yet, anyway, so long as we are neutral and the balance of trade with us is favorable."

"I really think they make more profit off of us now that they bear no responsibility for us."

"They certainly do off the shipping they capture and confiscate. That, too, could lead us into war if we are caught between two belligerent sea powers." Norton glanced at Daniel's leg. "Have you any unofficial dispatches?"

"Yes, here. I hope they are worth Trueblood's swim, but I could not afford to be caught with them."

Norton chuckled and plied his letter opener. "You are quite a pair, you and Trueblood. It would be a load off my mind if the British were planning nothing. Then I would have only the Canadians, the French and the Spanish to worry about. We believe they are all causing unrest on the frontier."

"Perhaps even Secretary of State Hamilton," Daniel suggested.

"Hamilton may be short-sighted, but the money for the war debts must come from somewhere. The whiskey tax is necessary. But is the tax the only cause of unrest? That is the question," Norton added, breaking the seal on the first dispatch and tossing the paper aside after a quick perusal.

"The Canadians have always supplied the Indians with weapons. There is no need to further incite them. Watching their land being nibbled away takes care of that."

"I see. You empathize with the natives as well. True-blood's influence?"

"No. This was not exactly a Garden of Eden before white men landed. We have merely given the native populations a common enemy."

"Or the Canadians have," Norton said, scanning the next letter and tossing it aside. He rose to pour them each another brandy.

"Prime Minister Pitt maintains that Britain wants peace."

"But what do the Canadians want?" Norton asked as he paced to the window, his frock coat gracefully slapping his thighs. "Simcoe seems a very unstable fellow to me."

"The governor of Upper Canada is afraid we'll encroach on his territory, hence all the forts."

"That's what makes him dangerous." Norton unrolled a map overtop of the letters. "There is even some talk of a secret agreement between the Canadians and Spanish now that Britain and Spain are allies again. With enough support they could split the country along the Appalachians and all the wealth of the interior would flow right down the river valley and out of American hands."

Daniel limped over to the desk. "There may be some temptation there. All the frontiersmen want access to New Orleans, but it will take more support and organization than what I have heretofore seen."

"So much for the British and the Spanish."

Daniel took a swallow and felt a satisfying burn, along with a numbing of the pain in his leg. "Where do we stand with the French now that they have declared war on England again?"

"Citizen Genet is causing a stir. The Federalists want nothing to do with him and the Republicans fawn on him."

"And you?"

Norton sat tiredly. "A reserved cordiality. He is, after all, the French ambassador, no matter how flamboyant. Besides, there is more to be learned from a man who does not regard you as an antagonist. Would you like to meet him? I should admire to know what you think of him." Norton took up his pen with renewed energy.

"If you can arrange a casual introduction."

"Come to dinner here tomorrow at seven o'clock," the older man said, scratching a note to himself. "Brace yourself to be opportuned to contribute money toward their revolution, seeing as how they gave us so much support."

Daniel laughed. "I will come. I am not easily imposed upon."

"Too bad you are not married. Two of you will put the numbers out—your brother will be invited, too, of course. But Elise will manage something."

"Something? Either a whey-faced chit who spends the whole evening blushing into her plate, or some spinster. I'll find my own dinner companion, thank you."

"Not another actress, Daniel." Norton looked sharply at him. "You know what happened last time—"

"No, a lady. She is newly arrived from England. Do not look at me like that. I met her on the way over on the ship."

"Of course, Daniel."

"Well, she is a lady and will take the shine out of any of the women in this town—except Elise, of course."

"I am saying nothing. Bring your paragon, by all means. I would be interested to meet a woman who has not washed her hands of you after knowing you for more than a few weeks."

Daniel had been busy most of the day obtaining the latest news, while Trueblood tended to their warehouse. Daniel returned with scarcely enough time to wash and change into clean linens and breeches. Someone had laid out his clothes and brushed and pressed his swallowtail coat.

When Nancy walked down the stairs, Trueblood smiled knowingly and Daniel breathed a sigh of relief. She was dressed in a peach silk gown of the latest fashion, with an ivory underdress edged in lace. A tiny knot of silk roses was tucked between her breasts at the top of her stomacher, and her hair, a natural honey blond, was swept up high on her head, with two long ringlets hanging down in back to caress her neck.

"Are you disappointed, Daniel?" Trueblood drawled as he took the lace shawl she held and placed it carefully around her shoulders.

"No, I am quite satisfied," Daniel said as he took possession of Nancy's arm and conducted her from the house and down the street, forcing Trueblood to walk on the other side of her.

"I take it your expectations were that I would turn up in a stuff gown and a pair of brogues."

"Now you are making game of me," Daniel said. "I could wish you would smile rather than scowl at me. It makes you look fatigued."

Nancy glared at him, since she had still to drag any real compliment from him. "As it happens, I am fatigued. Father invited home that Canadian, Dupree, and they played cards all night."

"Are you sure it was Dupree? Did you see him?" Daniel asked, almost pulling her into the street in the path of a carriage.

"No," Nancy said, hauling back on his arm until the way was clear, "but I have heard them talk together often enough on the ship to recognize his voice."

"What did he have to say for himself?" Daniel asked casually.

"Try as I might, even by holding a glass to the wall, I

could not make out the words,'' Nancy said in mock seriousness.

Daniel had opened his mouth to resume his interrogation when Trueblood burst out laughing. ''She really is making game of you now, Daniel.''

''Which would not be to my credit even if it were a challenge,'' Nancy replied. ''Sorry, Daniel.''

He shook his head. ''Bad enough I have Trueblood carping at me. If you are to start as well...''

''But you interrogate me about the man for no reason. If you want me to spy on him—''

''No! I do not want you to have anything to do with him.'' Daniel took a tighter grip on her arm.

''Well, I do not particularly like him. I keep thinking he is after father's prize money, if he has not got it already.''

''Yes, so do I,'' Daniel alibied. ''That is the only reason I was concerned.''

Nancy slanted a skeptical look at Trueblood, who shrugged. Then she turned her innocent face to Daniel. ''Then you think I have a right to keep an eye on Dupree— in a very subtle way, of course.''

''Dupree may be exactly what he appears,'' Trueblood said, taking Nancy's other arm and drawing her away from Daniel.

''Which is what?'' Nancy demanded. ''It strikes me as odd that such a rough man, one moreover who claims to be a fur trader, should be in England.''

Daniel glanced menacingly at Trueblood and dropped back to study Nancy from behind. He had suddenly lost all interest in Dupree and why the fellow had been in England. Even under the plumped-up side panniers of her polonaise gown, Nancy presented a trim figure and was attracting a deal of attention on the street. One of Daniel's acquaintances tipped his hat to her from horseback, getting a nod from Trueblood and a scowl from Daniel in return for his knowing grin.

Daniel envied the one curl that had slipped around her

neck and was glad Nancy did not hold with the old style of powdering her hair. Nothing should take the sheen out of those curls. Though he had little interest in fashion, he was a purveyor of cloth and had bought and sold enough in England and America to realize her dress was expensive. She should stay in Philadelphia and go to the theater, not be dragged to some crude frontier settlement where there were few civilized women and the men were all dangerous. He must think of a way.

At Norton's house, Daniel sprinted up the steps and was surprised to be greeted by Elise herself. Her flame red hair shone in the last rays of the sun and her green silk gown embraced her like a lover.

"Daniel, you have come alone after all," she complained.

"No, Miss Riley is with me." He reached down and firmly took Nancy's arm, drawing her up the last few steps to stand beside him.

Elise invited Nancy in, making her feel welcome. Daniel cuffed Trueblood on the shoulder as they jostled each other in the doorway, but drew no more than a smirk from him.

"I hope we are not to disappoint you," Elise said, "for Genet is not here yet and I will not hold dinner for him. Come, have some of your brandy."

Elise, Nancy and the daughters of the house, Penelope and Mary, were intimately occupied for a time with a discussion of fashion and hair. Nancy thought both girls showed future promise as belles of the town, but that neither would surpass their mother's beauty with her striking cast of hair. Though Nancy proclaimed herself a country dowd compared to London ladies, Elise graciously asserted she was closer to the pulse of the fashionable world than they in their backwater.

Trueblood was drawn into the conversation to give his opinion on the comparative merits of the open polonaise over the round gown, so that Daniel had a chance to convey to Norton his concerns over the Canadian, Dupree.

"I shall set a man on to follow him."

"I can manage it for the next few days," Daniel offered.

"You are too well known to him. If he has indeed detected your mission, your illustrious career may be at an end, Daniel."

"In other words I had best play the blockish merchant with intensity."

"To the hilt."

"It will not be difficult, with both Nancy and Trueblood cutting at me."

"I have seen that look before, Daniel."

"What look?"

"You are like a leashed dog whose bone has rolled just beyond his reach, watching another hound about to make off with it."

"Sorry, I will try to contain myself."

"No, do not. Jealousy becomes you. Just do not lose your head."

"I shall be hard put not to make a serious blunder tonight."

Norton did ask Elise to put dinner back, resulting, Nancy thought, in Daniel having one brandy too many. Or was that a ruse? Genet made a late appearance and apologized too profusely for his tardiness. Nancy had thought he looked French, with those sensual lips of his, even before he opened his mouth. Trueblood cast a tolerant eye upon him, while Daniel consulted his watch with a blank look. It was like a mask, Nancy thought, that face Daniel put on for company. No, not company— For an enemy. It was interesting to her that the voluble Trueblood, flanked by the daughters, was seated across from Genet, who had Daniel on his right and her on his left. Mr. and Mrs. Norton observed the party from either end of the elaborately laid table.

Had Daniel been across from Genet, that might have set them against each other as opponents. A man is more apt to trust a man at his side. How Nancy knew this she did not bother to consider. She had been at enough dinner parties to draw her conclusions from observation, setting aside her considerable instinct. Daniel had all the leisure in the world to observe Genet covertly, she thought, with that half-drunken smile loosely worn to shield himself from Genet's gaze.

Elise stirred uncomfortably, and it occurred to Nancy that the lady must think she had been looking critically at her table settings. "Such a lovely service of china, Mrs. Norton. I have been racking my mind to discover the pattern, which looks familiar. But if I ever knew it, I have forgotten."

"Why, thank you. It is a special order from Sheffield. It was a present from Daniel and Trueblood, a rather belated wedding gift."

"It was a rather belated wedding," Norton put in, causing his wife to blush.

Norton was not drunk either, Nancy concluded, but he was doing a good imitation of it.

They spoke of china and other elegances, the cost of obtaining them in America, and moved thence to trade, the deficit, America's debts to France, her apparent inability to pay. Daniel *tsked* over this, but could see no ready solution. He seemed such a selfish, complacent man even to Nancy, and she knew better.

If Daniel wanted to get something from Genet, she thought, he was going the long way about it. "I did particularly want to meet you," Nancy said to Genet. "You were so late, I feared I would miss the opportunity."

"And what a loss it would have been for both of us, Miss Riley," Genet leaned toward her to say. "You must let me explain the reason for my tardiness. I had business at the harbor. An English merchant ship has been brought in by the *Embuscade* and I was inspecting her. She will be recommissioned *La Petite Democrate*." Genet raised his glass as if he were making a toast.

"I prefer the *Little Sarah,*" Nancy said, taking a bite of capon.

"You know the ship?" Genet asked in pleasant surprise.

"I was on it." Nancy took another bite while Genet fumbled with his wine.

"A passenger?"

"Yes, until that pirate bore down and nearly sank us. You should speak to him about such lawlessness. It makes a very bad impression."

Genet gaped, as though a housewife had admonished him for his son throwing rocks at her chickens, then began to spout excuses in French, which she heard with only half an ear.

Nancy saw Daniel's eyes glitter with amusement, not brandy. He was neither drunk nor trapped. That meant Genet was here for Daniel's benefit, not the reverse. So this Norton was involved with Daniel and Trueblood more than socially. Well, if Daniel hoped to learn something from Genet, she had to throw them together as allies.

"*Vous comprendez?* He is a privateer, not a pirate," the ambassador was saying. "The ship was taken in the name of the Republic of France."

"*Privateer?* Is that the French word for pirate, the way *embuscade* means ambush?"

"*Non, non,* I say. He was commissioned by my government. You must understand, we are at war with England."

"France is always at war with England. That is no excuse for accosting civilians on the high seas. One sailor had his head taken off by a cannonball, and I would not be surprised if some of the wounded did not die from those vicious splinters. Daniel himself took a bad one. And poor Trueblood was knocked overboard."

"*Monsieurs,* forgive me for any inconvenience," Genet said over the shocked gasps of the other ladies.

"Inconvenience!" Nancy repeated in apparent astonishment.

Both Tallents made deprecating noises, as though the whole incident were forgotten.

"*Mais oui,* I forget, you are a woman. What do you know of such matters?"

"Apparently a great deal more than you. I was there. Even making allowance for them being French, I found your countrymen crude and offensive."

"Making allowance?" Genet sputtered.

Elise had turned away to bite her lip. Trueblood had his face buried in his wineglass, and Nancy thought she could detect bubbles. The girls looked expectantly at their father, who seemed oblivious to Genet's discomfort. In desperation Genet turned to Daniel, who shrugged in sympathy.

"*Monsieur,* you were on that ship. Surely you did not regard it as an inhumane act?"

"Why, no, luck of the draw, I would say."

"Was any disrespect shown to this woman?"

"Now that you mention it, the seamen did search her baggage, and you know how women are with their laces and…such." Daniel fluttered his fingers to indicate, Nancy supposed, frilly undergarments. "I expect that is why Miss Riley has taken such a pet. To have strange hands mauling her finery…" Daniel shuddered.

The daughters gasped even more at this ugly thought.

"Dirty hands they were, as well. Not to mention the language. I am quite certain the captain made an indecent proposal to me," Nancy said, nailing Genet with a menacing stare.

"Why, I do not comprehend how this misunderstanding could have happened. The captain said the only woman on board was a—a…"

"Yes, go on," Nancy prompted, her lips parted in expectation.

"*Non,* forgive me. I am sure he misread the entire situation. But he implied you were fluent in French."

"I speak it, of course, but not the crude jargon of sailors. I think I made them understand me, but I could not follow half of what they said, and no one appreciates being insulted in a foreign tongue,'' she said, disregarding her own brutal attack on Genet.

"Well, that is a blessing, if you did not understand. Even so, allow me to submit my most humble apologies.''

"Apologies? What good are your apologies now? I want your assurance that such an event will not occur again.''

"Impossible!''

"Ah, I see, you have no influence.''

"Quoi?''

"No power with your government.''

"Non—oui! I have power to act for my government.''

"Ah, you could do the right thing, but you will not.''

"La Petite Democrate will sail under the French flag as soon as she may be refitted,'' Genet said angrily.

"A grave mistake, I assure you, sir. For the first English ship it encounters will blow it out of the water.''

"They will not even know.''

"Once my letters reach England, they will. Though, now that I come to think of it, I should perhaps protest to the American government, as well. Trueblood, who is the American equivalent to our foreign secretary?''

Trueblood rolled his eyes in mock reflection, keeping his mouth tightly compressed.

"Oh, never mind,'' Nancy said. "I will write to the president. He will know who to forward the letter to.''

"President Washington?'' Genet asked in a panic.

Nancy saw Daniel's eyes flash at her in delight. Norton sat immobile, his chin resting on his fist as he gazed at her in fascination.

"I believe the ladies will withdraw now,'' Elise said with a prim smile, "and leave the gentlemen to their wine.''

"Mon Dieu, you do not really—'' Genet broke off as the women whisked out of the room.

"A trifle more wine?'' Daniel asked Genet, and filled his glass unbidden. The French ambassador drank deeply.

"Will she really...?''

"Perhaps I may be able to talk her out of it," Trueblood offered dubiously.

"I doubt it, brother." Daniel shook his head slowly. "She is a bit more headstrong than the English ladies you are used to. A loose cannon is what she is. Best keep your distance so you do not get blasted."

"My apologies, Monsieur Genet," Norton offered. "I had no idea the young lady would take things so amiss."

"Ah, I was forgetting." Genet tapped his forehead. "She is English. That explains it. An American lady would never take offense at our privateers."

"No!" the three men murmured in unison, shaking their heads and relaxing into a camaraderie of sex against sex.

"Unless, of course, she happened to be on an English ship," Trueblood offered.

"Yes." Daniel sighed sadly. "Those are the dangers of getting civilians involved in a war. One has no idea of the ramifications."

"But I apologized. Why would she not accept my apology?"

"I doubt there is any way to conciliate a woman whose undergarments have been mauled," Daniel said sagely, "whether she was in them or not."

Norton coughed and Trueblood turned to the sideboard to reach for a decanter of brandy.

"*Vraiment?* But I am the French ambassador, Citizen Genet, and she made me feel such a...such a maladroit."

"Do not give it another thought," Daniel said, thumping him on the back. "It happens to me all the time. Besides, it will never leave this room."

"No," the others murmured in assent.

When the gentlemen came into the parlor, Daniel glanced toward the door, and Nancy rose on that cue to thank the Nortons and take her leave of them. Genet, emboldened by the wine, came forward with another profuse, but tangled apology, swirling his French and English together like brandy and water in a glass. Nancy retrieved her hand and said, "I will...I will consider it."

They were not half a block from the Nortons when Trueblood's mirth bubbled over to the point where he had to lean against a hitching post for support.

"Daniel, I do believe you have let Trueblood drink too much."

"I keep forgetting these Indians cannot hold their liquor," said Daniel, taking him in tow.

"Daniel, have you ever seen the like?" Trueblood gasped. "I believe she could have had Genet on his knees if she had tried."

"And to a sergeant's daughter," Daniel taunted. "A lady would have graciously accepted his apology."

"That did cross my mind. After all, he is an ambassador. But then I remembered he is French. Even a sergeant's daughter must have some standards."

Daniel cracked into laughter and took her hand to draw it through his arm. "You will be wasted on the frontier, Nancy. Stay in Philadelphia."

"I am sure it would be more amusing, but I am a person who is used to employment. On that we will never agree, I know," she said as his grip on her arm tightened. "So it is very much better if I go where we cannot argue about it."

"Would you like to go to the theater tomorrow?" Daniel asked abruptly, interrupting Trueblood and causing Nancy to shake her head in despair. "They have just built a theater on Chestnut Street."

"I thought perhaps you were not best pleased with me tonight," Nancy returned.

"I put you in an awkward situation," Daniel said.

She cocked her head at him. It was not an apology. She decided if she were waiting for him to admit she had been some help to him she would wait in vain.

"You did not mind my making sport of Genet, then?"

Daniel's eyes glittered again, but only in amusement, not conspiracy. "I want to make it up to you."

"So tomorrow I am not to impress anyone or taunt anyone?"

"No, it will be for your pleasure alone. Do you want to take Trueblood for propriety?"

"No, you are harmless enough."

Trueblood chuckled, but Daniel cast Nancy such a skeptical look she thought she would pay for that remark.

"And who is that?" Nancy asked for the tenth time.

"That is Ellis, a banker. He handles my affairs. That is his wife with him and his eldest daughter...." Daniel trailed off. Sitting in a chair next to Nancy, he was being distracted by her low, square-cut neckline and the way her stays displayed the tops of her breasts over the lace trim of her ivory silk gown.

"You seem very well connected in Philadelphia."

"What? Oh, they all receive me for Trueblood's sake."

"You do not have to put on a performance for me."

"Why, Nancy, I do not know what you mean."

"You know very well— Oh, look, there is Genet. Daniel, this is too bad of him. He has the French pirate with him. And who is the other man?"

"By report, I would say it is Andre Michaux, the botanist."

"Like Trueblood."

"Yes, but by vocation only. What are you going to do? Looking daggers at them will only make them laugh at you."

"I think you are right. My instinct tells me that, as well. I think I will have a wonderful time and forget all about them."

"Not even acknowledge them?" Daniel whispered in her ear.

Nancy looked up at the men in the box, then gave a

delicious laugh and turned back to Daniel. "Will he think you have mollified me?"

"They are whispering. Clearly the captain still believes you are my mistress, and Genet is trying to convince him he is a fool."

"Oh, good, now we can enjoy the play and they cannot."

And they did enjoy it. Nancy could not remember such an intoxicating evening in her whole life. Even the grandest of her aunt's parties could not hold a candle to the theater, and with such an amiable companion. He took possession of her hand quite naturally and kept it cradled between his own throughout the evening. He leaned to whisper comments in her ear, making her giggle, and he breathed on her neck in the most seductive way, causing an occasional shocked gasp behind them. It did occur to her that he might only be trying to convince the French captain that they were indeed lovers, but she rather thought Daniel's attraction to her was genuine. He was a subtle man, but she had an instinct for the genuine article and thought he was being himself tonight.

As they walked home Daniel took her fan and plied it. The warm breaths of air were like caresses. "I'm glad you came with me tonight, for I must go away for a while."

"Away? To sea?"

"No, to Pittsburgh. I shall be gone five or six weeks, two months at the outside."

"I was forgetting, that is your business. I expect I will be gone by the time you get back. This might be the last we see of each other for a while. I will miss you—both of you."

"Trueblood is not coming. He has business here for the time being." Daniel ceased his fanning.

"I see." Nancy watched his profile as he walked arm in arm with her, trying to decide what she could say to him to let him know she wanted to see him again.

"I—I suppose you will be thrown together a great deal,

especially since you have the same interests, those con-
founded plants.''

"Yes, I suppose we will," she teased.

"I need not warn you—I mean he is a perfect gentleman.
That is…'' Daniel stopped and turned to her. His face
looked dark against the white of his cravat, but his blue
eyes caught the gleam of the moonlight.

"Does he come between you and many women?''

"Yes—no, not many. Hah, there is no good answer to
that poser. You have a knack for asking such questions.''

"Yes, ones I already know the answer to.''

"If he wishes, he can charm any woman he chooses.''
Daniel looked desperate and hungry for her.

"Not any woman.''

He dropped her fan, and when they both bent for it, they
collided. She was in his arms and he was lifting her up and
kissing her, suddenly, in the most ravenous way. As though
in a dream, she had hold of the back of his coat and was
letting him, more than letting him. He was not at all like
Reverend Bently. His mouth was possessive and urgent, his
arms demanding, his eyes wonderfully alive.

"Daniel, we must not,'' she whispered between kisses,
trying to think rationally.

"Why not?'' he gasped as he bent lower to kiss her neck.

She had never felt so wonderfully vulnerable in her life.
"We are in the middle of the street. We could get run
over.''

"Then come into the alley.''

She laughed at his solution as he pulled her into the dark
shelter of a doorway. "And in a few weeks I shall be on
the frontier and you… At best we will only get to see each
other a half-dozen times a year.''

"Unless you were to stay in Philadelphia,'' he countered,
nuzzling her earlobe to the point where she could scarcely
think straight.

"Daniel, I must go with Papa, at least for a while. He
has brought me all this way to be with him.''

"Promise me you will stay at Mrs. Cook's at least until I return."

"Daniel, I cannot. I do not know what I am doing."

He released her, nodded sadly and took her arm again in the most calm manner. There they left it. Had his impulsive lovemaking been by way of convincing her to do his bidding? Perhaps she could not read him as well as she thought. There was just the chance that he had very nearly found a way to confuse her into compliance. She would rather believe him merely impulsive. All she knew was that, if he had offered her marriage, she did not think her short-lived devotion to her father would have been proof against such a temptation. But he had not...or could not. Whatever he was doing in Pittsburgh, she thought, it had naught to do with trade goods.

The next morning Daniel was interspersing his packing with instructions for Trueblood, who made an occasional note with his pencil as he reclined on the bed reading. Even prone, he made an impressive figure.

"I have been to the docks, Daniel. They are beginning to refit *Little Sarah*, and Genet is openly recruiting in the newspapers."

"Then he is trampling all over Washington's statement of neutrality."

"The secretary of state is lodging a protest. President Washington is going to ask to have Genet recalled."

"That is good news, at any rate. I wonder if Genet will think our Nancy had anything to do with it?"

"Daniel?"

"Hmm?" Daniel closed one leather saddle pack and strapped it shut.

"About Nancy. She could be very useful to us."

"I do not want her involved in this mess any further than she already is."

"Then why did you invite her to dine with Genet?"

"I do not know. It was only that I wanted her to see that

Philadelphia is civilized. I had no idea she would go on the attack.''

"What were you expecting, Daniel?''

"That Genet would be distracted enough by Nancy to ignore us.''

"He was certainly that, but you might have guessed from her performance on the docks that Nancy would not simply sit back and be an object of admiration.''

"But that was an extraordinary happening—an adventure for her. I thought that she would behave herself at an ordinary dinner.''

"I have a better reading of her character than that.''

"I had assumed she had some company manners.''

"Admit it, Daniel—you miscalculated. Consequently you ended by dragging her into a highly charged political situation.''

"Dragging her? There was no way on earth to stop her.''

"You underestimated her, Daniel,'' Trueblood said, wagging a finger at him.

Daniel sighed and ceased his distracted packing to sit on the bed. "Yes, I know that now.''

"If you intend to stay in this line of work, with me assisting you, Nancy could be very helpful to us, if one of us were to marry her.''

"If you take advantage of my absence to get in her good graces—'' Daniel rose to shout accusingly at his brother.

"I was going to offer to go to Pittsburgh in your stead,'' Trueblood interrupted.

"No. It is my job. I should not even have let you carry that packet.''

"I was thinking of your wound.''

"A scratch. Besides, you get lost going across town. If you missed one river you would overshoot the city entirely.''

Trueblood lay back and put his hands under his head. "She reminds me a bit of the Loyalist lady. What do you think?''

"Who? Oh.'' Daniel thought for a moment, his outraged expression softening to one of abstraction. "No, not at all.''

Chapter Three

Trueblood and Nancy came in the kitchen entrance to Mrs. Cook's, Nancy carrying her basketful of lemons and packets from the apothecary shop, and Trueblood burdened with parcels from the butcher's.

"I thought this was supposed to be a free country where a person could speak her mind," Nancy argued. She plunked the basket on the table, tore at the ribbons on her bonnet and tossed the headgear carelessly aside.

"Not on the public street and not in front of a crowd sympathetic to Genet. Had I not been with you, I do not know what would have happened to you," Trueblood returned.

Mrs. Cook held her finger to her lips, warning them that the ill maids were asleep.

"It is stupid, this worship for a man who is no better than a pirate himself. Fitting up privateers, indeed!" Nancy whispered urgently.

"I cannot like the way you speak out in public against Genet, not with this French mania that has seized the people of Philadelphia. Washington himself is not safe from them."

"I give him a lot of credit for not fleeing the city," Mrs. Cook said, wagging her head as she stirred a kettle on the huge iron crane overhanging the fire.

"Were he to do so the government itself might fall," Trueblood said.

"Washington has the courage to stand his ground," Nancy declared as she removed a kettle of steaming water from one of the hearth trivets.

"He is the president. It is his job to take abuse."

"Should I rather lie and pretend to favor this stupid talk of war with England?"

"Nancy, dear," Mrs. Cook interjected, trying to mediate. "Are you sure you do not feel this way because you have so lately come from England?"

"Well, of course, I still have loyalties to England. That is no small part of my abhorrence for the present insanity. But looking at it objectively, it is stupid for a country to be drawn into a conflict where no offense has been given to it and there is nothing to be gained from fighting."

"Hold whatever views you like." Trueblood shook his finger at her. "Simply do not speak of them in the street."

Nancy shrugged and began to unload her basket. She neither wished to argue with Trueblood nor discomfit him, but she had a certain contempt for his powerless state where she was concerned. If Daniel had caught her taunting a mob of street rabble he would have... What? She contemplated the prospect of him tossing her over his shoulder and carrying her home, and was disturbed that the fantasy held so much appeal for her.

"Nancy, why are you so quiet?" Trueblood asked with foreboding.

"There is no point in talking to you while you are angry," she said, measuring some herbs into the teapot and adding hot water.

"I am not angry with you. I am afraid for you."

"I would not concern myself if I were you. If things go on as they have been, this Philadelphia rabble will succumb to a force more powerful than France, England and America combined."

"Yes, the yellow fever is getting worse by the day," Mrs. Cook agreed.

"Another reason you should keep to the house, since you are unwilling to take refuge outside the city," Trueblood argued.

"Not if there is work to be done here."

"Daniel would be extremely displeased."

"What has Daniel to say in the matter?" she asked with a pretense of coldness as she began to slice the lemons.

"He left me with the admonition to take care of you."

"I should not be your responsibility, either."

"Nevertheless—"

"Stir this, Trueblood," Mrs. Cook commanded as she went to check on the invalids.

Trueblood obeyed distractedly. "Nevertheless, Daniel asked it of me and I have never failed him."

"Really? Never?"

Trueblood thought for a moment, then turned an irritated gaze upon her. "Nancy, do not try to distract me."

"Where do you suppose he is now?" Nancy asked aloud. As often as she posed the question to Mrs. Cook, the kitchen maids or even the wall, Trueblood never failed to answer if he was within hearing.

"He has been gone a month. Most likely he is on his way back by now."

"You say he made it there and back in as little as a month?" Nancy asked, as though Daniel's arrival put a time limit on how long she had to cure the yellow-fever epidemic.

"And never more than six weeks."

She sat down on the kitchen stool and stared wistfully out the window. "Is it a very dangerous trip?"

"Not anymore."

"I know I should not worry about him. How many times has he made the trip?"

"Not more than fifty. Whereas your father has never

done it before. Here he has gone off with Dupree, and you have never asked after his safety."

Nancy turned and smiled at him. "What an unnatural daughter I am."

"If we are speaking of unnatural, Riley wrests you from your home, dumps you on a foreign shore and leaves you to fend for yourself, and with precious little money, is my guess."

"Oh, I have some of my own. Uncle gave me all the gold and silver coin he had by him. He reckoned it would be enough to buy my passage home if I should need to."

"In other words he had your father's measure. I hope you keep it in a safe place."

"It is sewn into the hem of my best petticoat."

"Good idea."

"I got it from a soldier's wife—the idea, not the petticoat. I have read over all your books again," she said, pulling a volume across the table to her, "and there is nothing here to help with this yellow fever."

"It would appear they either survive it or not."

"Yes, and that there is precious little we can do."

"So I have concluded."

"If I should get the fever, Trueblood, I don't wish to be bled. That is not the answer."

"I will not let the leeches get you, Nancy girl. I still wish you would let me take you to Champfreys, in Maryland. My mother and sister would love to have you, and it would guarantee that Daniel would go home."

"How could I leave Mrs. Cook in such a fix, with both her girls down with the fever?"

"Prudence is well nigh over it."

"But not much use yet. If she overdoes it now, she may have a relapse, and Tibby is still in danger. Why in the summer, Trueblood?"

"What?"

"The fever. Why only in the summer?"

"Bad air from the swamps."

"Why do we not all get it, then?"

"That may come."

Nancy pushed the book shut in defeat, but the cover flopped open to the flyleaf. It was a gift from Sir Farnsbey at Oxford.

She wondered why Trueblood had been the one sent to school and not Daniel, until she recollected what had been going on then. The rift between Daniel and his father went as far back as '77, when the sixteen-year-old Daniel, according to Trueblood, had left home after a blazing argument with his father to join the rebel army. No doubt Trueblood had been shipped off to England to turn him into a staunch Loyalist and to remove him from Daniel's influence. It had not worked, of course. For Trueblood had managed to get back into the country and rejoin Daniel by 1780. Now his greatest loyalty was to his brother, and that lent Daniel a great deal of credit in Nancy's eyes. If only he valued himself as Trueblood did.

When Daniel wandered into the kitchen the next day, Nancy, Trueblood and Mrs. Cook were all so intently watching a kettle simmering upon a pile of coals on the hearth that they did not immediately perceive he was not the boy hired to cut wood until he did not deposit any in the box under the window.

"Daniel!" Nancy leaped up and ran to him. She had just enough command of herself to merely embrace him and pull him toward a chair at the table, rather than kiss him as she would have liked to do. "You look so tired. I have some soup hot over the fire. Sit down. Tell us about your journey."

"Double, double toil and trouble," Daniel chanted as he sat down tiredly. "Fire burn and cauldron bubble."

Nancy laughed as she carried a steaming pot to the table and got down a bowl. "I suppose we do look like a trio of witches stirring a most unpromising brew."

"I sincerely hope that is not what you are planning on

feeding me, for the reek of it reached me halfway down the street.''

"Not unless you feel yourself to be coming down with the fever, for it is a rather potent purgative.''

"I was hoping this house had been spared. Trueblood, you should have taken Miss Riley away from here." Daniel touched the chicken broth to his lips, then sipped it gratefully, looking about for bread just as Nancy pushed a loaf toward him.

"I did suggest it, little brother.''

"How could you think I would desert Mrs. Cook?''

"Not you, too, mistress?" Daniel paused to look his landlady over thoughtfully.

"Yes, but I am better now. It was Nancy and Trueblood who pulled me through it. Prudence as well.''

"Now if we can just save Tibby," Nancy said, going to stare at the infusion in the kettle.

"Since it appears that those who survive are those through whom it passes the quickest, your idea of purging it may make the most sense," Trueblood said. "But why intersperse the doses of rhubarb with the Peruvian bark?''

"Only because it works for the ague. And I cannot believe the two diseases are unrelated. The symptoms vary, but the causes are the same.''

"The fetid swamps," Mrs. Cook said, drawing the great wooden spoon out and sniffing it.

"Do you mind?" Daniel asked.

"Sorry, Daniel. Are we disgusting you?" Nancy went and got a chunk of cooked beef from the larder and sliced it for him. He laid a thick piece on his bread and ate the two with one hand while he dipped up soup with the other. It made Nancy wonder how long he had gone without eating, and if he had done so to hurry back to her. She sat down to stare at him and only realized she must be smiling vacantly when he spoke with his mouth full.

"Yes. Moreover, I think you are enjoying mucking about with your herbs.''

"I am not. I would rather no one ever got sick."

"But it gives you a great deal of importance when they do." Daniel tore another chunk off the loaf of bread.

"That's not true. I only want to feel useful. Someone must take care of the sick."

"I am surprised you have not hired yourself out to the hospitals." Since this pronouncement produced a dead silence, Daniel could only think that Nancy had been performing some such service. "If that isn't the outside of enough." His fist hit the table. "Well, pack your bags, Miss Riley. I am about to escort you to meet your esteemed papa."

"I will not be hauled away like a child."

"Even if he sent for you?"

"You have seen him?" she asked excitedly.

"Yes, and he commissioned me to take you to Pittsburgh. He has bought an inn. Not much of one, but I take it he is in need of someone to manage it."

"Manage it? Me? But what is *he* doing?"

"Running the still."

"Oh, yes, of course. When do we set out?"

"Two days, if I can manage it."

"But that is plenty of time. By then Prudence will be able to help nurse Tibby."

"How convenient for you." Daniel wolfed the rest of his food and retired to his room, leaving Nancy and Trueblood in the kitchen, writing out their cures for Mrs. Cook.

"Damn!" Nancy said impatiently as she stepped out of one shoe and looked back to see it mired in the crossing. She hopped precariously on one foot, holding up her plain work skirt with the hand carrying the basket as she turned and reached down to pull the shoe free without muddying her stocking. Suddenly she was scooped up by a strong pair of arms, and was just about to raise her voice in complaint when she realized it was Daniel. She did not hit him with the muddy shoe, but wrapped her arm about his neck instead.

"When I recommended these lodgings to you, I did not think you meant to hire yourself out as a servant to Mrs. Cook."

"What on earth do you mean? I have only been helping since the maids have been ill. You can put me down now." Nancy stared about her to see if she knew any of the pedestrians.

"If I do you will only go on about the marketing. I am taking you back to Mrs. Cook's."

"But that is where I was going. I was just leaving a fever medicine at the Nortons'."

Daniel hesitated. "Is one of them ill?"

"One of the servants. Your friend has sent Elise and the girls to his plantation. He even offered to send me there for a visit."

"Which you declined in your high-handed way, I suppose." Daniel continued carrying her along the pathway, oblivious to stares from what few people still dared walk the streets.

"I wish you would put me down, Daniel," Nancy said, but without conviction. "You are causing a spectacle."

"Nothing like the spectacle of you exposing yourself up to the knee to fetch that shoe out of the mud."

"A gentleman would not have looked."

"Any man would have looked, even one staggering about with the fever."

"But what will people think?" Nancy asked, blushing at the backhanded compliment.

"That you have sprained your ankle. At least that is the story I suggest, but you are so inventive I am sure you can come up with something better."

They were within a block of home, so she left off arguing and thought about the strong arms under her thighs and around her back. "Norton seemed surprised you had not been to see him yet," she taunted.

"What did he say?"

"Nothing much, just raised one eyebrow in that way he has of indicating he cannot quite credit his senses."

"I was on my way to see him now. I shall tell him you detained me."

"I do not think that will surprise him," Nancy said, somewhat gratified that Daniel thought her safety of more moment than reporting to Norton.

"What? Bye the bye, are you packed yet?"

"Daniel, I am always packed."

"Yes, if the British attacked, you would be the only one poised to embark on a war. Here we are at Mrs. Cook's. See that you are ready to leave on a moment's notice."

"Well, Daniel?" Norton asked a half hour later as Daniel stood brooding over a small glass of brandy.

"You sound like Trueblood."

"That sounds like an accusation. I did not look for you for a week yet."

"I got back late yesterday."

"Rough trip?"

"Did you get any of my letters?"

"One. I swear, you may as well carry the mail. You do about as well as the post riders sometimes."

"I dislike sending information that way."

"You worry too much. It would never occur to the backwoods rabble that they have a spy among them. What pompous nonsense are they about now?"

"Well, they've burned one of the tax collectors," Daniel said.

"What?"

"In effigy, that is."

"Why didn't you say that in the first place?" Norton asked.

"Every inn and tavern is rife with talk of rebellion," Daniel added.

"Then an insurrection is imminent."

"Not immediately, and perhaps not at all, if something could be done to lessen the severity of the tax."

"Quickly, you mean? Not likely. Most of the representatives have fled. The government is scattered from here to Virginia."

"The president?"

"Will not leave, for the moment. It is the only thing preventing a mass exodus from the city."

"Washington must be able to do something."

"The law is the law. He cannot give any dispensations, even if he would. And the debts must be paid. Speaking of pay, when is the last time you had any money for your services?"

"I do not recall, but it does not matter. I never did it for that."

"I have never been quite sure why you do it, Daniel. I am only glad that you do."

"If only they had increased the taxes on imports it would have hit these rich city merchants in the purse, not the poor wretches on the frontier. They have nothing but the bit of whiskey they make. To tax it is inhuman, especially for the small producers."

"Compassion for the enemy, Daniel? That is likely to get you killed."

"They are not the enemy. They are our countrymen. Whether they remain so is another matter."

"You have found something."

"You remember us speaking of Dupree?"

"Yes."

"He has met with Bradford—twice, to my knowledge."

"Is Bradford in the pay of the French?"

"If he is they have most likely offered him something else."

"What?"

"Possibly governorship of the area, once it is no longer part of America."

"Do they mean to send troops?"

"I believe they mean to make the insurgents do all the killing themselves...and the dying."

"Why do they need France then?"

"They do not, but they do not realize that. I am wondering if there are other Duprees at work up and down the length of the frontier."

"Other than Michaux, the botanist, you mean? Do we have time to find out?"

"I suppose Trueblood and I could scour the frontier."

"That would take too long. I think it a better use of your time to keep your finger on the pulse of Pittsburgh and surroundings, but I do not like to run you ragged going back and forth. Are you sure you cannot trust your dispatches to the mail?"

"I am taking Trueblood with me this time. One or the other of us can bring news."

"Why did you not take him with you last time?"

"I had work for him here."

"More important work than this?" Norton raised a skeptical eyebrow.

Daniel opened his mouth to protest that his brother no longer worked for the government, but Norton waved a hand and said, "Do not explain. I have a feeling I know what you are going to say. Spare me."

Nancy pulled the candle across the large kitchen table and reread the letter from her aunt, who urged her, at the slightest inconvenience, to use the money her uncle had given her to book passage on the next returning ship. Nancy only hoped that Aunt Jane never found out that her ship had been captured by a privateer and that she had been nursing yellow-fever victims. A fine adventure and some useful experience, but aunts never saw such things that way. England was so far away. With any luck, they would never hear about the plague. Nancy sharpened her pen and composed her mind to write a comforting last letter before she began her journey to Pittsburgh.

Dear Aunt Jane,

You talk as though this is a wilderness. I assure you Philadelphia is quite civilized. Why, they even have hospitals here. And I have been to the theater and any number of other entertainments. I even dined with the French ambassador, and he kissed my hand. But enough of my society fling.

Tomorrow we set out for Pittsburgh, the roughness of which I am sure has been exaggerated. I have heard there are nearly two hundred houses there. Surely there are genteel folk among them. You need not worry about the journey. I travel under the protection of a family of merchants Papa and I met on the ship. What could be more fortuitous than that they run a regular trade with Pittsburgh? Papa has gone ahead and bought us a quaint inn. I can scarcely wait to see it. I will write you from my new home, unless there is an opportunity to mail a letter along the way.

With all my love,
Nancy

Chapter Four

Nancy stared at Trueblood's costume one more time, for that is what it seemed to be. Daniel was dressed in a rough coat and breeches with serviceable riding boots and sat his lean horse like a soldier, but his brother had donned a leather hunting shirt, which looked like it would be uncomfortably hot later in the day. Trueblood's breechcloth and leather leggings left a large expanse of hip and thigh exposed. His loincloth looked so much like the garment worn by women when they had their courses she could not help but regard it as indecent. Trueblood must have read something of her thoughts, for he smiled wickedly at her and basked in the stares of all the other women who passed the warehouse on their way to market. It was so unlike Trueblood that Nancy was on the point of demanding what he thought he was about when she remembered what she was going to ask Daniel and kneed her young mare to bring it up to Daniel's mount.

Daniel watched Nancy's approach with foreboding. He had been pleased to see that Trueblood had gotten her and her gear to the warehouse in good time. Moreover, her trunks had been got rid of in favor of somewhat more watertight saddle packs, and she seemed to be having no difficulty riding astride. She wore a leather hat, a thick linen skirt and a sturdy jacket and, it appeared, meant to lead her own pack animal. That would not last, but Daniel decided not to quibble over it. What worried him was the determined look on her face, and he could not be sure Trueblood's outrageous attire would distract her from whatever rub she meant to throw in the path of their departure.

"I forgot to ask. Did my father offer to pay you?"

"Why should he pay me?" Daniel asked. "The job is not done yet."

"Then I will pay you."

"Certainly not," he snapped, then bit back his anger when he saw her raise her chin.

"I do have money of my own."

"I am sure you—very well. You may hire us as guards."

"What is your price?"

"A shilling."

"Is that all my life is worth to you?"

"No, that is all I imagine I am worth at such a task, since I have no doubt you will be an enormous amount of trouble and I shall make a poor job of it. So you may stay in Philadelphia for all I care, or follow us if you choose."

With that, he led out his string of pack animals and proceeded northwest out of the city.

"Well, Daniel," Trueblood said, drawing level with him, "you did not handle that very well."

"Is she coming?" his brother asked apprehensively, without daring to turn his head.

Trueblood glanced over his shoulder. "Yes. She has fallen in between my string and Cullen's. What would you have done if she had not? Gone back and taken her by force?"

"Oh, no. I thought I would leave that to you."

"Such high-handed methods would never work with Nancy. She is used to being in charge."

"Then she had best accustom herself to taking orders. Do not laugh at me."

"I never laugh at you, Daniel."

"Not so anyone would notice, but you derive a deal of amusement at my expense."

"As you are so bent on arguing, I will frustrate you by agreeing completely."

It was some hours before they had passed beyond the environs of the city and the close farms that supplied it. Nancy gave a sigh of contentment as they left civilization behind for the sweeter air and breezier expanses of the country. After half a day's travel they passed through stretches of cool forest, where the ponies' shod feet thumped on the hard-packed road, the sound echoing off the leaves. Thousands of birds must be flitting about in the canopy, and the undergrowth, she was sure, hid all sorts of wildlife. As much as she was enjoying the new geography, she had the strangest feeling of foreboding, as if they were intruding where they did not belong.

When the serving girls had heard she was to travel to Pittsburgh, Prudence and Tibby had filled her head with tales of scalping and capture by Indians. Nancy tried to picture Trueblood in a killing rage, but she could not. He was too tame. She tried to picture being carried off by a war party, but the landscape seemed so benign. They were just foolish girls, after all. Daniel would never take her where there was any real danger.

She tried to picture being scalped, for the victims of such attacks were not always dead when this occurred, according to Prudence. They could, in fact, live some days in great pain, or even some years in great ugliness. That was the most appalling part. The horror, Nancy thought, was in being defaced, in being made ugly and in being made to long for death. She had only been thinking of war in terms of noble wounds. That headless sailor had put an end to any idea she might have that war was noble. Wounds would always be ugly to her now, and the foolish gossip of two serving girls had killed her complacency about their journey. Nancy had known fear on the ship but had found she could face it. She now knew that there were some fears she would carry to bed with her in her nightmares even if they were based in her own reality. These horrors had happened even if they had not happened to her. She empathized too much with the ghosts of those who had suffered. Even knowing she could still help the living did not lift her spirits.

They rested the horses at noon, but took time for no more than a few bites of bread and a drink of water. Toward late afternoon, when Nancy assumed Daniel would scout about for a likely campsite, he surprised her by pulling into an inn yard and negotiating with the proprietor for accommodations for them and their considerable string.

Over dinner—a hearty stew—he asked a subdued Nancy, "Are you still hungry? You may have anything you want from the groaning board, some fruit and nuts, or some cheese, perhaps." Daniel motioned toward the feast that was to be had at a slight extra expense.

"Nothing. The stew and biscuit were fine."

"If you are tired you can retire immediately, and we will make a late start tomorrow."

She shook her head, realizing she had to drive off the demons that haunted her if she were to live in this land. "The country is quite lovely, but rather tamer than I had anticipated," she said with mock bravado.

"And you are disappointed."

"Well, yes."

"What were you expecting?"

She decided not to confide the stories of the scalpings to him. "That it would be more difficult."

"Perhaps we will run into rain. Would that make it difficult enough?" Daniel teased.

"I suppose. Perhaps it is the time of year. One really cannot expect too many hardships in September, unless of course we were to be attacked by Indians." She glanced sideways at him.

Daniel laughed. "Always joking, Nancy. Why, such a

thing has not happened in what, Trueblood—two or three—''

"At least four weeks."

"Four weeks?" Nancy squeaked, as Trueblood mopped the last of the stew from his wooden trencher with his biscuit and filled his mouth with it. She stared numbly at him as he then flipped the wooden disk over and went to select a half chicken and a large cutting of cheese for himself. Cullen grinned and beckoned the landlord to refill their tankards.

"Four weeks," Nancy repeated. "And people live out here as though nothing has happened. How can they bear it?"

"You are afraid!" Daniel blurted out in surprise, his intense blue eyes searching Nancy's face.

"Yes, I am afraid," she said pathetically. "But I suppose I will get used to that just like everything else."

Daniel reached across the table and took her hand. "What I was going to say, when I was so rudely interrupted by my brother, was that such a thing has not happened for years around Pittsburgh. It is true that the Canadians are inciting the Indians to attack the more remote settlers' cabins, but those are isolated incidents."

"Oh, that makes me feel so much better," she said resentfully.

"And you will not be at some isolated cabin in the middle of the back woods, but at an inn on a well-traveled road. To be sure, you have nothing to fear from any Indian but Trueblood, and that is only if he bores you to death with his doltish behavior." Daniel nodded toward his brother, who was dismembering the chicken.

Nancy smiled at him and shook her head. Of course Daniel would never take her anyplace dangerous. She had been foolish to let those stories worry her.

When Daniel helped Nancy mount her bay mare the next day he noticed that she was smiling again and her hair was wet. As it dried it fell like a shimmer of gold about her shoulders. He started out at her end of the train so that he would be able to watch her without getting a stiff neck. But that only led him to contemplate an idyllic future with her, which he realized might be far from Nancy's expectations. That she liked him he knew, but he was very far from winning her. During a rest he traded places with Cullen to clear his head. He must get his mind back on Dupree and the fomenting rebellion or he would never get this job out of the way. That was odd in itself, that he would be impatient with an assignment rather than intently thinking of nothing else.

At their noon stop Nancy demanded, "See here, I have been talking to Cullen and he informs me that you do not always travel this way."

"What way?" Daniel asked, tearing off a mouthful of bread.

"From inn to inn as though you are on a tour. I wondered how you could make any profit if you were forever paying for food and lodging, especially Trueblood's food. Cullen tells me you normally make your own camp and hunt game along the way."

"I see no reason for you not to have a bed, if there is one to be had."

"Considering the number of fleabites I have gotten I would by far rather sleep on the clean hard ground."

"But you had warm water and a room to bathe in this morning. You won't have that if we travel rough."

"Yes, and now that I am free of vermin again I intend to stay that way. I can heat water as well as the next woman if you have a pot. Well, have you one?"

"Yes, at your disposal, Miss Riley," Daniel said, tipping his hat.

"I expect we can make better time also, now that you will not be forever looking for an inn."

"However did we manage without you, Nancy girl?" Trueblood asked.

"I have had quite enough of this delay," Daniel said, getting to his feet and preparing to mount.

"Delay? You cannot pretend that I held you up, for I can make more than fifteen miles a day even if I walk."

"How on earth would you know that?" Daniel asked as he lifted her onto her small mare.

"I practiced."

"Practiced walking fifteen miles a day?"

"Twenty, actually. I had to be sure I could manage it, don't you see? In case we should ever be on a forced march, or, God forbid, a retreat."

"Well, do not let us hold you up, Captain Riley," he taunted. "Would you like, perhaps, to lead the way?"

"The way, as you call it, is plainly marked and I suppose anyone could find it here. But I suspect it may become more convoluted when we reach the mountains. I am content for you to lead."

"Content, are you?" Daniel glowered at her, then set off with his string of ponies, pretending not to care if anyone followed him or not.

"Child, if you knew how much you bother him," Trueblood said with a chuckle as he brought his own string of ponies up level with her.

"I do know."

"Then why do you do it?"

"When he is competent and in control, he takes me for granted. He may even forget I am here. When I throw him off his guard, he can think of nothing but me."

"And how much he would like to give you the whipping you deserve."

"Did he say that?"

"Somewhat incoherently, but that was the gist of it. Does it worry you?"

"No, for I do not think he really means it," she said wistfully.

"You would never tolerate it."

''No, of course not. But if we were married, there is not a great deal I could do about it.''

Not for the first time, Nancy left Trueblood with a puzzled frown. Normally when a woman said something nonsensical he merely thought she was babbling. But Nancy was an intelligent woman, and here she was acting as irresponsibly as a moonstruck girl... That was it! She was in love, and Daniel had not the slightest inkling. There was nothing new about that. Daniel only wanted women who were ineligible. If a woman fell in love with him, he had not the acuity to realize it.

Trueblood hastened to catch up with Daniel. ''What do you intend doing about Nancy?''

''What the hell do you mean by that? I am delivering her to her father.''

''Well, Daniel, you have a reputation for impatience, especially with women. For using them rather hastily and leaving them in despair. If you—''

''Trueblood, what have you done? Have you fallen in love with Nancy?''

''In a manner of speaking, I have, but not in the way you imagine.''

''If there was ever a time to speak clearly, brother,'' Daniel threatened through clenched teeth, ''it is now!''

Trueblood blinked at him. ''I mean that I treasure Nancy for her talents, her loyalty, her...hmm...''

''What?''

''There is something even I cannot fathom about her. Nevertheless, believe me when I say that if you mean to seduce her and leave her weeping, I will nip this affair in the bud.''

''I believe you mean it,'' Daniel said in astonishment, taking in the determined set of his brother's brows.

''It is the only thing you could do that would make me turn against you.''

''She has made an impression.'' Daniel stared ahead at

a twist in the road, trying to picture Trueblood not at his side. It was inconceivable.

"I think she would also make you an admirable wife. No other woman we have ever encountered has been at all suitable for you."

"Is that why you relieve me of them so consistently?"

"As I would remove a poison mushroom from your plate, for your own good."

"If you have any such designs on Nancy…"

"Have I not already said she would make you an admirable wife?"

"But not yet. I must get this insurrection business out of the way."

"You talk about it as though you can will it to be over."

"That is the hell of it, Trueblood. If it was a war, there would be something I could do, but this waiting and watching is getting on my nerves."

"Nerves, Daniel? I thought you had none left."

Toward late afternoon Trueblood rode up to confer with Daniel, who nodded his head. Daniel then took charge of Trueblood's ponies while his brother turned off from the pack train. Some time later they heard a single shot. Daniel raised his rifle to fire an answering shot in the air and halted the train at the next small stream.

Nancy was about to slide off her horse when Daniel grabbed her about the waist and whisked her to the ground, letting his hands linger perhaps a moment longer than necessary. He looked at her in what she thought was a possessive way. She had to admit she hoped it was a possessive look.

"Trueblood's turn to hunt, I see. Does that exchange of shots mean he was successful?"

"Either that or he has lost the road and needed to know what direction we are."

Nancy gaped at him. "But the road is well-enough marked for even a novice like me to follow."

"But if you had gone some distance into the woods, you might get your direction turned around."

"I don't think so. One has only to backtrack and eventually one would come to the road. The sun would tell you which way to go then."

"I have no doubt you would not get lost, but Trueblood is another matter. He has the most abominable sense of direction of anyone I know."

"But—but he's part Indian," she said, undoing the cinch of her saddle.

"But he was not raised to that life." Daniel lifted the saddle off and placed it over a log to make a seat for her.

"You are making game of him?" she demanded. She began foraging for dried limbs and dumped an armload in the middle of the clearing.

"Certainly not. He is my brother and nearly perfect in every respect but this one. But do not quiz him about it, I beg of you. He is very sensitive on this point."

Nancy continued to stare at Daniel's back as he helped Cullen hobble the ponies and unload them. As she sought more firewood and some dried bark for tinder, she searched in her mind for some reason Daniel would malign his brother in this way, but could think of none. If it were true, it was not to Trueblood's discredit—not in her mind, anyway. If it were not, what did Daniel gain?

But her curiosity was aroused. She struck her flint and steel, taking many tries to get a spark that she could tease with dried glass into a small flame. She knew Daniel was watching her slow progress, but refused to be hurried into extinguishing the small blaze with too much fuel at once. She coaxed it as she would coax Daniel out of feelings of competition with his brother. There was no need. She already acknowledged Daniel as superior, but it was not an easy thing to tell a man.

Trueblood came down the road from the east, in due course, with a gutted doe slung across his saddle.

"How efficient of you," Nancy said, thinking of the good dinner she could make for them.

"A lucky shot," he said, sliding off his horse and carrying the doe to hang it from a tree for skinning. Daniel came and led Trueblood's horse to the picket line with the others.

"And modest," she added.

"To boast of my hunting prowess would leave me open to censure next time I missed."

"You and Daniel are not much alike," she said, watching him make expert incisions on the insides of the legs. Her scalp prickled and she gritted her teeth, but she did not close her eyes as he flayed the deer. She forced herself to stand and watch through the worst of it.

"No, he takes for granted he will hit the mark every time. It is almost a surprise when he fails." Trueblood winked at her.

"Are we still talking about deer?" she asked as he hacked off one of the haunches and carried it to a log.

"I am. What did you think I was talking about?"

Nancy swallowed. "I don't know yet, but there is a great deal more to both of you than meets the eye. Being a mere trader would never satisfy Daniel, and it would bore you to death."

Trueblood glanced at her. It was not an expressive look, but a calculating one, as though he were measuring something. Then he gave a rare smile. "Look—mushrooms, a ring of them. Go gather them."

"Are you sure they are safe?" she said, walking a little way into the woods to scrutinize the fairy ring.

"You have never eaten them?"

"I have never eaten any fungi, though I have tested many herbs in small doses. But it takes so little of that kind of poison to kill." Nevertheless she gathered them up in her leather hat and carried then back to him.

"You will be missing a rare treat if you don't try this

variety. Cullen, is that fire hot yet?'' Trueblood asked, pulling a pan out of a pack.

While Daniel built a rack over the fire, Nancy sliced steaks off the haunch of venison. Daniel showed her how to lay them so they would not fall in the fire. Trueblood thrust the pan under the rack to brown the sliced mushrooms in a bit of tallow from the deer.

"How much do you trust me?" he asked her as she was getting the tin plates ready.

"Enough to eat before you rather than after you," she replied.

"Courageous indeed."

Daniel and Cullen helped themselves to the mushrooms as well. "She's merely a realist," Daniel said. "Eating after you would mean she would get nothing."

Nancy laughed at the grimace Trueblood gave Daniel.

She did eat the mushrooms and also some of the venison when it was done. She tried not to think of the doe, but she did not believe she would get used to this part of her adventure. At least she would not take it for granted. She believed that if you were going to eat meat, you should be able to face killing it, but if she had a choice she would rather not.

She slept, happily enough, propped up against one of the packs, with her feet pointed toward the fire. She woke several times in the night to see one or another of the men awake and watching. When it was Daniel, he smiled, and his eyes glittered with reflected firelight.

Nancy had not even realized what she had been missing by sleeping at inns until the first morning she got to watch Daniel shave. Was it possible that he had no idea what a seductive act it was? It was as though he were undressing in front of her. This was how he would look if they were married, she thought, studying the skillful swipe that removed the dusky three-day growth from his face. She could not decide if she liked him better with a beard or no. When he shaved it off he looked ten years younger. But she had a strange liking for that desperate-looking character who alternately scowled and grinned at her, his blue eyes glinting in either case. It was mostly because he was so unaware of his affect on her that her eyes lingered on him. She shook her head to clear it of the vision of Daniel's naked back, dipped the leather bucket in the stream and went to prepare breakfast.

"I like this way of travel much better, Daniel," she informed him later in the day, where the road was wide enough for them to ride abreast.

"Washing in a cold stream?"

"I am trying to apologize for annoying you. After you saved my life and did me any number of favors in Philadelphia, it was very ungracious of me to spurn your help in getting to Pittsburgh."

"Damn right—I mean, I accept your apology."

"Good, and since I am convinced you will never get paid by my father, and you will not take my money, I intend to earn my keep."

"Whatever do you mean?"

"I can think of a dozen ways I may be of use to you on this expedition."

"Oh, really?"

"Besides making the fire, cooking and fetching water, I am a dab at sewing and—"

"Enough."

"Are you spurning my help now?"

"I simply do not want to arrive at our destination owing you money."

Nancy laughed, and Daniel did as well. Trueblood smiled benevolently on the couple.

Nancy was somewhat daunted at sight of the Susquehanna, but Daniel assured her they were fording it at the best possible time of year.

"Do you swim?" he asked with a grin.

"If the river is as shallow as you say, why are you asking

me if I can swim?'' she shot back at him, and clutched the saddle as her mare slid on a rock.

"Just making conversation." Daniel stayed on her downstream side, she noticed, which was touching and annoying at the same time. She did not like him to think her always needing help, but that he was sensitive to her fears impressed her and buoyed her confidence.

"As a matter of fact, I can swim...a little."

"Just in case you should have to ford a raging torrent in some godforsaken country, carrying a full pack on your back and dragging a wounded man with you?"

"Do not make game of me. I thought it was something I should know, but this is nothing like the millpond," she said as the water swirled up past her mare's belly and wet her boots. To her relief, the river, where Daniel chose to ford it, was equally shallow for its entire breadth, and the water did no more damage than wet the bottom of the woven pack baskets, which were slung across the wooden cross trees of the pack saddles. But these contained only durable goods. Anything that might be harmed by the weather was in the sturdy leather saddle packs.

When they reached the shore, the men checked and tightened the double cinches of the pack saddles, and Nancy slid off to do the same to hers. She reminded herself that all rivers might not be so benign. Still, she thought she had weathered that fear well, and her poise reasserted itself as they resumed their journey, oblivious now to town and farms. In fact, Nancy always hoped to be camping in the most desolate places. Except where briars were encroaching, the road was usually wide enough to lead two strings of ponies abreast, and Nancy would ride beside Daniel if Trueblood did not do so.

"Which annoys you more—'well, Daniel' or 'little brother'?" she asked, checking his profile to see what effect this comment would have.

Daniel smiled sheepishly. "Why? Are you thinking of some further way to try my patience?"

"Simply making conversation."

"His height. He outgrew me when he was twelve and I was fifteen. He has never let me forget it."

"'Little brother,' then, even though you are the older."

"What annoys you the most—'Nancy dear' or 'little sister'?" he countered.

"Never having had a big brother, I find Trueblood quite comfortable, as though I have always known him."

"What about me? Do I wear like an old shoe, as well?" Daniel tilted a skeptical look at her.

"You are the truly great mystery of my life." She looked ahead to where the road disappeared among the trees, in order to make him ask for more of an explanation.

"What do you mean by that?" he said eventually.

"Generally speaking, I know what men are thinking without them saying, but you are always nine parts under the surface, always thinking of something else."

"And you want to know what that something else is?"

"Oh, no. That would destroy the suspense of knowing you. When you open your mouth it is as though everything that was said before passed right over you, and you were merely waiting your turn to say something of importance."

"Which has no relevance whatsoever to the current conversation?" he guessed with a smile.

"It depends on the degree of your abstraction. If Trueblood wanted to turn a conversation, he would lead it gently by the string until he got it were he wanted it. You rip it loose from its moorings, spin it about and launch it in the direction of your choice such that it has no memory of where it was before."

Daniel chuckled. "But that is only when I am bored."

"Which is anytime you are not working."

"Working," he said with a frown.

"You seemed to melt into the conversation at the Nortons' as though you really were a simple-minded merchant. Do not gape at me in that stupid way, for you are nothing of the sort. But at Mrs. Cook's table you act as you please, for there is no one there you have to fool."

"If I am not a merchant, what am I, Nancy dear?"

"I have not put a name to it yet, but I will let you know when I do."

The road narrowed just then, and Nancy smiled and kicked her mare into a trot, to leave Daniel pondering.

Some hours later, Trueblood halted his string of ponies ahead of them and wandered off the track. Daniel groaned and pulled to a halt, flinging his arm up to let Cullen know they were resting. "I had thought pushing him rather than pulling him might work, but there seems to be no way to get him to Pittsburgh in good time."

"I am glad he has stopped," Nancy vowed as Daniel lifted her down. She waited for him to do this now, even though she was perfectly capable of sliding off her mare herself. There was something very comforting about those strong hands and the way he looked up at her. Nancy handed Daniel her reins and stepped into the cover of the woods to relieve herself. Then she went to see what Trueblood was digging up.

"Is Daniel extremely impatient?" he asked.

"No more than usual. If only he could appreciate herbs and plants as you do."

"But he does, or he did. I gained all my early knowledge from Daniel, who got it from my mother, Mara."

"But why then is he so intolerant of your occupation?"

"Daniel has a certain impatience with life now," Trueblood said as he finally got the specimen free.

"I wish I had known him when he was younger," Nancy said as she rose and dusted off her hands, "but then I would have been too young."

"He did smile more and…"

"And what?"

"And occasionally enjoyed the pleasure of a woman."

"What changed him?" Nancy demanded, as they made their way back to the horses.

"The war. Don't ask him about it," Trueblood warned as he caught his brother's menacing stare. Daniel was finishing adjusting the packs and tightening the cinches—or pretending to do so—when they came out of the woods. He led the strings of pack ponies up to them.

"Well, Trueblood?" Daniel demanded so much like his brother that Nancy burst out laughing.

"I thought it was bloodroot, but I was wrong."

"At this time of year? Of course not."

So Trueblood had not been joking, she thought, as Daniel lifted her up again. Daniel was the leader, the opposite of the way they appeared in public. How much could she trust them if they practiced their deception on everyone as a matter of course? Then she remembered that they had trusted her on the ship and in the confrontation with Genet. She vowed never to give them reason to regret their faith in her, however unspoken.

When Trueblood halted the train again, Daniel took the lead himself, not even looking around to see if his brother would catch up.

"Why are you so impatient with him?" Nancy asked, to slow Daniel's progress. "He will be only a moment."

"Because he has no regard for others, only his pastime."

"I do not think you realize that your object is different from his."

"What is to understand? We are all going to Pittsburgh." Daniel swept his arm to indicate the road. "I assume we all want to get to there."

"No, Trueblood and I are more interested in the journey, not just because of the plants. In my case, I may see this beautiful country only once. Cullen is paid by the day. You are the only one who really wants to get to Pittsburgh quickly."

Daniel chewed on the thought for a moment. "So I miss everything in between?"

"It does lead you to a restlessness to arrive at your destination that is at odds with our enjoyment of the trip."

"So Trueblood does not do this just to irritate me?"

"No—well, not entirely," she said with a smile. "Daniel, if you cannot feel the wonder anymore, at least do not fulfill Trueblood's expectations of your discontent with him."

"Pretend I am not impatient, so that he does not get the satisfaction of having irritated me?"

"Come now, you are such a good actor when you have an object in view. Your patience with Genet far exceeded mine. Surely you can pretend well enough to dupe your own brother."

Daniel shot her a suspicious look, but met only sincerity. "I will endeavor to disguise my justifiable impatience."

"And enjoy yourself?"

"Now you ask too much," he said with a grin. "I will, however, pretend to do so."

Chapter Five

The days of splendid sun passed with Nancy enjoying the excellent weather and glorying in her newfound knowledge of native plants. Daniel warned time and again that she had seen only the gentler side of the wilderness, that she would be glad for a roof over her head, even a leaky inn roof, if it came on to rain. But nature perversely proved him wrong, and the sun smiled on their expedition through Carlisle, Bedford and Ligonier. They were as likely to pass through a settlement at midday as at evening. Daniel always asked if she wished to stop. She always answered that she would rather camp, much to Cullen's chagrin. She suspected he would like a chance to drink an evening away at an inn. But Nancy did not want some strange innkeeper and his wife fussing over her. Mostly she did not want to be secluded in the ladies' parlor and be put at risk for sharing a bed with strange women, not when she would far rather...

"Walking again?" Daniel asked of her. "I bought you that mare so that you would not have to walk or ride a jerky pack pony."

"But I am tired of riding, and I am sure that Tess is tired of carrying me."

"If you are tired, you should have said so." Daniel raised his hand to Trueblood, indicating that they would rest.

"What was that you said, Daniel?"

"That we could rest when you felt tired."

"No, before that, about buying Tess for me."

"I did buy her for you. She's too light for a pack animal. But considering our inauspicious start, I did not want an entire horse thrown back in my face, as well as my fee for the journey."

"You mean I can keep her after we get to Pittsburgh?"

"Only if you do not offer to buy her."

"Oh, Daniel, thank you so much!" She hugged him and was on the point of kissing him when she realized they were not alone. "I was wondering how I could bear to part with her. But why did you do it?"

"You must know you were a help to me in Philadelphia...on more than one occasion. And I had the strangest feeling you would not accept a necklace or a bolt of silk."

"Of course not, but a pet is an entirely different matter."

Nancy led Tess off the road to the stream, telling her what a grand time they would have when they reached Pittsburgh.

They went on quite amicably for that day, but the peace lasted only until Nancy decided it was her turn to procure their dinner. Usually either Trueblood or Daniel went off to shoot some game close to day's end. The other would help Cullen unload and water the ponies, while Nancy started a fire. Until now she had contented herself with this task, and with drawing water and cooking, but she could shoot. She had only to borrow a rifle. And no one was willing to lend her one, least of all Daniel.

Daniel and Nancy continued to argue so vehemently after they had chosen a campsite that Trueblood stayed to start the fire, afraid to leave them alone together. They still had some corn cake from last night that they could stretch, but the woods abounded in fat deer at this time of year and they had not had any for a few days.

"Well, Daniel," Trueblood drawled. "Are you going to kill something or not?"

Daniel spun and fired, sending Trueblood flat against the ground and stunning Nancy to silence.

The chittering squirrel, too, was reduced to silence as it fell from its limb.

"What I had in mind," Trueblood said calmly as he pushed himself up and brushed off his leather shirt, "was venison."

"If you wanted venison you should have specified venison," Daniel snapped as he stomped out of the camp.

Cullen came up from the creek, looking questioningly at Trueblood, who merely shrugged.

Nancy picked up the dead squirrel and carried it to Trueblood, who proceeded to skin it. "Is Daniel coming back?" she asked, suppressing a shudder at the sound of skin being pulled off flesh. She should be used to it by now, but it always made her scalp prickle when any of them skinned an animal. She would simply have to get used to it and forget her silly fears.

"Eventually," Trueblood replied, "when he has gotten over his anger. If we are lucky, he may even bring us some venison. If not, we will make do with roast squirrel, though it will be a meager meal."

Daniel sought to puzzle the situation out by walking, but he was beyond thinking rationally when fatigue overtook him. The weariness was a reaction to his anger, and when it came over him he curled up by a tree and nearly dozed, disregarding dangers or responsibilities. Why did he not like the idea of Nancy hunting? Was he merely worried for her safety, or did he actually resent her competence? In a world full of helpless women, he should applaud one willing to take on any task a man could do.

But this particular woman was the one he wanted to marry, and he disliked the idea of her doing his job. She was not like other women. That was what had attracted his

attention. But there was a limit to what he was willing to
let his future wife do. Or was he only dreaming to think
that she might someday marry him, with the more-
handsome Trueblood so available?

He had, during the war, been so necessary to its success
that he had never adjusted to the normalcy of peace. There
had always to be some trouble or intrigue to keep him going. This rebellion, as much as he dreaded it, was the only
thing besides Nancy to spark his interest in many months.

He usually did court a woman when he got in a state of
utter boredom and ended by making a damn fool of himself
when she chose someone better able to supply her needs.
So often that other was Trueblood, who always took a
woman away from Daniel with the admonition that she
wasn't right for him, as though he were removing a dish
of sweetmeats from the reach of a child.

It had happened again in England with Miss Helen Barr.
He had waited for the instant when Helen had realized
Trueblood was not serious, but that she had lost Daniel by
flirting with his brother. It was absurd that he should enjoy
her moment of regret so much. That was all he kept from
the relationship for himself. He tried to call to mind Helen's
face, but it melted together with all the other faces of need-
ful women he had known.

What he could call to mind quite clearly was Nancy's
innocent countenance, the impish smile that she wore like
a shield for her heart. What man could hurt her if she did
not take him seriously, did not let him take himself seriously? She was different. Why then had he expected her to
be like all the others? He had made a grievous mistake,
and it might cost him Nancy. He had acted like a stupid
fool and left her with his brother at the very moment when
his own anger might turn her toward Trueblood's sympathetic shoulder.

Daniel leapt to his feet and began running unerringly in
the direction of the camp. If only he could capture Nancy's
so well-guarded heart. Beyond getting back to her he did

not think as he ran full tilt along the deer trail, his rifle balanced in his right hand, his left keeping his shot pouch and powder horn from flapping. No doubt he would be too late. She would ignore him and turn her attention to his brother. Eventually, when Trueblood was through with her, Daniel would see that look of regret on her face. That he would not enjoy.

He smelled the smoke of the campfire before he was within calling distance. In his haste he didn't hear the rustling in the underbrush until he had collided with the source, a young buck in early rut. The animal hit him sideways, bowling him over. They nearly embraced, cracking heads together, but the deer had antlers and one sliced Daniel's jaw. The other caught in his jacket, and as the buck scrambled to his feet, Daniel was dragged with him. Fortunately, he realized what had happened quicker than the animal. Just as the beast flung his head to rid himself of what was blinding him, Daniel slid his knife across the animal's throat. He held on to the creature then, to keep it from killing him in return during its death throes. When all was still he disentangled himself, shedding the mangled coat and holding a handkerchief to his cheek until the blood had clotted.

He then proceeded to gut the animal out as though he had not just narrowly escaped death. He was feeling far from well, and he had no idea how much of the blood he was looking at was his victim's and how much was his own. His mind reared dizzily back to the worst of the fighting during the Revolution, when a man's life had been worth so little. Almost losing his again made him value it as he never had before.

He saved the liver in a cloth in his pouch, and tying a thong around the animal's antlers, he picked up his rifle and began dragging the deer toward the camp. It occurred to him that he could call for help, or even fire a shot, as Trueblood would. This close, they would certainly come to carry back the kill. But there was something most important

to him about making it back on his own this time. It had
to do with Nancy, with providing for her. Beyond that, his
befogged mind did not analyze.

His reappearance in camp caused all three of them to
gasp.

"I did not hear a shot," Trueblood said, looking his
bloodied brother up and down. "What did you do? Wrestle
this one to death?"

Daniel merely sent him a smoldering look and jumped
when Nancy appeared at his elbow with a leather bucket
of water and a cloth. "I can clean up myself," he said,
propping his rifle against a tree and ridding himself of his
shot pouch and powder horn.

"Of course, but I can see better than you," she said as
she persuaded him to sit and let her sponge off the gash
along his jaw. "I think you will not be able to shave for a
while. Will you let me put some stitches in this? It will
take Trueblood and Cullen some time to skin and cook
dinner, anyway."

"I do not care what you do," Daniel replied belligerently, knowing all the while that it mattered very much to
him that she cared. Each of her touches sent a small shudder through him.

"I am sorry to be hurting you," she said as she soaked
her needle and thread in a cup of brandy and then tried to
thread it. He saw her hands shaking and regretted his
brusqueness. He wondered if she would be equally rattled
if it were Trueblood she was sewing up.

"Would you like me to thread that for you?" Daniel
asked softly.

She looked at him with pain-filled eyes. "No, I can do
it." She took a deep breath and got the thick thread through
the eye, then bit her lip and set to work, holding the skin
down so as not to pull it.

"May I have the rest of that?" he asked, motioning toward the flask of brandy.

She handed him the amber bottle and paused in her stitching until he had drained it.

Once she had done with that wound she began cutting away his ruined shirt. Daniel had never known such exquisite torture. This sent a different set of chills through him, and Nancy misinterpreted the groan he emitted. He was the next thing to embarrassing himself in front of her. He bit his lip in concentration, trying to think of her as a child and not as a woman he desired very much.

"He's gored you," she announced in shock, when she had stripped the bloody shirt from his torso and washed him.

"Where?" Daniel asked in confusion, as Trueblood came to have a look at him.

"Under the collarbone," his brother said. "How deep is it, Daniel?"

"How the hell am I supposed to know?" Daniel tried to look down at the wound, but moving his head at all made his face hurt and his eyes blur.

"You did not even feel it?" Nancy asked worshipfully.

Daniel stared at her, trying to remember what the animal's rack had been like. "It cannot be more than an inch deep. That is as long as his point was after it branched."

"Oh, well, nothing to worry about then," Trueblood said with bravado as he watched Nancy put a poultice on the puncture. Daniel was surprised at his own compliance in letting her wash the gore off his body, bandage him up and get him into a clean shirt. She asked him more than once how he was feeling, a question he took to mean was he about to pass out?

"Fine," he whispered each time, but he always did manage to reply. The brandy was doing its work, the wounds had taken on a distant numbness, like his heart after one of his affairs, and he was beginning to feel more himself, with one important difference. He had not lost Nancy as he thought he would.

Daniel moved over to lean against one of the packs, and

Nancy brought him some of the freshly roasted liver and some bread, which he managed to eat, though he no longer felt hungry. He declined any of the steaks. He looked on in amusement as Trueblood discoursed between mouthfuls on the specimens he had collected that day. When the tea water was ready, Nancy sprinkled in some fragrant mint she had gathered and presented them each with a cup. Daniel received his most gratefully, since it sent a comfortable calm though him. There was another flavor as well—subtle, but not bothersome. He realized with surprise how much he trusted Nancy. Were she to hand him a cup of poison he would calmly drink it down. Nothing mattered except that she was still his, and he very much wanted to tell her so. But he was more tired now than desperate, so he said nothing.

"Ah," said Trueblood, and sighed. "There is nothing so aids the digestion as a strong cup of mint tea."

"Especially when one has as much to digest as you do," Daniel remarked in a slurred voice.

"It has many other properties as well," Nancy said to stop their bickering.

"Yes, one of the most harmless and wholesome of herbs," Trueblood agreed.

"Must you two ruin my enjoyment of this by discussing its medicinal purposes?" Daniel asked, bringing the cup to his lips again with his left hand.

"Sorry, Daniel," Nancy said sadly.

They fell into silence, and Nancy stirred the fire despondently, making Daniel regret that he had snapped at her after all her care of him. There was some whinnying among the ponies hobbled near the stream. Both Trueblood and Cullen took their rifles and went to see to them.

Daniel also took up his rifle and checked the priming. He got up carefully, making sure the dizziness was not going to overtake him, walked stiffly around the fire and came to sit beside Nancy.

"You are strangely quiet tonight," he said.

"But I thought you did not want to hear me. You must have a terrible headache."

"I merely wish you two could save your medical talk until I am not around."

"I suppose we take such things as a matter of course."

"For a woman you have too avid an interest in wounds and illnesses for my taste."

"But that is what I trained for. What use would I be to my papa if I could not dress a wound or dispel a fever? Do you need a fever medicine?"

Nancy reached for the coarse linen bag with the strings and sorted through it. Daniel realized she must have taken it off to better get at the contents, which amounted to much more than a needle and thread.

"And all out of your capacious pocket," Daniel said. "I am amazed at what you manage to carry under that petticoat of yours."

"Under my…" Nancy laughed outright.

"Damn! You see why I am such a risk in a drawing room."

"Is that why you pretend to be half-drunk? To excuse your behavior?"

"No, one can find out— I mean, yes, that is why."

"I see. You and Trueblood play off each other very well. If one did not know you, one would think the rivalry between you was serious."

"And what makes you think it is not?" Daniel asked, thinking again of Miss Helen Barr.

"If you suddenly decided to strike off the road in a completely illogical direction, Trueblood would follow you, would he not?"

"Yes, he would," Daniel answered, trying to comprehend her thoughts.

"He acknowledges you as the leader."

"No, he just has such a deplorable sense of direction he knows he shouldn't wander off alone."

"I see. Trueblood acknowledges many things you will not."

"Such as?"

"My competency, for one."

"Somehow I knew we would arrive back there."

"Where?"

"At you not being allowed to hunt."

"I was not purposely heading in that direction, but I think you might let me try. My feeling is that if you are going to eat flesh, you had best be up to doing the animal in."

"And skinning it out and butchering it, as well? I see."

"Of course."

"But you are a lady. Where did you learn army cooking, anyway?"

"I made it my business to learn it. I always expected Papa to come take me off to the wars the way he had Mama."

"And he disappointed you?"

"I suppose," Nancy drawled. "I know he must have fought bravely as a soldier, but he is not everyone's idea of a hero."

"And what is your idea of a hero? Someone like Trueblood? Some all-wise being who only walks the earth because heaven is not good enough for him?"

"No," she said softly, taking a stick and stirring the coals into another fire sculpture and creeping a little nearer to him. "A real hero would be quite unaware of himself, never satisfied with anything he had done, no matter how foolishly courageous he had been."

"What has Trueblood told you?" Daniel asked, staring at the embers she was turning.

"Nothing. A real hero would, I think, be rather impatient with the world and a hopeless idealist."

"A pure man?" Daniel asked, taking the stick from her and poking at the fire sadly.

"Only in his ideas. Shall we say an uncompromising man."

"And could you love such a man?"

"I think I could not help myself."

He turned his head suddenly to discover her face mere inches away. He kissed her tentatively and when she responded, he locked her in his good arm, letting the gun fall clumsily away. He forgot all about his wounds, the fire, Trueblood, the ponies and the rest of the world.

Some fragrance stirred his brain, like a wisp of fog reaching out to him, cooling and calming, to bathe away the feverish night horrors. Daniel raised an eyelid and realized it was Nancy's hair, the clean scent of her snuggled against his chest. She must have slept beside him to keep him from thrashing in the night, for her arms enfolded him still. She was awake, watching Trueblood build up the fire, waiting for Daniel to wake up as well.

He felt a strange reluctance to do so, to break the spell of her caring. Sleep was all he wanted so long as she was beside him, yet he greedily kept himself awake so as not to lose one moment of her nearness. He shut his eye gently and concentrated on feeling the pressure of her hands, the feathering of her hair against his cheek.

Cullen dropped a pan with a clang and Daniel jerked. Only the dead could have slept through that, he thought, as Nancy turned to look at him.

"How long have you been awake?" she asked.

"Since that clap of thunder." He threw off the blanket and groaned as Trueblood came to help him to his feet.

"This is such a pleasant spot," his brother said. "Perhaps we should rest the ponies here a day."

"Do not be absurd," Daniel grumbled. "Lose a day when the rains could overtake us at any time? Help me load up the horses."

"Trueblood and Cullen will have to do that if you want

to leave soon," Nancy said, bringing him his breakfast. "I must change your bandage and poultice."

"I see," he said, as he fortified himself with some of the oatcake Trueblood had cooked and a mug of tea. Daniel was getting used to the light touch of her hands—not that she would ever cease to set a wave of desire racing over him, but he could almost enjoy it now. And she had not turned to Trueblood. She had quite blatantly declared her interest in him. That was worth all the pain in the world. Daniel even let her fashion a sling for his arm, though he had no real need of one.

The day continued rainless, but the heat from the baking sun was such that the cool night had not been long enough to dispel it. Nancy knew they must be close to the end of their journey, for they had crossed two ridges of mountains and were once again in a muggy river valley. By late afternoon she was feeling sticky and impatient to make camp so that she could wash.

She saw Daniel wave Trueblood up to talk to him. Trueblood took the lead then, and Daniel dropped back beside her. He shook the sling away as though it were an annoyance and glanced toward his rifle in its holster. There was a tenseness to his face she had never seen before. Something was wrong, and he was not going to tell her what. She searched for any weakness in him, a pallor that might suggest his wound had broken open. If anything, he was like a coiled spring, more alert than she had ever seen him. Thirty yards in front, Trueblood sat his horse stiffly, his fall of black hair sliding across his shoulders as he looked from side to side.

She looked around her. Something was different. The forest looked the same—darker, perhaps, because the sun was about to set. Normally they would have chosen a campsite by now. Perhaps Daniel had some particular destination in mind. She looked sideways at his set profile and noticed his eyes scanning around him. He never moved his head, but he was watching. Then it hit her that the only sound was the thud of the ponies' feet on the packed trail. There were no birds fluttering in the trees, no tentative scuttling in the underbrush. Someone had passed this way before them and could be waiting.

The sound of running water came at her around a bend in the road. She had the most ominous feeling that something terrible was about to happen and that she could do nothing to stop it. Daniel reached for her bridle, a thing he had never done before. Trueblood splashed into the shallow, wide river ahead of them. His horse slipped and stumbled over the round rocks so badly that he slid off to wade in the knee-deep water rather than risk being pitched headlong into it.

At the first shot Daniel grabbed Nancy and pulled her into the stream with him. He snatched the rifle from his horse as it bolted. The men were all running, using the scattering ponies as a shield of confusion. Daniel had a tight hold on her arm and dragged her the rest of the way across the river and toward a pile of rocks partway up the embankment, from which Trueblood was already firing. The ponies had floundered downstream, trying to get away from the noise. Nancy and Daniel jumped in beside Trueblood, and Nancy flattened herself out of the way as Daniel took aim and fired. Cullen was within a leap of safety when a shot cut him down. There was still enough light to see the red stain spreading on his back.

The fire was heavy for a time, producing such a cloud of powder smoke that Nancy could scarcely see the trees where their attackers must be hiding. Cullen had been alive just an hour ago, joking with her, and now he was dead. She was certain of it. It was her worst nightmare sprung to life, but now that it was happening, she must think what to do about it. During a pause in the shooting, when both Trueblood and Daniel were reloading, she sprang out from behind the rocks to run to Cullen's body.

"Nancy! Are you mad?" Daniel shouted as he fired prematurely at the targets they could not see. Trueblood held his fire until she had stripped off Cullen's shot pouch and powder horn, then grabbed the rifle. She flung herself back among the rocks as Trueblood released his shot. She remembered Cullen had not fired, and handed the weapon to Daniel, who held it at the ready until Trueblood reloaded.

"He's dead. There's nothing you can do for him," Trueblood said.

"I know it. I wanted the gun and bullet pouch."

"To what purpose?" Daniel demanded, firing and hearing a satisfying yelp of pain.

"I can load it for you. Three shots are better than two."

"Just keep down," Daniel warned.

"I can see them now, Daniel," Trueblood said as he took another shot.

"What tribe are they?" Nancy asked.

"White Indians," Daniel said.

"What kind?" Nancy asked.

"Renegades," Trueblood answered. "White men who have taken to living like animals. They are far worse than any savages you might imagine."

"Does that mean they will scalp us?" She had her answer from their silence. "If they wanted the goods, they would have just taken the ponies, right?" Nancy finished loading and passed the rifle to Daniel.

"They may want you, as well," Daniel said. "Women are not all that common in these parts."

"You told me Indians were not, either," she accused.

"I just said—"

"I know, white Indians. That hardly matters, as they can kill us just as dead as any other kind."

"They are creeping up, Daniel," Trueblood warned.

"I see them."

Four leather-clad figures had been working their way through the sparse growth at the edge of the woods, then from bush to bush. As she reloaded, Nancy wondered why Daniel and Trueblood did not fire, then realized they must

be waiting for a definite kill. Finally the savages sprang out
of the last trace of cover and rushed their small redoubt.
Shots stopped two, and Daniel and Trueblood locked with
the others, thrashing about among the rocks. Nancy laid
one gun at the ready, not trusting herself to fire into the
melee, and was frantically loading another when a war
whoop came at her from behind. She fired prematurely and
ejected the ramrod, which she had failed to remove from
the barrel, into the man's chest.

Trueblood turned from the fray, wiping his bloodstained
knife, to find her staring at her handiwork, and went to pull
the implement out. He presented it to her with a flourish.
"Yours, I believe, Miss Riley."

"Thank you," she whispered through trembling lips.

Daniel had pushed the two bodies down over the rocks
and turned to gape at her as she calmly reloaded, amazed
that her hands were not shaking at all.

"How many do you reckon are left?" Trueblood asked.

"Five, but two of them are wounded," Daniel answered.

"We are evenly matched, then."

"Except I am nearly out of shot."

"There is some in Cullen's pouch," Nancy said. "Why
have they broken off the attack?"

"Too dark. They'll come again at first light, or later in
the night if there is a moon," Daniel replied with a dry
mouth.

"Then we can sleep by turns," she decided.

"I thought you were going to let me give the orders
here," he joked.

"It does not matter, Daniel. I could never sleep anyway," she said wearily.

"Enough adventure for you, Nancy?" Trueblood asked.

"I must confess, I have had my fill for a lifetime. Is it
certain they will attack again?" She rested her head against
the rifle she had reloaded.

"We have killed five of their own and the two wounded
may die, if I mistake not. I know they will try to finish us

off. Am I to assume that you can not only load like a seasoned soldier, but fire as well?'' Daniel asked to distract her.

"I can hit the mark four of five times—not a moving target, though," she said with a quaver to her voice.

"How about a living one?"

"I think we need not worry about that, Daniel," Trueblood said. "She already killed her man."

"Nancy, listen to me. You may load for us tomorrow, but I do not want you to fire," Daniel continued.

"Why not?" she asked.

"If Trueblood and I should both be killed, it would be better for you if you had not been seen to dispatch any of these fellows."

"Oh, we are going to die then," she concluded, thinking of her long blond hair adorning a savage's belt. "They will scalp us." She blurted it out when she had not meant to let the thought escape. It was like letting Daniel watch it happen, and she shuddered. She never wanted him to see that. Never!

"Nothing is certain," Trueblood said.

"Thank you for telling me." She raised her chin and took a deep breath.

"They will never kill you, Nancy," Daniel assured her, taking her hand. "You are worth too much to them. If we should be killed, you must surrender to them. They will carry you off and you may get a chance to escape in the future. It is the sensible thing to do. Don't you agree?"

She stared at him, at his blue eyes pleading in the last of the twilight. How could he think she would care about living if he were dead? The notion was absurd. Then it occurred to her what would happen—something Daniel had been so careful not to mention. "But they will rape me. Am I right?"

"We do not know that," Trueblood said.

"I know it," Nancy returned. "It is the way in war, to complete the victory."

"They may only hold you to ransom," Daniel said.

"Do not lie," she said gruffly, then regretted it as he turned his face away.

"If you cooperate with them," Trueblood offered, "you may be able—"

"There may be some sense in what you say, but there are things worse than dying," Nancy interrupted.

"I know you now," Daniel murmured, his weary voice hoarse with tears. "There is nothing you cannot bear."

"You do not speak from experience in this case. You are a man. You would not know that particular pain."

"Do you agree to give yourself up to them?" Daniel asked desperately.

"But what would be the point if both of you... No, I would as soon die with you."

"Do not be a fool, Nancy," Daniel pleaded. "You are a survivor. You can survive that, too."

"I will surrender to them on one condition."

"What is that?"

"Daniel, I want it to be you."

Trueblood chuckled.

"What?" Daniel asked.

"I do not want the first time to be horrible, even if every other time is. I do not want—"

"What in God's name are you suggesting?" Daniel demanded, recoiling from her.

"I want you to make love to me tonight, to cheat them out of that, at least."

"Do you realize what you are asking?"

"Yes, I know it is a lot to ask—"

"A lot to—! Why do you not ask my brother? I am sure he would be happy to service you."

"I swear you two will be arguing to the last breath," Trueblood said with another chuckle.

"Trueblood and I are friends. I think only of you in that way. It would save me a deal of pain if it were you, but if the prospect disgusts you so much..."

"But like this, without marrying…"

"I hardly think one of them will offer me marriage. If you make love to me tonight, I will do as you order. I mean to cheat them out of my virginity, at least."

"She has a point, Daniel. You will hurt her far less than all of them."

"I will not do it. I will not be coerced into such an act."

"Then I will die with you, and you cannot stop me."

"No!"

"I am sorry, Daniel. It was too much to ask of any man, even you."

"What do you mean, even me?"

"You are the only man I have ever loved."

"Brother," Trueblood interjected, "this may be the last thing you do on this earth. Let it be an act of love, not killing."

"I do love you, Nancy," Daniel vowed.

"I will sit on the other side of the rocks and keep watch," Trueblood said as he slithered into the darkness.

"They will shoot you," Nancy whispered.

"There is no moon yet. They will never see me."

Daniel stripped off his coat and threw it down on a flat table of limestone that presented itself like an altar. He would have only unbuttoned the flap of his drop-front breeches, except he saw that Nancy meant to disrobe, to take this last act in her young life to its fullest. He could do no less than make it all that she hoped.

"This is insane," he said, helping her with her petticoats. She surprised him by having secreted a pair of leather breeches under everything else. So that was why she never got saddle sore.

"Even if they come in the night, what difference does it make if we are naked or not?" she asked.

"Precious little. You are not wearing stays," he commented distractedly, then laughed at the absurdity of worrying over that.

"They lace up the back and I could never…"

"Never do it yourself. Of course not."

"Daniel, I did not even know you were wounded," she said, regarding the gash on his upper arm and reaching for the large pocket sack he had untied from her waist.

"A scratch—no more."

She knelt to tie a bandage around it. The only articles he now wore were his bandages. Then she lay down under him like a sacrifice, and he kissed her, gently at first. He wanted to do this properly, but the prospect of imminent scalping caused him to hasten his kisses to the breasts he had coveted for so many miles.

"Did you mean it on the ship, what you said about the ring?" she asked languorously, twisting a lock of his hair around one finger.

"Yes, I meant it."

"Then it does not matter about the rest of it." She stroked his back.

"There should be a bed and flowers," Daniel said hopelessly.

"I want no other marriage bed than this."

"All women are not the same," he said in amazement. "Some are sadly wanting in expectations."

"And conduct?"

"I am proud to be your husband," he said, taking her hand. "I take thee, Nancy, as my lawful wife until death do us part," he said softly in the way of the frontier. He knew the words would bind them together as legally as though a minister had said them.

"I take thee, Daniel, as my husband until death us do part." Her voice was tearfully brave.

He lowered himself over her and was surprised when she coiled her legs around him. They felt so warm and alive. He entered her as slowly as his pounding heart allowed. One convulsive surge penetrated her and wrenched a gasp from her that stopped him.

"I am sorry. My damned impatience again."

"Now I know," she said in awe.

"Know what? Have I hurt you?"

"No. Now I know why women have children. There is a hunger, a wonderful hunger. It is irresistible," she said, wriggling her hips under him. "Is there more?"

"More," Daniel said with a chuckle. "Yes, much more." His member sought all the soft, secret places he knew a woman contained, and he was met not with softness, but with hot, strong surges of muscle contractions that made him groan. He stopped her gasps with a kiss—his last, he thought. These same shivering contractions might in the course of nine months deliver to them a child, if the world were a just place. But the world was cruel, too cruel to imagine being happy in it for more than the time it took to love a woman.

"Daniel, you are amazing," she whispered. "How long—"

"For once, Nancy dear, do not ask any questions."

When the sounds of lovemaking had died away, Trueblood turned and looked on the sleeping couple like some benign god. Seeing them entwined under the cold moonlight like a couple of alabaster statues, he spread Nancy's cloak over them and laid their wet clothes out on the rocks to dry. "Peace, Daniel. Sweet dreams, Nancy dear."

Chapter Six

Nancy opened her eyes to sunlight dancing through leaves and the smell of something good cooking. She looked at Daniel and smiled. In sleep his dark lashes were even more entrancing. She could hear Trueblood moving about, she could see Daniel's rifle propped ready for the attack, she could hear a pony munching grass on the other side of the rocks. She knew that at any moment the peaceful morning might be split by a scream, the world torn asunder by shots, the reek of powder and the flow of blood. But just at this moment she would not have traded places with any woman on earth. Daniel was beside her and alive still, and this moment would be with her in this world and the next.

He had pillowed his head on his arm, and she lay likewise, watching him. His dark growth of beard made him look roguishly desperate. She wondered if she would ever enjoy the suspense of watching him shave again. His eyes moved under his lids and he rolled onto his back with a sigh of satisfaction as though he, too, could die peacefully after the previous night. Her cloak had fallen away to reveal the bandages wrapped around his tan shoulder and arm. She smiled and, unable to resist any longer, stroked his cheek.

He jerked awake, his lips parting as he remembered. "Nancy!" He kissed her briefly, then leaped up to scramble into his clothes. She watched his hard-muscled form greedily until it was hidden by boots, breeches and shirt. He crawled to the top of the rocks and searched the clearing with his intent gaze. Nancy came out of her reverie, hastening to dress herself, and sorry now that she had disturbed his rest.

"Anything?" Daniel asked Trueblood.

"I could not tell if they were there or no. But we must eat and drink. I did venture as far as the river to get water."

"And no one fired at you?"

"No."

"That means nothing."

"I know. Eat. Then we will reconnoiter."

As Nancy came to wash her hands and face with the water in the leather bucket, Daniel took time only to grab a piece of yesterday's venison Trueblood had seared. Then he took his rifle and slipped out of the rocks through the back way into the woods.

"Tea, Miss Riley?" Trueblood asked in the grand manner of an English butler.

"Yes, thank you," Nancy agreed, feeling wonderfully refreshed and rested. She seated herself primly on a rock near the fire Trueblood had built on the river side of the outcropping and accepted the tin cup from him. She was enjoying being served her wedding breakfast and sprinkled some extra herbs from her pocket into her tea.

"If our alarm was false yesterday, I apologize for making you think your life was in danger." He tossed another piece of gray driftwood onto the fire and squatted on a rock.

"But I, too, considered the alarm genuine and our fate sealed." She took a nibble of oatcake, marveling at how good it tasted. She would never again take even the smallest pleasure for granted.

Trueblood stared at her, his dark eyes intent under furrowed brows. "Then you meant to break your promise. You did not mean to give yourself up."

She lifted her eyes to stare proudly back at him. "How could I let another man spoil that? And, in spite of playing tea party, the alarm is still very real,'' she said, staring at the edge of the forest from which yesterday's attack had come.

"You may be carrying Daniel's child now. You must think of that."

"Do not worry. He has not got me with child.'' She looked shyly down into her tea.

"How can you know that? Unless…you took precautions…. Not a sponge, surely, but the right mix of herbs in your tea?''

"As it happens, I do know a mixture that works without doing any permanent harm.''

"Not pennyroyal, then?''

"No. I will give you the recipe if you like.''

"I should be used by now to your preparing for any eventuality. But you could not have anticipated last night—''

"Trueblood! What are you thinking? That I planned to seduce Daniel?''

"No, but why else…?''

"You tell me you are taking me to a land with few women and I am to be at an inn with the worst of men. I had to prepare for the possibility of rape, just as I intended to prepare myself if I had been following a war train.''

Trueblood smiled. "Is there anything you have not thought of?''

"Women are usually raped when an army is overrun.''

"But that is not always the way it happens.''

"No, but I have found that being prepared for the worst case means that nothing shocks me so very much.''

"And that you are not afraid. I know, but really—''

"No, I am still afraid, but that passes quickly. Surely other women consider such things.''

"No, I believe you are unique in that respect.''

"Trueblood,'' she whispered. "Someone is coming!''

"It is Daniel with the rest of the horses and ponies.''

Trueblood rose to take the broken ropes and begin to string the ponies together again.

"They were grazing around the bend of the river," Daniel said darkly.

"I do not understand," Nancy said. "If they attacked us for our goods, why didn't they take them with them?"

"Most likely they could not find them in the night," Daniel lied, without meeting her eyes.

Trueblood gently carried Cullen's body to load it onto his horse, then began to tighten the pack saddles on the ponies. The enemy dead were still laying where they had fallen, and Nancy was shocked that she had not even noticed them until she thought of Cullen. She hoped Daniel and Trueblood had no intention of giving them a Christian burial, for they did not deserve one. She assumed Daniel's thoughts must be running along those same lines, for when he turned to her he was looking as black as thunder.

"Where, if I may ask, did you learn to load rifles with such speed?" he demanded as though it were an accusation.

"I got Uncle's gamekeeper to teach me. Well, he taught me how to load. I practiced doing it fast on my own. I had heard it would be useful for a woman in an army train to know."

"Do you have any idea what your station would have been if you had convinced your foolish father to take you to war with him?" Daniel tightened the cinches on their horses and propped his rifle nearby, ready to take up when he mounted.

"I suppose I would have cooked and done washing for him."

"The officers have their ladies, the sergeants their wives and the soldiers their women," Daniel recited.

"But I would not have been any of those."

"You would have soon enough," he said, coming toward her to help her mount.

"And which category would I have fallen into?" Nancy demanded, her hands on her hips.

"I would have hoped you would have had the sense to marry an officer." He whisked her off the ground and tossed her up onto her horse.

"A captain, perhaps," she teased, as she gathered up the reins. "But I meant to go to help, and I would have."

Trueblood walked toward them, making placating motions. "It is not all that easy to keep these ponies calm after last night with you two shouting at the top of your lungs."

"Just because I did something useful," Nancy declared, then dropped her voice, "Daniel has to get on his high horse...."

"Well, Daniel. You must admit we would have been hard-pressed without her."

"Next you will be wanting to let her hunt as she demanded," Daniel hissed as he mounted and gathered up the pony leads.

"Can you?" Trueblood asked.

"Well, of course I can. What would be the point of knowing how to load one if I could not hit a target?"

"Then you should carry Cullen's rifle," Trueblood said, handing it to her. "How is your arm, Daniel?" He was clearly doing his best to distract the two from their dispute.

"It hurts. Now may we finally leave this place?"

Nancy sighed impatiently and replied, "The ball passed through and there was a deal of bleeding, but no vital spot has been touched. In any case a good bit of bleeding helps cleanse the wound."

"Do you think so?" Trueblood asked, staring at Daniel's retreating back as his brother led his string of ponies onto the track.

"Oh, yes, for a healthy man, a little bloodletting does no harm." Nancy raised her voice. "It relieves the spleen, or so they say."

"Spleen?" Daniel demanded, twisting his head around and then grimacing at the pain this caused. "I have every right to be angry."

"Why?" Nancy urged her horse and pack beast to come alongside Daniel.

"Because you trapped me into making love to you."

"If, upon consideration, you do not wish to ally yourself with a sergeant's daughter, I am sure I will not hold you to a promise made under duress."

"Not hold me? Let me tell you this, Nancy Riley. I have every intention of making you my wife before the world, and it will be a proper wedding."

"Where is our difficulty then? I agree with you."

"If you do, it will be the first time."

"Not quite the first," Nancy said more softly, but Daniel took no notice of her, so she dropped back from him. The brothers had each to lead six animals now, plus Cullen's. Nancy thought of demanding that they give her two more ponies, but they could be haggling all day if she did, so she let it pass. She knew what Daniel would whisper to Trueblood later on the trail—that robbery had not been the motive for the attack. Someone did not want one of them to get to Pittsburgh. The question was, had they shot up the band so badly that they had given up or had they only moved down the road to a more advantageous ambush point? She unslung Cullen's rifle and carried it across the saddle, as the brothers did, checking the priming to make sure there was enough powder and that it was quite dry.

Daniel led the way, with Nancy in the middle. Where the road was not overgrown, Trueblood moved up beside Nancy and they rode along the two wagon ruts rather than the center hoof track. They had gone only a few miles when they turned south off the main road onto a deer path. Nancy looked inquiringly at Trueblood, but supposed this was some subterfuge to evade those who might lie in wait for them. The deer track crossed another river with narrower banks. The footing was treacherous, but the water not deep. It took all Nancy's poise not to gawk about her, but to keep her mind on the slippery rocks and lead her horse by the safest ford. It wasn't until they had regained a main road that Trueblood could ride up beside her and inform her that they had left Forbes's Road and come south to finish their journey by Braddock's Road.

"Why is Daniel so angry at me, Trueblood? We might have been dead and we are not. I should think he would be joyful."

"I thought he took it rather well," Trueblood replied.

"You expected Daniel to turn surly?" She looked up at him in surprise, then forced her attention back to the road and the surrounding forest.

"Yes, as soon as he perceived we were out of danger. I knew his mind would gnaw away at his decision and convince him he had done the wrong thing."

"Does he often second-guess himself?"

"Yes, he always has regrets no matter how the business turns out."

"Ah, well, it is fortunate then that you are only engaged in trade, not something earthshaking."

Trueblood gaped, then grinned and chuckled, drawing a dark look from Daniel some thirty yards ahead. "It is part of your charm, Nancy, that you remain unconscious of your effect. You amuse, startle, shock even, to the point where my normally impassive face must show it...."

"Who says I am unconscious of my effect?" she asked with a superior smile. "It is stupid for him to be angry that we were not attacked again."

"That is not what is grieving him. He is blaming himself for ruining you."

"How absurd, when it was my idea."

"Nevertheless, it would be unwise to speak of it."

Nancy considered Trueblood's advice in thoughtful silence until they came to another ford. The river was broader here, but shallow at this time of year. Nancy stared around her suspiciously, but neither Daniel or Trueblood showed any unease. They merely led their ponies across and began to ride uphill. Nancy pushed up beside Daniel to ask, "When will we get to Pittsburgh?"

"We are not going to Pittsburgh. I am taking you directly to your father's inn."

"Is that not in Pittsburgh?"

"No, it is on the south side of the river. I do not know my—"

Nancy did not wait for him to finish, but plagued him with all manner of questions about the inn. After two hours of fending off her interrogation, he finally said, "There it is, the White Horse." He nodded at a two-story stone building with a central chimney stack. The windows were deep set with green-painted shutters, and the wood shake roof had been newly repaired. The building sat solidly fifty yards off the road, with such an aspect of complacency Nancy was hard-pressed to find anything wrong with it.

"I had thought it would be in town," she quibbled.

"Well, it is not," Daniel replied tiredly as he dismounted with a grunt.

"And I thought it was an inn, not a tavern."

"What difference does it make?" Daniel snapped.

"I do not mind running an inn, but I draw the line at being a tavern wench."

Daniel gaped and looked suitably horrified at this thought.

"I see your point," Trueblood intervened. "I shall repaint the sign for you."

"Is it a good location?" Nancy persisted.

"I rather doubt your father picked it for location," Daniel said. "I would not think you would get much more than local custom here."

Riley appeared in the doorway, lighting his pipe, and Nancy slid off her horse unassisted to run to him. "Papa, you will never guess what happened!"

Daniel stared at Riley, who had come to embrace his daughter. It was late afternoon and the man had already imbibed. Daniel rubbed his eyes tiredly, prepared for Riley's anger.

"We were attacked by renegades, but we managed to fight them off."

"Are ye hurt, Nancy girl?"

"No, but Daniel is wounded, and one of his men was killed." This last recollection subdued Nancy's excitement.

"Come inside, come in. Luce will take care o' the ponies and the body. Poor fellow. And what a fright for ye, child."

When Trueblood saw the sullen hired man who lounged out from under the oak tree, he waved Daniel toward the inn and led the animals around the back toward the un-chinked log stable himself.

"What a bad bit o' luck," Riley said, pouring Daniel a whiskey and very nearly doing the same for his daughter as they seated themselves at the table closest to the fireplace. "Ah, Nancy, ye would like a nice spot o' tea, I expect. Ellie, if there's any water hot, make up a pot o' tea," he commanded to a pregnant girl who stood on the broad hearth stirring a cauldron over the fire.

Daniel watched Nancy appraise the state of the girl's pregnancy, calculate that her father could have had nothing to do with it and turn her attention back to the Irishman.

"I do wonder if 'twas the same bunch wot attacked Dupree," Riley mused.

"Dupree was attacked?" Daniel asked skeptically. "Where?"

"Not but five miles from here, by wot he says. But he lost a bit o' blood. So there's no telling how far he wandered. Have ye yer bandages by ye, Nancy girl? He lies in the common sleepin' room, above."

Nancy made her way past the settle and other benches and tables to the precarious corner stairway that spiraled to the upper level. Daniel was amazed the man could send his daughter to deal with such a mess alone. He rose to follow her, suspicious that Dupree might have been one of their attackers.

"Can I get ye a drop more whiskey, Tallent? I want ta thank ye for gettin' my Nancy here. I been that worried."

"Later, perhaps. I want to have a word with Dupree," Daniel said as he absently carried the tin tankard up the steps with him.

Nancy had already exposed an ugly wound on the man's side, making the semiconscious form shiver and groan. "There is a rib shot through, but I cannot tell if the bullet is still in there or not."

Daniel looked dispassionately at the buckskin leggings the man still wore and asked, "How many attacked you?" as though it were a command.

Dupree focused his eyes on Daniel and flinched.

"I have scarcely touched you yet," Nancy chided.

"What did they look like?" Daniel persisted.

"Could the interrogation please wait until I am finished?" Nancy asked.

Daniel left Nancy to her work and went to see what he could get out of the hired man. He had rather not reveal to Riley that there might be some reason for the attack other than robbery.

Trueblood entered the newly built stable with a half-dozen of the ponies he had been watering at the stream. "If you are looking for the hired man, he went off to tend to the still as soon as he saw I was doing his work, but he knows nothing. Someone dumped Dupree at the doorstep early this morning."

"I did not think Dupree could have run far like that," Daniel replied.

"Nancy is preparing for surgery. I will finish feeding and watering the ponies if you have a mind to go help her."

"No stomach for it, Daniel?" Trueblood asked.

"Not where Dupree is concerned. I might slip up."

* * *

Getting seventeen head of stock watered and fed to his satisfaction took most of an hour. When Daniel went back into the inn, Nancy and Trueblood were sitting at the table nearest the fireplace being served by Ellie, who filled another porringer with venison stew and set it before Daniel.

"Why are you not eating with us, Ellie?" Nancy asked the girl.

"I've no appetite just now, miss. I'll be hungry later."

"You look tired, child. I think you should lie down for a rest."

"Do ye mean it, miss?"

"Yes. Where do you sleep?"

"In there, the storeroom. 'Tis…handy." Ellie wandered in that direction, looking back over her shoulder to make sure her new mistress was serious about letting her rest. When Nancy merely smiled at her, she went into the room and closed the door.

"And there is a lock on the door," Nancy said to the brothers, "though she must have been caught without once."

"You can minister to Ellie at your leisure," Daniel said. "How is Dupree?"

"Barring infection, he should survive."

"Did he say anything?" Daniel demanded, causing Nancy to cast him a suspicious look.

"Something about paying when the job was done," Trueblood replied.

"Nothing else?"

"The gray horse and rider," Trueblood said ponderously.

"What did he mean by that?" Daniel wondered.

"This place, of course," Nancy said, as she went to get hot water for more tea. "Because of the gray stone of which it is built. And that huge chimney stack squats on it like a rider on a horse. Oh, yours, I believe," she said, producing a misshapen lead ball from the pocket under her skirt and plunking it down on the table in front of Daniel.

Daniel stared at her. He was a fool to get Nancy involved in this. She was far too perceptive for her own good. Why could he not remember that about her?

"Actually, I believe it is mine," Trueblood said, picking it up from the table and rolling it between his fingers.

"Where is your father?" Daniel demanded. "I must speak with him."

"Tending the still, which I take it has been rebuilt at some distant, secret place, since the one across the road was burned. He went back there as soon as he had eaten." She poured the water in the teapot and sat down on the bench by Daniel.

"Tax collectors?" Trueblood inquired.

"No, according to Papa, the previous owners paid the tax. It was the Whiskey Boys who burned them out. They said next time it would be the inn. Even made of stone I suppose they could set fire to it inside." She glanced up at the broad oak beams of the ceiling.

"Explains why someone gave up such a good location. Did you take it from your father that this was a common occurrence?" Trueblood asked.

"It has convinced him it would be safer not to pay the tax, but that would be his tendency, anyway."

"I must speak to him," Daniel repeated.

"You are going to stay the night, are you not?" Nancy asked.

"Yes," he replied, wondering if she was going to demand he perform his husbandly duty again.

"Besides the common sleeping room, there is a large bedroom upstairs you and Trueblood may have. I shall take the small room over the storeroom." She could feel Daniel's stare upon her.

"It might be well for one of us to keep an eye on Dupree," Trueblood cautioned as he picked up some of their baggage and started toward the small twisted stairway.

"I can hear him through the wall," Nancy replied. "Besides, I am pretty sure that common sleeping room is infested with fleas. I shall have those straw ticks out and burned tomorrow.''

"I knew how it would be if she ever got the tiller in her hand, Daniel. May we know the charge for a night's lodging, Mistress Riley?'' Trueblood teased as he stood poised on the bottom step.

"Nothing, of course. You are our guests. Truth to tell, I do not think Papa is at all interested in making money off the inn. I have a feeling he spends all his time at that still.''

"Leaving you to take charge here,'' Daniel brooded. "I do not like it.''

"Well, I am needed, at least.''

"There must be someone in Pittsburgh who can marry us,'' Daniel said possessively. "Come with us tomorrow.''

"I have been thinking about it, and I think we should wait awhile before we formalize our vows.'' She had the courage not to cringe at the anger that flared in his blue eyes.

"Why in God's name would you want to wait?''

"If it is known that I am your wife, someone trying to get at you could use me against you.''

"Who would be wanting to get at me?'' Daniel asked lightly, avoiding eye contact.

"Dupree, for one.''

"She is right, Daniel. She is much safer as plain Miss Riley for now.'' Trueblood continued up the stairs.

"How long?'' Daniel demanded, leaning across the table toward her.

"As long as you were going to wait when we were in Philadelphia, until this business is over.''

Daniel shot her a reproachful look.

"That is what you were waiting for, was it not?''

"Yes,'' he said with resignation. "Just how much do you know about this business?''

"Very little.'' She poured him a mug of tea, knowing the mint would calm him. "And the less the better. What I do not know cannot hurt you.''

"And you will stay here and keep that Lucifer fellow at bay? How the devil are you to get him to work for you?"

"His name is Lucius, and if he does not work, he does not eat. Some things are very simple, Daniel."

"I still do not like it."

"Daniel, I have been used to running my aunt's household in Somerset, and there were twelve servants there."

"Here, take this pistol. It looks dangerous, anyway."

"Why, thank you. I may need it, as it appears my first customers approach now."

The three men came in noisily and seated themselves at another table, each casting a furtive glance at her and Daniel. Nancy was on the point of rising to see to their wants when Ellie reappeared from the storeroom, automatically went to the board where the whiskey was kept and poured a quantity into tankards for them. There were jugs of whiskey lined up on the trestle table by the end wall, along with two sideways barrels with taps that Nancy surmised would contain small beer and ale. Not cider, she thought, in this wilderness. There probably were not mature orchards here yet. Other than a table near the storeroom for cooking and one settle by the fireplace, the three tables and sets of benches comprised the only furniture of the room. There was an equally rustic area on the other side of the double fireplace that squatted in the middle of the house, but since no fire had been kindled there Nancy thought it was only used if a party sought some privacy.

As Trueblood thumped back downstairs, he drew stares from all three men, and one of them motioned to Ellie. She came to refill his tankard and answered a whispered question.

"So ye're the Nancy we've been hearin' about?" the man said as he strolled to the table. "I'm John Spode. This is Hiram and Ned Johnson."

"Yes, I am Nancy Riley. This is Daniel Tallent and—"

"Trueblood!"

Nancy gaped as Trueblood raised a hand in greeting, then

sat stoically staring at the teapot as though he had never seen one before. He had said his name so gutturally she had scarcely recognized it, and she wondered if he had interrupted to keep her from revealing that he and Daniel were brothers.

"I am a trader from Philadelphia," Daniel explained, shaking hands with Spode and the other men as they came over.

Nancy leaned back from the table to gaze raptly at the impassive Trueblood and wondered what part he was playing.

"Trueblood is my guide," Daniel explained.

Nancy turned away to hide her smirk at this unlikely claim and revealed the small pistol she had thrust into the waistband of her skirt.

"What on earth is that for?" Ned Johnson asked.

"This little thing? Why, I must keep order somehow. In case someone should not wish to pay." She drew the pistol out and sighted along the barrel. "Then he will have to pay another way."

Ned took a step back. "Ye'd shoot him?"

"Only as a last resort. I would prefer to put him to work chopping wood or some such thing."

"Well, we all have a running tab," Hiram said defensively.

"Yes," Ellie piped up, holding a piece of board for Nancy to see. "I keep a count here."

"Well, I assumed regular customers would have an account. My papa is an easy and likable man, do you not think so?"

"Yes, a very merry fellow," Ned agreed.

"But not what one would call a careful fellow. That is why he needs me, to collect his accounts."

"I see. We usually barter with Riley. Is he at the still, then?" Hiram asked.

"What still?" Nancy asked coyly, with a prim smile.

"What still? Ye're a right one, Nancy," Ned said with a grin.

"If by 'right one' you mean I am sharp, yes I am."

"And a better-than-average shot," Daniel interjected, causing Nancy to raise an eyebrow at him. "We were attacked by renegades a day from here and they killed one of my men. He lies out in the stable."

"Attacked?" Hiram gasped. "'Tis years since the Indians, yerself excepted, sir," he said with a nod to Trueblood, "have been a problem. Now they have taken to raiding the outer farms again."

"They were white."

"Renegades! Scum o' the earth. Neither white nor Indian will have aught to do with 'em. Did they take yer goods?"

"We managed to save those," Daniel said sullenly.

"Ye should be glad then."

"Trueblood's pride is wounded, too. That always makes him surly."

"To be sure, to be sure."

"And Dupree lies above us with his ribs shot up," Daniel added.

"What's the world coming to? I thank ye for the warning. We'll be sure to bar our doors this night."

There was stomping and a rumble of talk from the back door that led in past the storeroom. The three customers tensed as though they expected an attack.

"Well, well, gentlemen, a good evening ta ye," Riley said, as he tossed his hat on a peg. "Ye've met my dotter and the good men who brought her to me? Luce, the woodpile's low. Get some and build up the fire fer us." Riley rubbed his hands together. "Wot are we drinking, gentlemen?"

"Good Monongahela rye, sir," Ned replied, raising his mug.

"Let's all have a refill on the house, then—I'll get it, Ellie. Sit ye down."

Nancy took the opportunity, while the men toasted each

other, to withdraw to the hearth, where Ellie sat on the settle, and confer about their bill of fare.

"I've put some barley on ta soak for breakfast, though yer da likes a bit of ham fried up, too. I was meanin' to put a big venison stew on tomorrow for dinner that'll do for supper as well. We don't have nothing fancy, but we don't serve a lot of meals unless they be to travelers. Mostly men comes here to drink."

"So I see."

"Miss?"

"Yes?"

"Will I be turned out?"

"Whatever makes you ask that? You seem to be managing rather well under trying circumstances."

"Luce said when the new mistress came I would be turned out if he did nay put in a good word for me."

"Luce must think me unusually stupid."

Ellie blushed and pushed her limp brown hair behind her ears.

"Is it Luce's child?"

"Aye, miss."

"Do you want to marry him?"

"Aye. But he won't. He says he has nay money ta raise a child."

"Typical male logic. Would he have you if you had a dowry, a bride portion?"

"Where am I ta get any money?"

"Never mind that. The only question is, do you want him?"

"I've always wanted him. That's why I..." She looked furtively toward her room.

"Very well, I shall see what I can do."

They were interrupted by Luce, stomping through the back door and dumping a pile of wood in the box near the fire. He shot Nancy a triumphant smile as though he had done something extraordinary. Ellie got up to close the door behind him.

Nancy could see why Ellie was attracted to him. He was handsome and masculine, though not of Daniel's height. She might have let his insolence pass had not Luce, once he had built up the fire, said, "What shall we do with her, mistress, now she has gone and got herself in trouble?"

Both women colored up, but Nancy's blush was impelled by rage, and the Tallents watched raptly as she rose to blast him.

"What do you mean we, boy?"

"I'm not a boy."

"You have spoken out of turn. If you have any wits about you, you will be silent now."

"I don't know wot she's told you, but I'm innocent."

"Innocent of what?" Nancy demanded sternly, crossing her arms and letting him see the pistol.

"O' gettin' her with child."

"No one has accused you of that, boy. I would not think you capable of it. Now go on about your work."

"But—but wot will you do with her?"

"Treasure her for the hard worker I can see she is. Nothing else counts for much with me."

"Mayhap she'll lose the child," Luce warned.

"That is hardly likely. I have delivered fourteen babies and all but one safely. Her child will be the joy of our household until I find her a husband."

"Not likely!" he scoffed.

"I am nearly as good at matchmaking as I am at delivering babies," Nancy boasted. "With the right bride price she will have her pick of men. After all, she has already proven her worth as a mother."

"I'll not be forced into marriage with her," Luce said.

"Most assuredly not. You were never under consideration, boy."

Ellie gaped at her until Nancy gave her a wink. Daniel guffawed from his table, provoking chuckles among the Johnsons and Spode at the other table. Riley nodded approvingly.

"Well...well, just so you know."

"I told you, Luce," Riley said. "You'll have to tow the line now that my Nancy's in charge."

Luce shot his employer a disbelieving look.

"If you have finished tracking in mud for the night, you may sweep that floor."

"I'll not. That's woman's work."

"As I am well able to do a man's work, you had best be able to do a woman's, especially as you are the one who undid Ellie's scrubbing. A man who has no respect for women's work has no place in this house. I cannot make myself clearer than that, can I?"

Luce glared at her, but did take up the twig broom and begin raking mud and pieces of bark toward the hearth as he grumbled to himself.

"Mistress Riley," Ned Johnson said as he approached the settle, tugging nervously at the shapeless lapels of his rough coat. "Did I hear ye say ye had birthed babies?"

"Yes, I helped deliver so many of my nephews and nieces, it is an avocation for me."

"My wife's on the point o' havin' our first child. Mother's there with her, but feeling very uneasy, her bein' so old and Dora bein' so young...."

"I should be glad to come when her pains start. Is it far?"

"Not but a few miles. I will bring a horse for ye...and pay ye."

"My fee is small. You can well afford it."

"Miss Riley," Daniel said warningly, "may I have a word with you?"

"Yes, Mr. Tallent, what is it? More whiskey, perhaps."

"I have had quite enough."

When she approached the table, he demanded in a low voice what the devil she meant by hiring herself out as a midwife.

"Daniel," she whispered, "you have no idea how much

I can learn if I get to talk to some of the women of the community. I can be your agent in Pittsburgh.''

"But I want no such thing!" he said vehemently.

The others looked up at this, and Trueblood eyed Daniel and Nancy with mischief dancing in his eyes.

"Well, if you will not let me treat your wound it will have to be Trueblood," she warned in her new voice of command. "Let me give him some lint and some hot water for washing it."

"Come, Daniel," Trueblood said in the blunt, guttural tone that made Nancy stare at him again.

"Good Lord," Riley said, "I was forgetting Nancy said ye was shot. Where did they hit ye, boy?"

"Just a scratch," Daniel said, glancing toward his arm.

"Well, there are scratches and there are scratches. Best have it cleaned. I should know. I was a soldier."

Trueblood silently picked up the small pot of steaming water and the roll of bandages Nancy thrust at him and looked suggestively toward the stairs.

Trueblood pulled a rough stool toward the bed where Daniel sat. "For an intelligence officer you seem rather sparse on intelligence, little brother." He undid the bandage and began to wash away the dried blood.

"I will not have my wife working at a common tavern and selling herself as a midwife— Ouch!"

"Too hot? Unless I miss my guess, she will be safe enough here. She is already lording it over the men, including Luce. Ellie has become instantly devoted to her, and if word gets around that she is a skilled midwife, she will be esteemed in a community that at my last remembrance boasted only a few doctors for nearly...what? Nine hundred or a thousand people?"

"It is too much to ask. I cannot see her work like this."

"You will not be here to see it. Once we have sold our goods, bought whiskey or pelts and gathered what information we can, we must hie us back to Philadelphia."

"Trueblood, I cannot leave her," Daniel said desperately.

"Hmm. Your arm is worse than I thought."

"Do not be absurd." Daniel glanced at the wound. "The bullet only tore through the muscle. I shall be fine in a few days."

"Not if I say you will not, and you are observed to be wearing a sling. I see you would be no use to me at all on the way back to Philadelphia. I shall hire Luce to help with the ponies. You will just have to stay here until we return." Trueblood wrapped the gash with finality and rifled through their packs until he found a length of cloth for a sling.

Daniel's eyes lit with understanding. "I suppose I could malinger just this once. I could certainly gather more information if I had an excuse to stay. But, no, Trueblood. What if you were to get lost again?"

"I think it most unfair for you to bring that up. So long as I eventually deliver your report to Norton, you should have no complaint. Well?"

"I do not think they would believe me wounded that badly." Daniel tested the sling. It was on the same side as the unfortunate encounter with the deer, and he remembered how much more he had enjoyed having Nancy dress his wound than his brother. Why then had he been so disgruntled? Perhaps he was not used to having someone care about him—not a woman at any rate.

"I shall have Nancy tell them the bullet grazed the bone and she has grave fears about you keeping your arm. They will believe her. Why, if you play your cards right, you could stay the winter. With me carrying news to Norton at regular intervals, all will be well...Daniel...Daniel? If worse comes to worse she can always cut your arm off."

"I suppose there is merit in what you say."

"You have not even been attending me. For once your duty jumps with your inclination. You will not be on tenterhooks about Nancy since you can look after her yourself."

"Mmm," Daniel said, and Trueblood knew he had won his brother's agreement, however passive. Trueblood did not bother to mention that looking after Nancy was a great deal more disquieting than a journey to Philadelphia in the foulest of weather. Indeed, he would be able to travel back with a light heart, knowing he had stuck his brother with the more onerous task.

Chapter Seven

The next morning after breakfast, Riley read a short service and they buried Cullen in the grave Luce had been prevailed on to dig in the family plot behind the inn. The fine autumn air was pungent with the warm smell of dying leaves and the smoke tailing out of the inn's chimney. Trueblood began to lead out the ponies he had loaded for the trip to Pittsburgh. Daniel pretended to help him, though Riley thought he was more in the way with his bad arm than any use.

"Where might yer brother be goin'?"

"Jackson's warehouse in Pittsburgh," Daniel answered.

"Could ye bring back a load o' barrels fer me?" Riley asked Trueblood. "I've had 'em made at a cooper there, but can nay leave the still long enough ta go fer them."

"What about Luce?" Daniel asked.

"I can nay trust him ta get there and back sober, or ta watch the still. I had some hopes ta train him in the makin' of a good punch, but his mind is elsewhere."

"I will do it," Trueblood said. "I come back tomorrow."

Riley nodded.

"I begin to wonder if we will be able to get a load of legal whiskey to take to Philadelphia with us," Daniel stated with a sad smile.

"Whiskey drinks the same whether it's paid the tax or no."

"But if no one has paid the tax, anything we carry across the mountains will be known to be contraband and liable to be confiscated."

"I see yer problem. There are some big producers who've paid for this year. Ye could buy some from them. Inferior stuff, though." Riley shook his head.

"And make up the rest of the load along the way?" Daniel suggested with a twist of his eyebrows.

"It's a possibility. You've seen a still working, haven't ye, lad?"

"Never had the time. I'm a simple trader. The making of anything is a mystery to me."

"Come along with me, then. That is, if a bit of a walk will nay bother yer arm."

Daniel wandered off with Riley, causing a slow smile to spread over Trueblood's face.

"What are you pondering?" Nancy asked, making him start. "I was able to creep up on you without even trying."

"How Daniel can be so hotheadedly incautious when you are around and cool enough to get your father to show him the location of his still."

"Patrick Riley is not the most canny of souls. I find I cannot help myself loving him, no matter how impatient he makes me."

"Are you still speaking of your father or Daniel?"

"It could apply to both. Is there a chance that my papa will end up in prison because I have let a couple of...unsteady characters gain his confidence?"

"I think we should be able to shield him from any repercussions along that line."

"Trueblood, you have become rather sullen of late, brooding almost. Certainly not your usual voluble self." Nancy paced around him, with her shawl drawn about her shoulders against the morning chill.

"Ugh," Trueblood grunted, straight-faced.

"Ah, a disguise. I see. If they all think you have little English, they will not bother to guard their tongues around you."

"Correct, as usual."

She held out a sack to him. "I have brought you some bread and cheese. The former owners knew how to keep house. The cold cellar is well stocked with potatoes and all manner of squash and pumpkins. Ellie has turned all the keys over to me, much to Luce's chagrin."

"Except the one to the storeroom."

"Yes. He did not take her by force, but by seduction and false promises."

"Is that any better?"

"Yes. He did not hurt her and she does love him, or so she thinks. I will not make it easy for him, but I do not consider him hopeless."

"A terrible thing to have thrown at you."

"How so? It is an intriguing puzzle, but not at all daunting. If he thinks her unattainable, especially if someone else pays court to her, he may see marriage from a different angle. If he does not, then there is always the someone else."

Trueblood nodded at the simplicity of her logic. "You are going to use part of the money your uncle gave you."

"It was not a great sum to him, and even when I took it, I knew I would not use it for the purpose he intended. I have written them again, telling them of our idyllic journey and safe arrival. It takes so long to get a letter back, but they will be agog to hear of my adventures."

"You did not tell them everything." Trueblood looked askance at her as he took the letter from her.

"I did omit my marriage."

"Yes, of course, but I was speaking of the attack at the ford."

"I gloss over anything worrisome and concentrate on essentials—food, plants, local customs, particularly anything that will make them think it is not so very different from Somerset. At any rate, please see that my letter gets into the mail. They say the rider gets to Philadelphia in two weeks, depending on the weather. By my count we were not much longer than that on the trail.''

"Yes. We could carry more in wagons. But they are forever being shaken apart on those corduroy sections of road, or breaking a wheel in the worst possible defiles. We find we make much better time with ponies and mules.''

"And if one should lame up, you simply leave it for your return.''

"Or turn it loose to fend for itself. Speed is of the essence for someone as impatient as Daniel.''

"Has he always been so?'' Nancy looked down the valley toward the woods Daniel and Riley had disappeared into.

"Yes,'' Trueblood replied. "Do you expect him to change?''

"A man as old as Daniel, or even as old as yourself, has a fully formed character. Any woman who sets out to change such a man is going to make herself miserable. I like Daniel just as he is. I could wish he were not so hard on himself.''

"Such a realist. Hold the fort, Nancy dear. I shall be back anon, with news.''

"Can you manage all these ponies yourself or do you want Luce to come with you?''

Trueblood looked back to laugh at her. "You cannot get rid of him that easily yet.''

Nancy started back to the house and intercepted Ellie coming from the stream. She relieved the girl of the two buckets of water and delivered a stern lecture on what she was and was not allowed to do.

"But miss, someone must carry water. 'Tis nay fit work for ye.''

"It is certainly not fit work for you. Luce can do it when he has finished burning that bedding. Did he move Dupree to a clean bedroll?''

"Aye. He seems better. He was complainin' when I carried his breakfast up, but all in gibberish."

"Probably French. I will take care of Dupree. I do not want you up and down that cramped spiral of steps. It would be the easiest thing in the world to lose your footing."

"I don't understand, miss. Everyone acts like my baby is a terrible thing, but you want it ta be born."

"Every baby is a precious thing. Someday I hope to have some of my own. But for now you cannot blame me for wanting to pamper yours, now can you?"

Ellie smiled at her, and Nancy emptied the buckets into the cauldron hanging in the yard to start the water boiling for the wash.

Luce approached, dragging the empty tick mattress covers. "Where do ye want these?"

"In the pot with two more buckets of water. Then get a good fire going under there. We will boil them."

"'Tis a pure waste o' time. The bugs'll be back in a few weeks."

"Yes, but not as many. By washing frequently, and I mean bodies as well as clothes and bedding, we can keep them in check."

"You'll catch your death o' cold washing in this weather," Luce said, then scratched. "July and August, them is the bathing months."

"If you wish to sleep in the house rather than the stable, you will bathe. Once winter comes and the fireplace dries the house out, the fleas will not be much of a bother."

"I've noticed they're never as bad in the winter," Ellie said.

"Like many insects, they need dampness to breed. If we get the house dry there will not be as many. For now we will lay down tansy rushes throughout the house and stuff some into the bedding. I saw a huge patch of tansy growing right by the doorstep. When you have the pot boiling, Luce, cut as much of it as you can carry and bring it into the house.''

''I've other work ta do, ye know.''

''Such as?''

''I've ta feed and water the horses that are left.''

''Yes, of course, and muck out the stalls. You can use the wheelbarrow to start bringing some of that good manure down by the garden. We will need it for next year.''

Luce opened his mouth to protest, but could only see himself getting mired deeper with chores he had not intended to do. He picked up the buckets and went to the stream.

Nancy and Ellie grinned at each other, then went into the house to spend a comfortable morning trading recipes and getting acquainted.

Daniel came back at noon with the announcement that Riley could not leave the batch. So Nancy fed Luce and him, then sent Luce off with a basket of food for her father and Ellie off for a nap. The girl blushed at this consideration and withdrew to her room.

''I suppose that plate is for Dupree,'' Daniel said. ''I shall come up with you.''

''I may learn more from him if you do not. Remember I speak French.''

''Vividly. I will go see to our horses, then.''

''Luce has taken care of them. At least he said he did, though I do not imagine taking care extends to any currying. If you do not mind, Daniel, could you give the cauldron in the yard a stir on your way by?''

''That sounds like woman's work,'' he said in gruff imitation of Luce.

''Oh, lower yourself to it, Daniel, just this once,'' she taunted as she started for the stairs.

''I have a feeling that if I become connected with you, I will be hobbled to a hearth for the rest of my days.''

''I can promise you they will not be dull days.''

* * *

"Well?" Daniel asked impatiently when he heard Nancy's footfalls on the stairs. He had been stirring the stew over the fire and carefully hung the spoon back up to watch her carry the tray of dishes to the cooking table.

"I cannot make up my mind if he is delirious or if he rationally believes that he can lead a rebellion and set up a separate government here under Bradford. With men, it is sometimes hard to tell."

Daniel sent her a measuring stare, then shrugged. "Much as it sounds like pride talking, it is not out of the realm of possibility, if..."

She turned from the cooking table at his hesitation and shook her head at him. "Oh, Daniel, I have no time for your international intrigues. I have to see to my washing."

"You are right. I should never have involved you in this."

"I consider it a compliment to be trusted by a spy."

"I am not a spy. I am a merchant."

She looked askance at him.

"We would have to be at war for me to be a spy. I am an intelligence officer. I gather information for the government if it comes my way. Any loyal American would do the same."

"What sort of intelligence?" she asked provocatively.

"The sort that will keep us out of a war if I do my job right."

"So, during the Revolution you were a spy then?"

"No, I was a captain."

"Who always wore a uniform?"

"Except when performing other services."

"What sort of services?" she goaded.

"Secret services," he finally admitted with a grin.

"Oh, well, that makes it all right then. I do not know where I got the idea you were a spy," she said over her shoulder as she went out the back door to the yard.

Daniel chuckled as she left him. If ever there was a woman for him, it was Nancy. How he had been fool enough to thrust her into what looked to be turning into a war he did not know. But he would protect her at all costs. Besides, she was his lawful wife. It was going to be very hard not to reveal that.

By the time the evening meal was over, and Luce had been dispatched to take care of Dupree, the usual crowd of half a dozen had arrived for a hand or two of cards and a few rounds of whiskey. Riley remarked on Ned Johnson's absence and invited Daniel to sit in. They had not played more than one hand when Ned rode up to the door.

"Miss Riley, can you come? Dora's in labor for certain."

"I will get my cloak."

"I shall saddle the horses," Daniel said, tossing his hand in and rising.

They kept the horses to a trot in order to keep Johnson in sight and came to his farm in less than half an hour. There were nerve-shattering screams coming from within, but Nancy calmly followed Johnson into the house, leaving Daniel to find the stable on his own.

"You are much advanced for having a first child," Nancy said after a brief examination. "It will not be long at all now."

Daniel entered to discover Ned wringing his hands in the middle of the single-room dwelling, as his wife let out a prodigious groan. "We will need to keep the fire going and water hot," Nancy warned. "Could you and Daniel, perhaps, chop some more wood?"

"I've a kettle of hot water all ready, miss," the elder Mrs. Johnson said as Ned and Daniel fled the noise.

"Oh, we do not really need any more wood or water, but men tend to be a little underfoot in these proceedings. Dora, I am using a salve to stretch the tissues so the baby will not tear you. But you are a fine, strong girl. I do not think you will have any trouble, and if there should be a bit of tearing, that is easily mended."

"Can ye nay give her something fer the pain?"

"That would slow the baby down. We need these contractions, strong ones to get him out. And you can scream as much as you want, Dora. It helps to push the baby out."

"Ned says you've delivered many babies?" Dora asked between gasps.

"Yes. It is rather odd, I suppose, even where I come from, for an unmarried woman to know so much about it. But we are each shaped by our lives and must make best use of what knowledge comes our way. Push really hard this time, the head is crowning. It should take no more than one or two more strong pushes. Breathe deep—that's it. Now, when the pain comes again, push very hard." Dora grunted and pushed heroically. "That's it, Dora, the head is out."

Nancy gently turned the baby's head sideways to clean his air passage, and his shoulders slipped out. With very little effort she eased the baby out to lay him on the rough blanket. A shuddering wail filled the room, accompanied by Dora's ragged laugh of relief.

"There we are, and you are not torn in the least."

"What is it?" Dora asked urgently.

"A boy," Nancy said, smiling at the perfect, albeit mucus-covered infant. She wrapped him in a clean cloth and laid him on his mother's stomach while she gave her attention to the umbilical cord.

"Did you boil that knife?" she asked the mother.

"Was I supposed to?"

"Yes. I must cut the cord now that I have it tied."

While Mrs. Johnson went about this task, Nancy cleaned the worst of the birthing from the infant with warm water. Only when he was vigorously squalling did she wrap him in another clean blanket and lay him in his mother's arms for his first meal.

"We got more wood," Ned said as he stumbled into the cabin. Daniel followed him in and closed the door, keeping a discreet distance.

"I should not have sent you off. You have missed it."

"Look, Ned, our son," Dora said in awe.

"Thank God. I mean, I'm sorry I missed it."

Nancy kneaded Dora's belly. "We have still the after-birth to wait for. Ned, can you get me a slop bucket?"

"Yes, o' course."

Nancy waited until he went out before she cut the cord and bound the baby's hips and belly in clean cloth. She knew that Daniel was watching her.

"The end of this cord must be kept clean. Do you understand?"

"Yes, miss."

"Here's the bucket," Ned said, then looked away from the blood on the rough blanket.

"Nearly finished," Nancy said as she scooped the mass Dora expelled into the slop bucket and covered her patient warmly. She carried it outside with a lantern, and when Daniel found her, was spreading the afterbirth out in the yard.

"God, I thought you meant to bury it, not read it like some augury."

"You need not look, Daniel. But if any of this tissue stays inside the mother, she will surely die."

"What if it is not complete?"

"Then I must go in after it, but it is all here."

"How can you tell?" he asked, looking at the tissue she was probing with a stick.

"I told you that you need not look on it."

"I want to know," he said desperately.

"Why?"

"I may be in the position of needing to know someday. There may be no one to assist you when your time comes."

"I suppose I will be able to manage on my own."

"I do not want you to have to." He folded his arms around her from behind and rested his head beside hers.

"Very well then, observe...."

* * *

When they came back inside, Ned served up tumblers of whiskey all around. Daniel accepted gratefully, but Nancy took it away from the mother. "Remember, whatever you drink your baby gets through your milk, so you must avoid anything stronger than tea or water until he is done nursing, especially these first few weeks. I have brought you some tea if you have none."

Nancy stayed only to make sure the baby was nursing off both breasts and the mother not hemorrhaging, but exited with such a running stream of instructions and a promise to come the next day that Daniel thought they would never get away.

"Do you think she will listen to all that?" he inquired as they rode home.

"I shall be satisfied if she observes the half of it. Perhaps we should have borrowed a lantern," Nancy said, as her mare picked its way beside Daniel's.

"The moon is nearly up and the road is not that rough for this hilly country."

They rode in companionable silence for a time before Daniel asked, "Where did you acquire all your knowledge of babies and matters medical?"

"I was sworn not to tell."

"What?" He turned to face her, but she was not smiling.

"Daniel, little more than a hundred years ago I could have been burned at the stake for what I know, as could my teacher."

"Healing knowledge? Surely not, for that is to everyone's good. Mara was always highly respected among the Oneida for her skills with herbs."

"But the native cultures here were still matriarchal to some extent when we arrived."

"What has that to do with it?"

"European cultures were matriarchal once, too. Women were reverenced because they could produce children and men could not. Once those men figured out they had something to do with it, they took over."

"That's absurd."

"It is what my teacher said. And any woman with some knowledge, some power, even if it was beneficial, was eliminated."

"Burned as a witch, you mean? But such women were accused of absurdities, crop failures, causing cattle or women to be infertile...."

"What would a man think if his wife bore him a dozen children and suddenly no more? Having a baby takes nothing from a man. Too many children steal a woman's bones. If she had more than she could care for already she might go to a wise woman for an herb that would free her of that particular enslavement."

"So there may have been something behind those accusations."

"It is very likely."

"Would you ever give a woman such a 'cure'?"

"No, but once she knows the herbs to bring on women's courses she may use them to avoid becoming pregnant, and if she knows what to take to expel a dead baby, she will guess that the same medicine might rid her of a live baby. That is her decision."

"And the way you love babies, it cannot be easy for you to give that knowledge."

"I give all medicines with the warning that incautious use of them is poisonous."

"Except mint."

"What?"

"Except mint, of course."

Nancy recognized his attempt to lighten the conversation. "Yes, there are a few exceptions."

"I will make you some mint tea when we get back."

They rode for some minutes in silence. Nancy finally said, "Well, Daniel?"

"You sound like Trueblood. What is the 'Well, Daniel' in aid of?"

"Do you mean to make me give up my occupation?"

"Which one? Innkeeper, laundress, gardener...?"

"You know very well which one—midwife."

"If I asked you to, would you?"

"I would try, but if a frantic man came to our door in the middle of the night and you knew I might make the difference between a healthy baby and a dead one, could you turn him away?"

"I suppose not. I just wish you had not advertised your skill so freely."

"That was not my fault. Luce goaded me into it."

"And into defending a girl you hardly know."

"It is my instinct to have more sympathy for her than for Luce, especially now."

"Now that you have been seduced yourself, you mean."

"Seduced? We met on equal terms. I needed less persuasion than you, if you recall."

"Vividly!"

Nancy stared at him suspiciously, but by the slow smile that spread across his face in the moonlight she realized he was looking back on the incident with pleasure. The memory of that coupling, which she had truly believed would be her first and last, brought an ache deep inside, and jogging along on a horse only enhanced the urge to repeat the act. She wondered if their next meeting would be fraught with the same excitement, seeing that their lives would not be on the line.

"Well, Nancy."

"What?"

"You were saying..."

"Now that I know the strength of the desires that drive women...and I assume they are as strong or stronger for men?"

"Mmm," Daniel assented.

"I cannot find it in me to condemn Ellie, especially since she was misled by a false promise."

"Men are a perfidious lot, I admit. What makes you trust me?"

"Unlike most men, you do not lie to yourself. Why would you lie to me? I see no reason—"

"Wait! You deliver a facer like that and simply pass on. What do you mean, most men lie to themselves?"

"They do not know it, of course. Take my father, for example. He thinks he has done right by me."

"And you do not bother to correct him."

"Most men do not like to know the truth."

"I do."

"That is what sets you apart. Whatever part of a man that can be played upon, fooled as he fools himself, has all been stripped away from you somehow. Perhaps it was the war."

"We will not speak of how I got the way I am, but it occurs to me you are equally without illusions, except perhaps for a damned dangerous liking for adventure."

"That is why I trust you. We two meet on a level where there is no room for pretense, no time for lies."

"Not when we were about to be tomahawked. Would you think it such an exciting adventure to make love to me if we were absolutely safe?"

"I do not know. I have been wondering that myself."

Daniel chuckled, but said no more until he helped her down from her horse in the stable.

"Go up into the loft. I will take care of the horse. Can you see well enough?"

"The moon comes through the cracks between the logs," she said over her shoulder.

When Daniel came to her he found she had made them a comfortable bed with her cloak spread atop a nest of hay. She had stripped down to her shift, her pocket sack of medicines and bandages laid aside for the moment. He knelt and ran his hand slowly up her thigh, then teased at the hairs of her mound until she was tugging at his clothes in impatience. Finally he stood up to throw off his garments, watching as she slid the shift over her head.

The bands of moonlight coming through the log wall

played temptingly over the curves of her young body, first picking out a breast, then a thigh as she moved. They danced across her buttocks like a caressing hand, his hand. He could not help but wonder what she was seeing of him. Her eyes, when they came into the light, were bright with wonder. No woman had ever looked upon him with wonder before. She turned deliberately in the bars of light and laughed at the play over her body, as though they really were drawing a response from her. One moonbeam slid across her young face, leading Daniel to her lips. He could feel the aroused tips of her breasts nudging him in the chest. Never had a woman so wanted him. She writhed under his hands, and the more she rubbed against him the more erect he became. He took her hand to place it on his member. She explored him gently and tentatively.

"I still say it is extraordinary," she whispered.

"You asked me if there was more to it. There are many ways to make love and one I think you will find particularly to your liking." He lay down on the cloak and pulled her astraddle him. She knelt over him, then bent to kiss him, her thighs hot against his sides. "When you are ready," he said, then set to nuzzling the young breasts suspended over him. He suckled one breast until Nancy was moaning deliciously, then transferred his attention to the other. His fingers moved lightly over the insides of her elbows, then down her ribs, to her buttocks to position her over him.

"I cannot wait," she begged as she let herself down onto him. She gasped as she shifted to take in his full length. She felt hot and wanting inside and knew in her deepest desire that he could complete her, fill that void she had only just discovered. Instinctively she moved up and down, aided by his bouncing thrusts, then she tried leaning to the right or to the left, unable to decide which felt better, as he gently probed her. "Oh, Daniel. I never imagined anything to equal it."

"Are you quite sure you would not be happier if someone had a gun to your head?"

"No, this is even better. How long can you…?"

"I do not know. Are you exhausting yourself?"

"I could never get enough of this. I mean to outlast you," she said, kissing him savagely on the mouth.

"We shall see." Daniel gripped her breasts gently and thrust deep inside her, drawing a small scream from her.

"Unfair tactics, sir," she gasped.

"Do your worst, then, m'lady."

Nancy realized she had been concentrating on her own experience, using Daniel like a tool to satisfy her own needs. Without moving any external part of her body she squeezed with her internal muscles, drawing a grunt from him. She had never known a woman could have such power over a man. She began a rhythmic assault on his manhood, biting her lip with the effort to keep her muscles tight. Daniel was groaning and sweating as he supported her by her arms. Suddenly he rolled her onto her back as though they were in a wrestling match, and stroked in and out of her with fervent vigor until she arched her back to receive his seed. He gave a shuddering sigh, then fell down beside her.

"I am a brute," she said, "to be asking this of you when your wound must still be hurting."

"What wound?" he asked with dry lips, as he pulled her to him, his flesh burning hot against hers.

"Your arm."

"I am feeling only one thing just now."

"Is it not amazing how—"

He silenced her with a kiss. "No more observations, just at this moment."

"I think I did not best you, sir, at least not this time."

"Are you challenging me to a rematch?" His hand slid over her hip to grasp the tantalizing curve of her buttock.

"At any time and place of your choosing."

"I shall remember that. But if this was a contest to see who could give the most pleasure, I think we have both won."

"That is as it should be."

"So, the baby came quickly for a first child?" Daniel asked, pulling Nancy close and wrapping her cloak over her.

"Yes, sometimes it takes hours," she said sleepily.

"What is the longest labor you have ever attended?" He nuzzled her neck, and she seemed to be having difficulty answering.

"Oh, all night once. I assure you we got off easily this night. We might have been there till dawn."

"So your father will not look for us for hours?"

"Why, Daniel! You intriguer." She looked up at him with delight.

"What would you expect from a spy?" He kissed her longingly, wishing the night would never end.

Chapter Eight

Daniel was lingering over a second mug of coffee, still trying to figure out exactly what was in it. The game had developed between them quite naturally. Nancy never said what was in her tea or coffee concoctions, or even in her stews. He had to guess. If he did and she smiled, saying "And?" he knew he had got some of the ingredients, but not all. He did, in the end, manage to figure it out, though sometimes it took him all day. It brought back memories of Mara and Champfreys, the infant Constance, and roaming the woods with the so-impressionable Trueblood. Daniel found the memories, like the tea, sometimes sweet and fragrant, or like the coffee, occasionally bitter, but all with a familiarity he could wear like an old coat. If only there was a way for Nancy and Mara to meet. But that would mean going back to Champfreys, and he could not.

Perhaps a plantation not far removed from there, with enough work to keep Nancy busy, and close enough to Philadelphia in case he should be needed again... But first they must get through this business. He realized with a pleasant start that he had never actually thought in terms of having a future. Now he could engage in such pleasurable daydreams with the feeling that he was looking forward to settling down, not dreading it. He even had a righteous excuse for lounging about the kitchen.

Since there was heavy lifting to do at the still that morning, Riley had taken Luce off with him and told Daniel he looked half-dead and should go back to bed. Since neither he nor Nancy had gotten to their beds until nearly dawn, Daniel was surprised at how sprightly his wife looked. Her midwifery calls, if they came in the middle of the night, could provide them with many other opportunities he had not heretofore considered.

"I believe you enjoy playing the invalid," Nancy chided as she stirred some batter in a bowl and came to stand beside him.

"Chicory and fennel." He waited for her approving nod. "It gets me out of an enormous amount of work. Now that I have taken care of the horses and hauled in your wood and water, I have nothing to do but sit about the inn and pinch comely serving wenches on the cheek." He reached around her waist to pull her down for a kiss.

"They might pinch back," Nancy warned.

"I did not say which cheek." He made a grab for her derriere, but she spun and evaded his arm, hampered as it was by the sling, and he nearly overset the bench backward.

"Harumph." The dour man in the doorway consulted a small pocket notebook and demanded, "Is this the White Horse Tavern?"

"Inn," Nancy corrected.

"If it's the White Horse, I'll come in. Otherwise—"

"It is the White Horse Inn, I said."

"That's not what the sign says."

"Then why did you ask if you meant to contradict me, sir?"

"My name is Coggins. Is your still registered for the tax?"

"My name is Riley. What still and what tax?"

"The still tax. I have this place down as producing fifty gallons last year."

"Do you see that blackened ruin across the road?"

"Yes."

"That is what is left of the still and the old barn. The tax was paid and that is the result."

"The tax was paid by Williams when he was here. And I didn't burn your still."

"A moot point since it is burned. If you have no further business..."

"I'd like some whiskey."

"Are you serious?"

"Yes," he said, sitting at the table by the door.

"Very well, I suppose you have money?"

He thumped a coin down, and Nancy went for a noggin and filled it.

"Daniel, I have to feed Dupree."

"I shall look after things."

Daniel raised his mug to Coggins but made no move to join him. To be caught drinking with a tax collector would damage his reputation in these parts beyond repair.

"And who might ye be?" the man inquired of Daniel.

"Tallent. I'm a trader from Philadelphia."

"Ye trade for whiskey?"

"Sometimes."

"Best make sure whatever ye buy has paid a tax or I'll confiscate it."

"How am I supposed to know if it's paid a tax?"

"Almost none of it has. That makes my job easy."

"And mine close to impossible. If I go asking a man if his whiskey has paid the tax he will either lie or shoot me for the insult."

"The law must be maintained."

"You know, I can remember during the Revolution what happened to the British tax collectors who were overzealous about their work."

"Wot might that be?"

"They were tarred and feathered or burned in effigy, and occasionally strung up to a liberty pole—by the belt, usually."

"I am not British. I am American."

"More's the pity," Daniel said sadly.

Nancy ran back down the stairs. "Dupree is gone. Did you see him leave?"

"No, but it never occurred to me he could walk. I was out of sight of the front door while I was tending the stock. He might have slipped away then."

"Who's Dupree?"

"What business is it of yours?" Nancy demanded of Coggins.

"He has not paid his shot," Daniel confided to Coggins in an undertone.

Suddenly the door was flung open and Trueblood entered. "Well, I have the barrels," he said, then hesitated as Daniel's eyes flicked meaningfully from him to the gruff man by the door and back again. "If you can show me where the gristmill is, we'll go for the flour now," Trueblood finished valiantly.

"The horses must need water. I'll tend to that while you have your breakfast."

As though on cue Nancy began to slice away at a butt of ham and throw pieces into a three-legged skillet set over some coals on the hearth. She looked suggestively at Coggins as she raised her knife again. "We have no eggs, but do you want some breakfast while I am about it? Now or never."

"I could do with some ham."

As Daniel had walked out the door in his shirtsleeves, and had obviously been in no particular hurry, Nancy only thought he was going to warn her father. But when Coggins went out twenty minutes later he came back in shouting that there was not a pony in sight, either in the yard or in the stable.

"Where's he gone?" demanded the tax collector.

"The gristmill, I suppose," Nancy replied. "Did you not hear him?"

"Aye, I heard him. Lying bastard!"

"Who's a lying bastard?" Trueblood inquired, looking

none too pleased about being disturbed at his prodigious breakfast of ham, porridge and corn cakes.

"Any o' those barrels have whiskey in them?" Coggins demanded, sucking a bit of ham from between his teeth.

"All new, clean, dry," Trueblood said proudly.

"Well, if any o' them was to end up with whiskey in them, ye had best buy it legal from Inspector Neville."

"Why Neville?"

"He's paid the tax on his still."

"What tax?"

"Aye, ye're all of a feather, you backcountry thieves."

"First you call Daniel a bastard, now I am a thief?" Trueblood started to rise with his eating knife in hand.

"Easy, Trueblood," Nancy warned, laying a hand on his shoulder. "Remember what happened last time you lost your temper. I still have not got those bloodstains up."

"But he did not pay." Trueblood pointed the knife at Coggins.

The man nervously added to the coins on the table until Nancy nodded.

"I know, and neither has Dupree."

"Dupree's gone?"

"Yes. Now, Trueblood," Nancy warned as the big man lifted a chair.

Coggins scuffled out and mounted his horse, kicking the skinny beast into an ungainly trot.

"Do you think Daniel will be able to get away from him?" Nancy asked with a chuckle.

"If Daniel cannot lose him, I do not know my brother. He is probably taking a roundabout way to the still. Where is it, by the way?"

"I have no idea. They always go down the valley in that direction, but they never seem to take exactly the same path into the woods."

"Very wise. To be sure, if I looked hard enough I would be able to see some smoke, but then, if I tried to find them

I might get lost. Best I just wait here with you. Was Dupree fit for travel?''

"Not to be jogging along on a horse. He might have walked a few miles without doing himself harm.''

"He has probably gone down the hill to take the ferry into Pittsburgh. It will be easy enough for him to get to Bradford then.''

"Yes, the man who is inciting the rebels.''

"Did I say Bradford?''

"Never mind. I do not care about the stupid whiskey or the ridiculous tax. Seems an absurd reason for all this commotion.''

"No doubt you are right. Certainly nothing to lose one's temper over.''

Trueblood grinned at her and she remembered the joke. "We deal nearly as well together as you and Daniel.''

"Yes, too bad we have not more scope for our acting talents. How can I make myself useful, since it appears the rest of the men will be occupied for some time?''

"Since we have Dupree off our hands, you could kill something—for dinner, I mean.''

Ellie came out apologetically, only just then able to face the rank cooking smells in the main kitchen. Nancy threw open both the front and back doors to clear out the burned-fat odor, and the two occupied themselves with shaping the risen dough into loaves for the two great ovens built into the right side of the fireplace. Nancy shoveled red coals from the hearth into the bottom of each oven so that they would be hot enough to bake their bread once it had done its final rising. Then the two women commenced cutting carrots and potatoes for the daily batch of stew.

Trueblood came in later to present them with two large squirrels and to share the remains of last night's soup with them. He then ate an entire loaf of bread new from the oven, had a glass of whiskey and went off to busy himself about the stable.

* * *

When Riley and Luce finally came back from the still they had Daniel with them, and he looked much the worse for wear. His shirt was ripped, he was limping and there were fresh briar scratches across his face. Moreover, they had all been drinking in celebration of Daniel giving the tax collector the slip. Nancy shook her head, while Trueblood put the now-unburdened ponies in the stable. They were like three boys, joyously unconscious that their cause was not noble. Was Daniel really drunk, she wondered, or only pretending to be?

When the nightly customers arrived, her father recounted the adventure for them in what she considered to be an indiscreet way. One or two of them looked suspiciously at Daniel, but finally succumbed to Riley's trust and good-natured offer of free drinks.

She wondered what Daniel was playing at. Had he really been trying to help her father or was he using this incident to get into the confidence of the rebels? Somehow she could not think of Spode or the Johnsons as rebels. But one or two of the others? She would not put it past them to burn a still, then come back to the place they had done it.

Riley had no such suspicions. He started singing a ditty she had heard once or twice before from him when he was drunk. But now, unfortunately, they could all make out his exuberant rendering of "Nancy Whiskey," punctuated at the end of each chorus by a toast to her. She was not sure she liked the new name he was saddling her with and looked at Daniel, expecting to see disapproval on his face. A wicked light gleamed in his eyes as he, too, toasted Nancy Whiskey, and she knew then that he was truly drunk and not pretending.

She sent him the most disapproving look she could manage, then got her sewing out of her workbag and pretended to ignore them all. She did get Ellie to make sure Daniel ate something, but was not at all surprised when he fell asleep on the table. Trueblood left the others toasting their own ingenuity to escort an uncoordinated Daniel up the

winding stairs. A few minutes later he returned to say,
"Wound broke open. Needs Nancy."

"I shall go up. Do not leave Ellie alone with this lot."

Nancy found Daniel lying on the bed and woke him by
pulling his shirt off and washing his scratches. So he really
had been asleep.

"Where am I?"

"The White Horse. Where did you think you were?"

"Home."

"And who did you think I was?" she asked suspiciously.

"Mara, Trueblood's mother. When we would not get up,
she would douse us with water."

"What a cruel woman," Nancy said with a chuckle.

"No, she was the kindest... I passed out. That is not like
me."

"No, but I think you have had rather a busy day," she
said, undoing the grubby bandage. "Daniel, there is nothing
wrong with your arm. It is healing nicely."

"Yes, I know."

"So what was the point of..."

"Getting you to come up and take my shirt off?"

"Daniel! Was this your idea or Trueblood's?"

"I do not like to take credit for another man's work, but
you must admit it is a good idea." He ran his free hand up
under her petticoats so neatly he surprised a gasp of delight
from her as he cupped her buttock.

"Not a good idea. The door has no lock. Anyone could
step in."

"I think we can trust Trueblood to prevent that. But if
you are worried, we can make love with our clothes on.
Except I would like access to these treasures." He tugged
at the ties of her shift until her breasts were freed, and she
willingly lowered herself to be nuzzled and suckled in the
most lascivious manner. She wondered idly what it would
be like to have a babe nursing at her breasts, and suddenly
the hunger in the cavern of her stomach took on a new

urgency. She wanted a baby and wanted one quite desperately. The fact that there was no way for her to get one at the moment did nothing to quell that hunger. She undressed herself as Daniel watched appreciatively from the bed. He was drunk, no doubt of that, and she wondered how that would affect his lovemaking. She came toward him and undid his breeches, then tugged at his boots. She thought he derived a strange delight at bracing one foot against her backside while she slid each boot off.

"Now if we are caught out, we will be equally disgraced," she said, crawling onto the bed beside him.

"I should think the excitement of the risk would inspire you to even greater heights of passion," he mumbled as he stroked her tumbled hair.

"I do not need danger to make me want you."

"I want you always." Daniel sighed heavily and was asleep.

Nancy knew a moment of disappointment, but his failure stole nothing from the joy of loving him, of watching him as he slept. She ran a finger along his bearded jaw, then pulled a blanket over them and snuggled against his hot flesh. If she should fall asleep as well, Trueblood would wake her. There was really nothing to fear.

Nancy had already fed Trueblood and Luce breakfast and sent them off to see to the horses when her father crawled downstairs, begging for coffee. She saw that he had some bread and ham as well, wishing they had some butter or honey to put on the bread. She must have been looking rather thoughtful, for he asked, "Nancy dearie, are ye sorry now I've brought ye all this way?"

"Sorry to leave a comfortable home and my imminent wedding?"

"Aye, they told me about yer vicar. Was the fella handsome?"

"I would rather describe him as large."

"And did ye love him?"

It seemed a strangely intimate question coming from this father she hardly knew, but she turned to smile at him. "Not at all. Of course, he assured me that would come in time."

"The liar."

Nancy giggled.

"Aye, and a cradle robber. Yer not but a child. I have nay got ta know ye myself. I will nay have some man steal ye away from me."

She looked down into her teacup. How was she ever going to be able to tell him that a man already had stolen her, that it was only a matter of time before she did leave her father?

"Listen to me, lass. Never marry until ye've found the right man. Yer heart'll tell ye."

She smiled at him. When the time came he would accept Daniel.

"Ye're not sorry ye came then?"

"Not a bit of it," she said in imitation of his brogue, and he hugged her.

He smelled, as he always did, of whiskey. The scent permeated his person even when he had not been drinking, but she was getting so used to it now that it was almost a comfortable smell. She could see why her mother had fallen in love with him. Beneath all the bombast and drunken bravado, beneath even the charming tongue and well-meant promises, there was a caring man. And here Nancy was, aiding two spies in a plot to entrap her own father.

"Aye, but it does grieve me to see ye turning yer pretty hands to hard work. It was not what I wanted for yer mama, and not what I had in mind for ye."

"But out here I must keep myself busy, Papa. It is my nature."

"Aye."

"Please try not to talk so freely of rebellion in this place. What if you were arrested?"

"There's no law here ta speak of."

"That is hardly something to be grateful for."

"No, but it's a fact, Nancy dear. I'm not a man who likes it too civilized."

A boot fell on the floor above, and as Trueblood had already breakfasted and gone out, she realized it must be Daniel.

"How's our boy this mornin'?"

"A bit feverish, but that may have been your whiskey."

"I told him not ta lift anythin'. He's a ripe one fer adventure."

"I'm sure he would be delighted to hear that."

"Take care o' him, Nancy girl. I must find Luce and get ta the still."

"What's that?" Daniel asked as Nancy entered the bedroom with a steaming mug. He was sitting with one leg still in bed and gave his head a shake to clear his vision.

"I recommend a cold cloth after the tea."

"God, what was I drinking?" He moved his tongue experimentally inside his mouth and shuddered, then took a gulp of the strong, minty brew.

"One of Papa's best batches, according to him. And I thought you could hold your liquor."

"Did I really send for you last night?"

"Yes, you said your wound had broken open and needed immediate attention. Do you mean to tell me you remember nothing?" She hung his discarded breeches on the rickety chair.

"Vaguely. And did I...I mean, did we...?"

"Daniel! You do not remember!"

"It will come to me," he said defensively. "I was simply wondering..."

"If you had a good time? What is the point of asking me, Daniel? I could tell you anything and you would have to believe me."

"But I want to know. Tell me the truth. Did I make love to you or no?"

"I will not tell you, and if you have the nerve to ask how it was, I shall pour that tea over you."

"Why are you so angry?" He held the cup out of her reach just in case and downed the rest in one swallow.

"Because you have forgotten last night," she said tearfully. "You must promise never to drink like that again."

"Most definitely, unless it is in the line of duty."

"Daniel!" She turned on him with a determined look.

"What?" he answered as he pulled his breeches off the chair.

"Whose side are you on?"

Daniel sighed heavily. "I work for the good of the country."

"That tells me nothing. Will you betray those men you were drinking with last night?"

"Who the devil were they, anyway?"

"Do not play games! They are farmers. They are the country, at least this part of it. Will you betray them?"

"It is my duty to report the true state of affairs here. Would you have me lull Washington into a false sense of security if the frontier is about to go up in flames?"

"No, you would look a proper fool then." She stood with her hands on her hips.

"Do you think I care about myself?"

"What I want to know is do you care about me and Papa?"

"You know I care. You are my wife."

"Not to put too fine a point on it, Daniel, but are you sitting and drinking with those men so that you can infiltrate the rebels and find out what they are planning?"

"I could drink in any tavern in the country and find that out." He pulled his shirt over his head and emerged with delightfully tousled hair. She looked away so as not to be distracted. "They are not, any of them, overly discreet."

"I am asking if you will use information gained in such a way against them."

"Not...personally."

"What do your mean by that?"

"I will name no names."

"Not good enough, Daniel. I think it perfidious to gain information in such a way and to pretend you are a friend when you are none."

"You thought it a rather pleasant ruse when we toyed with Genet." Daniel struggled to his feet and pulled on his breeches.

"That was different. This is my own papa. Do you expect me to betray him?"

"And you are my wife." He shook his finger at her. "You are supposed to have some loyalty to me. God, why did you make me yell? I feel like my head is about to split." He held his skull with both hands as he sank back onto the bed.

"It serves you right," she said, flouncing away.

"How dare you leave? We are not finished arguing yet—ouch."

"Then get up!" she shouted as she wound her way down the stairs.

By the time Daniel had washed, shaved and dressed, Trueblood was slicing bread and applying himself to the remains of the previous night's stew. He seemed to need this second breakfast to sustain him until the midday meal.

"Eat this, you will feel better," Trueblood commanded.

Daniel wrinkled his nose at the bowl his brother thrust toward him. He merely broke off a chuck of bread and began to chew it.

"Is that why you came to my bed then?" he asked Nancy morosely, ignoring Trueblood's presence. "To convince me to save your papa from his own indiscretions?"

"I came to your bed because I wanted to," she shouted from the hearth. "Nothing else would bring me there. And you do not even remember it!" She flung a glob of porridge down on a wooden trencher and thrust it in front of him, nearly making him wretch.

"Are you going to eat that, Daniel?" Trueblood asked.

"Not likely," he said, shoving it away. "Because if you use yourself to save him," Daniel continued as though he had not heard her, "you are no better than—than…"

"Than what, Daniel? Spit it out," Nancy demanded, stropping a rather large carving knife almost under his nose.

"Than the Loyalist lady, Daniel?" his brother asked.

"Stay out of this, Trueblood," Daniel complained.

"Stop it, both of you." Nancy shook the knife at them. "If Daniel is going to drink himself into a stupor, there is no more to be said, but nothing will make me regret any of the nights we have spent together."

Trueblood rolled his eyes at this revelation.

"I did not say I regretted it. I merely want you to understand I have my principles."

"If you have any principles, I should like to know what they are, Daniel. Do you not eat at a man's table and see him hanged on the same day?"

"No! I mean, no harm will come to your father."

"You cannot promise that, Daniel," Trueblood warned. "If Riley persists in flaunting the law, if he gets involved in harrying tax collectors—"

"As you two helped him do yesterday!" Nancy reminded them, slamming the knife down on the table in such a way that they both eyed it warily.

"Well, that was just a harmless joke," Trueblood said. "I mean, if he does violence…"

"I give you my word that I will warn you if he is in danger," Daniel promised. "Beyond that I cannot help him."

"I see. I have work to do. I wish you would either eat your breakfast or—"

Daniel bolted for the back door, and Trueblood looked sympathetically after him.

"Now where…?"

"Getting rid of last night's lot, I expect. Daniel always did have a touchy stomach."

"Serves him right," Nancy said over the retching sounds coming from the backyard.

"Daniel seems a little troubled."

"You mean he is not normally so irritable?" Nancy asked, beginning now to regret her verbal attack on a man in no way prepared to defend himself.

"No, until this year I would have said he was better-than-average company."

"It is not me who has changed him." She left off chopping the carrots.

"Not on purpose. But he has fallen in love with you. I know the signs. It has taken him hard this time."

"That cannot be it. If he were only in love, he would be more loving and not so disagreeable. He is acting like a man in a struggle with his conscience. I think he has taken to heart what I said about him using my father—and me, for that matter—to get into the rebels' confidence."

"If you were Daniel what would you do? Advise the government to send troops, or take a chance on this insurrection coming to naught?"

Nancy sat despondently. "If only he could warn them what will befall them if they do not stop this talk of rebellion."

"He cannot, not without giving himself away."

"I think he is feeling old, Trueblood."

"What do you mean? He came out of our last fracas with no more than a scratch."

"Yes, I know he is only using his wound to give himself an excuse to stay here."

"To be with you."

"Only to be with me? You do not expect me to believe that, do you?"

"No, but I would appreciate your making a pretense of believing it."

"It is dangerous, this work you do."

"More boring than dangerous."

"If some of these men knew you were connected with the government…"

"Yes, I know, a coat of tar and feathers or a noose. Daniel would never let such a threat disturb him."

"Think back. Before, when he went off to fight in the Revolution, he was rebelling against his father more than against the king, was he not?"

"Yes. I do not know what passed between Father and him, only that there were very hard words on both sides."

"Daniel now finds his position strangely reversed," Nancy mused.

"How so?" Trueblood asked, munching on a carrot. "He is still loyal to Washington, in support of the Revolutionary government. It is Father who has done an about-face. According to Mother he is no longer a staunch Loyalist, but a moderate Federalist."

"I comprehend that, but I am not sure Daniel does. No matter how devotedly he works for Washington he cannot help but see things from the rebel point of view."

"Be sympathetic to their cause, you mean?"

"Yes."

"I am quite sure he is only considering that you have a father who is the closest thing to a rebel."

"I do not think Daniel even likes Papa. I think Daniel would much rather be on the other side himself."

"That is absurd! Turn his back on everything he has fought for?"

"It is not just a matter of principles, as he says. It is a matter of being used to always struggling, always fighting. To find himself in the position of turning someone in, or calling down government troops on folk ill prepared to defend themselves against a sizable army, is weighing on him. He will do the right thing, of course, but it will cost him a great deal. And he will be sorry."

"He has got to get out of this business," Trueblood said flatly.

"So you would not object if he stopped this kind of work?"

"I have begged him time and again to give it up. Mother wants us home, both of us. Father is so ill the running of the plantation has fallen on her."

"But can Daniel afford to give it up? Will his life have any meaning, otherwise?"

"It may if he has you. Yet you are the very thing he may lose if he does the right thing."

"His dilemma is worse than mine," Nancy said, staring out the window at Daniel, who was making his way to the barn.

"I wish I could help you, both of you, but I leave for Philadelphia as soon as I have a load of whiskey. Is there anything you want me to bring you?"

"I shall think about it. Do you mean to go alone?"

"As I am leaving Daniel here, I thought I would hire Lucius. Would that bother you?"

"You are welcome to him."

It was still pitch-black the next morning when Trueblood and Lucius were ready to set out.

"We should be going," Trueblood said, grasping Daniel's shoulder. "I want to be well on our way before anyone is about."

"Here is my letter for Norton. There is no very important news to send back just now."

"So if I should take my time it is no loss. You must stay in case something of moment happens. Then you can ride post as fast as horses can bring you."

"After yesterday, I would as soon trade places with you."

"What would you solve by running away? She is your wife. You should be with her."

"But we are on different sides. I am a Federalist and she is a rebel, or the closest thing to it."

"A rebel's daughter. It is not the same thing at all. And

she is a reasonable woman, when she has not been provoked."

"No other woman ever made me feel guilty about the work I do. I was always so sure…"

"Yes, and always the mysterious hero, Talon, who dared anything for his country."

"What is your point?"

"Nancy is not interested in a hero. It is you she loves."

"She has a damned odd way of showing it."

"This little tiff will blow over. Any woman would be offended if you mislaid an entire night. What bothers her most is our dilemma."

"I already said I would name no names."

"But others will."

"Whose side are you on, Trueblood?"

"Yours. Whose side are you on?"

"America's."

"You had better practice saying that with a little more conviction if you mean to convince Nancy."

"Leave me to my fate. Mind you do not miss the way."

Chapter Nine

Daniel was restless for the first few days after Trueblood left them, and Nancy feared there was no way to make him feel less torn about the situation. He might even bolt after his brother. She did regret now that she had brought on the crisis, but she was still feeling rather torn herself. So she simply did not refer to it, but tried to lighten his mood with kitchen talk and prattle about England. Fortunately, one of the things Riley had brought back from Pittsburgh that day was a letter from Aunt Jane, which Nancy read out loud to them that evening.

"Wot does she mean, that she can nay like ye ta be on the frontier?" Riley asked. "'Tis a very settled and civilized area."

"So I have told her in my letters. But from my recipes she deduces we are without a good many things, such as sugar, which she has come to regard as a necessity."

"You send her recipes?" Daniel asked. "That seems a rather odd use of the post."

"It may seem like a terrible waste of correspondence to you. I am sure all your letters are of great moment," Nancy taunted. "But when I discover something entirely new it seems the most natural thing to tell her about it, such as boiling these wonderful sunflower roots. I also told her how to make soup inside a pumpkin roasted whole on the hearth.''

''She'll be thinkin' you have nay cookin' pots,'' complained Riley.

''Yes, I see now I have teased her with such novelties into thinking ours a hand-to-mouth existence, when we have storerooms packed with food beneath us. Come, everyone, and help me enumerate the advantages of our situation to Aunt Jane.'' Nancy took up her pen.

Ellie and Riley alternately named all the really good dishes they made and extolled the virtues of the inn and its environs. But Daniel did not believe a strong-flowing spring or molasses and beans would impress Aunt Jane with anything but the privations of Nancy's situation. Here was a girl who had been used to dinner parties and silk dresses. How did she manage to fit in so comfortably at a frontier inn where her wool apron got scorched if she stood too long stirring a kettle over the hearth? How did she even know how to cook on an open hearth? She had taught herself, of course. What she did not know when she came, she learned from Ellie.

Adaptable though Nancy was, Daniel vowed to contrive some ways to make her life easier. He had asked Trueblood to bring back some cones of sugar and some real tea, also some plates. The inn had only wooden trenchers and bowls, tin and leather tankards, a surprising number of coconut-shell mugs and a few chipped cups left by the former owners. Someday he would see that Nancy had all the luxuries, but they were not appropriate here. He wanted to give her so much, but he could not until they could be publicly married.

Daniel did the chores in half the time it took Luce and helped Riley at the still daily while the rye lasted, but he never repeated his drunken spree. And he did not again, to Nancy's disappointment, call her to his room to change his bandage. She wondered how long his sense of duty would keep his frustration in check.

She began to think of all the preparations she would normally be involved in for winter and tried to apply them here. Firewood, water and food were their three chief needs. If the spring should freeze over, they could always melt snow, but that would take extra wood.

"How bad are the winters usually in this area?" she asked Daniel one morning after breakfast. He had been puzzling over the ingredients in her tea and she thought he was nearly ready to guess them.

"They vary. Why?"

"How much firewood will we need to make it through the worst of them?"

"We can get wood in the winter and slide it over the snow. That is when most of it is cut anyway."

"But will it be properly dried by then? And what if we were to have a dry, cold winter, with no snow or rain and everything frozen?"

"You do think of the worst possibilities," he said with a crooked smile.

"We are going to have an infant in the house soon. We must be ready."

"I will see to it."

"Also, I would like to have a smokehouse."

"Do you know anything about smoking meat?"

Nancy cast him an admonitory look.

"Of course, you know all about it. Why did I even ask? I will see what I can contrive. Is there anything else?"

"The hog will have to be slaughtered, but that need hardly concern you."

This arrested the mug halfway to his mouth. "I see, you could manage that by yourself, could you?" he teased.

"If I must. But pork and ham alone would provide rather boring fare for the winter. If we are to serve any respectable dishes I require a quantity of venison. I would like to try smoking some of that, as well. If there are any fish to be had, I could pickle those. And I will need a chicken pen for the hens Ned Johnson has promised me for delivering their baby.''

''Is that all?''

''For now. It is very like setting up winter headquarters for an army, do you not think?'' Nancy asked, looking up from her list. ''Except, of course...''

''What?''

''We will not be obliged to live in tents. I was so particularly looking forward to that. But the inn is here, so I suppose it cannot be helped.''

''Tents?'' Daniel squeaked before he caught the twinkle in her eyes. Then he laughed outright. ''I fear I cannot supply you with the inconvenience of a tent, but if you would like to be under attack, or perhaps even a siege, I will see what I can arrange.''

''Ordinarily that would be a great adventure, but as we are preparing for a baby, I can see that would hamper us. We will just have to contrive with what excitement we can garner from surviving the winter.''

''Comfrey, mint and chamomile,'' he said, looking up at her with those keen blue eyes.

She nodded with a bright smile and watched him walk gracefully from the room as he went off to do her bidding. The ache was back, and it looked as though Daniel could hold off from her with much more endurance than she had against his unconscious charm. She closed her eyes and waited for the waves of desire to pass, but they only made her think of him more and how easy it would be for him to satisfy her. She had had no idea how suspenseful marriage could be. Certainly marriage to anyone except Daniel would have been a dead bore. She could make it through another day, but what about the next?

While Daniel hauled out the previous night's ashes and lit each new day's fire, Nancy threw open the doors on even the chilliest days. She swept the hearth clear of ashes and the floor of dust as the dew-drenched morning breeze carried away yesterday's smoke and replaced it with the scent of the doorstep herbs—mint, tansy and chamomile. The dust motes in the sunbeams had begun to settle when she closed the kitchen up again, and the morning brew of coffee dispelled the last of the previous night's cooking odors. The smell of oatcakes baking on the frame in front of the fire drew her father from his bed, and Nancy smiled at him, since she found this sent him about his day more contented than any nagging on her part about the amount of whiskey he had consumed the night before.

She had to remember to cut her recipes in half now that Trueblood was gone. She missed him, right down to the grumbling of his stomach when he had not been fed promptly. She wondered if Daniel missed his brother as well. Perhaps that was why he paced from window to window of an evening, unless she had worn him out with work.

Daniel had accomplished nearly all of the tasks set him by Nancy, including building a small log smokehouse where pork, venison and fish were now being cured. She was racking her brains for some other labors of Hercules to throw at him to keep him occupied. She was delighted by each new accomplishment of his and showed her appreciation as a proper wife would. She cooked for him, but she did not give herself to him, only because he did not ask her to. She supposed she could go to him in the middle of the night, but she did have some pride. She would never again be in a position where he could accuse her of using her body to influence him.

As Ellie grew greater with child, more of the work was thrust on Nancy, and Daniel took over the most odious of the tasks. If Norton could have seen him hauling water and emptying slop buckets he would have laughed. Yet every chore Daniel did was something Nancy did not have to do, and that made it worth the doing. For him she devised all manner of new dishes, new ways to fix the same pork and venison, the same potatoes, carrots, onions, barley and beans that he had eaten the day before. He never failed to be amazed by her ingenuity and the tastes she could achieve with her store of herbs.

Daniel wanted to make something special for her. What he had in mind—a springhouse—could not be a surprise, of course, but it was something she had not thought of herself, busy as she was preparing for winter. When summer came she would be glad of a place to keep food cool, and eventually milk and butter. That put him in mind of going into Pittsburgh to see if he could come by a goat, or perhaps even a milk cow.

The new structure would be a log building, straddling the spring where it came out of the hill, with shelves on one side over a hard-packed floor. When Daniel started laying the stone he merely informed her he was improving the spring.

She brought him lunch the day he set the first logs in place, and she compared it favorably to the springhouse they had in Somerset. Much of the adze work, squaring up the logs, he did shirtless in the last warm days of autumn. Nancy could not but wonder if this was for her benefit. But much as she wanted Daniel, she decided he would have to come to her.

The day he completed the lapped-wood roof she came out to admire it and invite him inside for a particularly fragrant batch of gingerbread to go with their tea. Afternoon tea was a custom she would never forego so long as she could concoct any infusion, even her homemade teas. The brick tea she had found in the basement storeroom was so old as to be undrinkable even when ground and mixed with some mint to lighten it. Today they were having spearmint tea, no challenge for Daniel to identify.

He watched her empty the coals from the lid of the cast-iron pot and scoop the pan of gingerbread off the nest of rocks inside. He then ate his fill of a treat he had seldom had since his stepmother Mara had made it for all three children.

"It has frosted hard for two mornings now," Nancy said,

staring at the remains of the gingerbread. "Do you suppose a hive of wild bees would be dormant yet?"

"They do not go dormant. They are active all winter, perhaps not in full force, but if you were to cut down their tree they would definitely come out and sting you."

"Oh, I had assumed they hibernated or something. Now why would I think that?"

"I do not know. Besides, I have no idea where there is a bee tree. They are rather hard to find. I'm surprised you have not asked me to tap the maple trees. There is a good stand not fifty yards away. The spring flow is better, of course, but with these warm days and cold nights we should be able to get some sweetening for the winter." He took another satisfied swallow of tea.

"What on earth are you talking about?"

"Will wonders never cease?" he asked impishly. "Have I in one morning hit on two things you know nothing about?"

"Yes, tell me," she demanded with a delightful laugh.

He got a stick from the wood box and began to whittle a spout as he described the buckets they would need. "For now we can use ordinary firkins with covers. All we need then is a brace and bit to drill the holes. You see how the tap also has a notch to hold the bucket?"

He got the required tool and a wooden water bucket, then showed her how to tell the rock maples from others. "You can get sap out of any maple, of course, but these yield the most sugar." He tapped one tree to demonstrate, and Nancy half thought he was just toying with her, trying to see how tall a tale she would swallow, until he returned the next morning with a bucket of sap and demanded a copper kettle to boil it in.

"We have none. I had not even thought of that. Sugar does not do well in iron kettles. We will not be able to try it, after all." Her disappointment was touching.

"Oh, I have one." He went to his room and returned

with a brand-new copper pot with a bail. Nancy could not have been more amazed if he had produced a rabbit.

"Of course, I was forgetting you are a trader."

"Actually, this was to be a wedding present."

"For me?"

"Do you know anyone else who is getting married?"

"Unfortunately, no."

"Does her lack of a husband weigh heavily on Ellie?" Daniel asked as he positioned the kettle's handle on the crane and poured the sap into it. "When it begins to simmer, we must stir it. We want evaporation, not a hard boil."

"I will remember. Young Spode has been courting her, but only after I said she would be dowered. He has once or twice asked in a roundabout way how much money that would be."

"You suspect his motives?"

"Yes. I informed him that would depend on the quality of the husband."

"Hah! I bet that threw him into a quandary. You would be setting a price on his worth then, not Ellie's. Very nicely done."

"I thought so, but I do not think she will have him, no matter how desperate she is for a father for her baby. She is still in love with Luce."

"He is the father, I take it."

"Yes. He may yet come about."

"If they ever return. It has been seven weeks. Trueblood must have gotten lost."

"Take heart. Perhaps he has only been stopped by the tax collectors and had his whiskey confiscated."

"You lighten my mind. My brother may not be wandering the woods, but languishing in a jail somewhere."

"At least they will feed him, and considering the quantity he eats, they will not want to keep him long."

"There is that."

"Why did you take the risk of buying Papa's whiskey, knowing he had not paid the tax?"

Daniel stared at her to see if she meant to bait him into another argument, but she was not looking angry, just her innocent self. "A challenge. It tells us much if that false receipt I wrote out for Trueblood gets him past the tax collectors."

"It tells you that the tax is ineffectual," Nancy surmised. "That it can be easily evaded."

"Yes," Daniel said with a shrug as he pulled more hot coals under the kettle.

"Then you do care about the rebels. You mean to see what you can do about the tax. And because you know the most about it, the government may listen to you."

"But can I do anything to help in time? I have drunk with these men—untaxed whiskey, I might add—all these months. I have a strange liking for some of them. I would do much to keep them from rushing off a cliff's edge in their ignorance...." He left the statement uncompleted, suspended in the air between them.

"But if they insist upon it," Nancy finished, "you cannot stop them. They are, after all, grown men."

"Yes," Daniel said, satisfied at last that she understood his position. "Even if it means losing you, I must do my duty." He stared at the liquid in the kettle.

"Do not be absurd," she said, touching his arm. "There is nothing you can do that will lose me. You will not get out of our marriage so easily."

He smiled at her, for he knew he was permanently ensnared by her charms, had been since they crossed the sea together. He had been happier here, slaving for her, than he had ever remembered being in his life. Not the thrill of battle or the danger of intrigue could compare with spending the evening watching her cook, sew and perform the hundred tasks that kept her household running smoothly. "I wish you would come to my room tonight," he said, and was surprised to hear the words, when he was intending only to think them.

"Is your arm bothering you again?" she asked with a mischievous smile.

"Yes, along with every other part of me."

"I will come to you, then."

"And it is only midday! Where can Trueblood be?"

Daniel strode impatiently to the window, and Nancy wondered if there was not some way for them to lie together sooner. Her father was at the still, but they might have guests at any moment. And now that she knew she was to have Daniel, the fire of her desire, so long banked inside her, was sending a torrent of heat through her that would have boiled the maple sap without a fire.

"Nancy? Are you feeling unwell?"

"No—yes. I mean, I expect it is my fault he is taking so long, but he did ask." She went distractedly to the table and sat down, pressing her knees together until the waves of desire subsided.

"Ask what?" Daniel wondered, turning from the window to watch her begin to peel the potatoes.

"Ask if he could bring me anything."

"And?"

"And I said yes, there was one thing I particularly wanted."

Daniel came to loom above her and stare. His eyes glittered with suspicion when she looked innocently up at him.

"Spit it out. I am picturing him laboring over the mountains with a bedstead or some such thing attached to a pony's back."

"Oh, Daniel, do not be so silly. You know me better than that."

"Nancy!" he threatened, reaching across the board to still her hands. "What have you done?"

"It seemed a simple-enough request, but now that I consider it, if there is a calf involved, which there very well might be, it would be sure to slow them down."

"A calf?" He seized her arms, disregarding the knife

she still held. "I cannot stand the suspense. What did you ask for?"

"A milk cow, of course. We will eventually need one anyway, and not just because of the baby."

Daniel gaped at her. "A cow? Trueblood is leading a cow all the way from Philadelphia?"

"Well, yes, I suppose so, unless he could buy one on the way."

Daniel twice opened his mouth to say something, and she waited for his anger. But he let go of her and broke into hysterical laughter.

"But Daniel, how else would a cow get here? And if she is fresh with milk, she will probably have a calf. I am quite sure that is what is taking so long."

"So any instructions Norton may have for me from President Washington concerning the fate of this country must wait on the convenience of a cow," concluded Daniel, pacing again.

"President Washington is a farmer, first and foremost. I am quite sure he would understand."

"Yes, of course. I just lost my head for a moment there." Daniel's lips twitched again.

"Now you are making game of me. Are you angry? I wish you would not glare and laugh by turns. You make me fear for your reason."

"I am angry with Trueblood, but then I picture him cozening this cow to follow him and I simply cannot be serious."

Nancy laughed then, too. "I suppose he could carry the calf if he had to, but then, he might have to carry the cat."

"The what?"

"We need a cat, Daniel, and a big one, to face down the brash squirrels that have taken over the basement. It is the only way we will be able to keep any grain."

This set Daniel off again. "Trueblood hates cats." He paused long enough in his laughter to wrap Nancy in his arms and kiss her longingly. "I must go chop some more wood now."

"Daniel, I think even I am satisfied we have enough to get through the winter."

"No, I need an outlet for this energy if I am to wait until tonight."

"Perhaps you could dig some holes for me instead."

"Whatever you like. What size holes?" He was already at the door, reaching for his coat.

"Oh, apple tree-size holes," she said as she turned back toward the table.

"Drop the other shoe, Nancy." Daniel strode back to turn her around to face him again. "What else have you asked Trueblood to carry back?"

"Just some apple trees. Daniel? Why are you staring so? What is the matter?"

"Just picturing Birnam Wood moving to Dunsinane Hill."

"Nonsense, it will be nothing like that. They will be little, like sticks practically."

"And just how did you order these apple trees?"

"Mrs. Cook recommended Bartram's nursery, and he is not so very far from Philadelphia."

Daniel sighed. "Not more than a day," he said with an indulgent smile. "Nancy dear, I do not see how Norton and I are to conduct this business if you keep waylaying my courier."

"But you just said he will lose only a day."

"But that road puts him on the way to Champfreys. Mara and Constance will not let Trueblood away from there in fewer than two days."

"Oh, well, then I have ruined your plans. Daniel, I am sorry."

"You could not know. Perhaps we would be better off if we were obstructed."

"Your heart is not in this work."

"Not anymore." He looked at her and seemed on the

point of kissing her, but they both knew that would make it very hard to wait until the night.

"The fact is you now know these men. It is different when you have eaten and drunk with the enemy."

Daniel shrugged. "I wonder if Mrs. Cook conspired to get Trueblood a chance to see his mother and sister."

"She favors Trueblood over you. Did Mara do so as well?"

"No. She treated me like her own son," he said softly.

"Then why will you not go back there?"

His haunted look silenced Nancy more effectively than his anger ever could. "Do not ask me to explain." He turned and left, and she began to wonder how far he had gone, until she heard the comforting sound of his axe thudding in the yard. She knew that no matter how much she pushed Daniel, no matter what she demanded of him, she should not ask him that question again until he was ready to answer it.

The arrival of Trueblood, Luce, the string of ponies and the rest of the livestock might have put an end to their plans for a tryst. Nancy began doubling the quantity of stew she was making for that night and stirred up an extra batch of sourdough pan bread from the starter she kept in a crock on the cooking table. To be sure, she thought Daniel would be even more relaxed now that his brother was safely back, and with no very disturbing news or instructions that she could tell.

Trueblood and Luce were putting the stock away and doing the feeding and watering, while Daniel read a short letter and Nancy got acquainted with the large orange tabby who was preening itself against her legs. When Daniel looked up, Nancy was watching him expectantly.

"I am to stay here and use Trueblood as my courier, seeing as I am so deep in the rebels' confidence." He waited for her reaction to this.

"I am glad...that you are to stay."

"It still leaves me on the horns of a dilemma," he said, approaching the worktable and nearly tripping over the cat. The afternoon sun flooding in the window lit his desperate blue eyes.

"You have already decided what you must do. Now I have decided that what is between us must be above politics and men's silly games."

"Men play some pretty deadly games."

"Which makes them seem all that much stupider. If we were fighting over religious freedom or survival, if they had taxed bread, then I would say it would be a worthwhile fight."

"You do not consider whiskey to be essential?" he probed.

"What is used for medicinal purposes should not be taxed, but that is so little it is of no consequence."

"I do feel something of what these men feel."

"Enough to play devil's advocate?" she asked as lightly as she could.

"Yes. You see, it is their only luxury. When they drink, they can forget for a few hours how very brutal their lives are. It is their only escape, their only freedom. I do not think you can grasp that, for you plunge into work as though it is meat and drink to you.... What are you thinking?" he asked, as she silently put down a bowl of venison scraps for the cat.

"Picturing how it would be if I could not have my hot Saturday-night bath in the washing room. Yes, I would feel deprived. You have convinced me, Daniel. The rebel cause is just. Where does that leave us?"

Daniel was staring at her, picturing her naked. "What?" he asked stupidly.

"I said you have made a rebel of me."

"Oh, I was only demonstrating that I can see their side of it. But the law must be upheld."

"I know, even if it is an unjust law." She turned back to the hearth.

"Do you bathe in the washing room every Saturday night?"

"Yes. Sometimes on Wednesday night, as well." She looked provocatively over her shoulder at him as she stirred the cauldron of stew.

"Mmm."

"I must see to the supper now. I have started some venison steak on the rack. Can you watch it while I set the table?"

"Yes." He sat down on the settle to do his assigned task and look forward to the night.

"Where's Ellie?" Luce asked when they sat down to eat.

"I already took her some supper. The baby is due any day now, so I have not been letting her carry anything and have been making her rest."

"I've a present fer her."

To Nancy's surprise, Luce got a bundle and went across the room to knock on the storeroom door. Nancy looked inquiringly at Trueblood.

"I may have dropped a hint here and there."

"You threatened him?" Nancy accused with a twinkle.

"Never. A man should not be forced into marriage."

"Oh, really?" Daniel asked with mock resentment.

Trueblood shrugged. "But when I dwelt on all the advantages—having a helpmate, not to mention strong children to work the land, and the fact that he could take her into his bed every night for the rest of his life…"

Daniel stared rather miserably at Nancy, his blue eyes troubled with desire. She looked sympathetically at him, regretting all the nights they had missed because of her stubbornness.

"Yes, I am sure you emphasized all the nicer parts of marriage," Nancy said. "I wonder if I should thank you or no. Just wanting her does not make Luce good husband material."

"But 'tis a start," Riley said eagerly.

"Yes, I suppose."

Luce returned to the table to say, "She likes it."

"That was very thoughtful of you, Luce," Nancy replied.

The man blushed and went back to his meal.

The remains of the considerable feast Nancy had prepared for their return were hardly cleared away when the usual crowd of half-a-dozen men showed up. She wondered that their womenfolk did not object to their absence night after night.

The talk tonight was all of Philadelphia and the wonders Luce had seen there. He remembered belatedly that he did still work at the White Horse and took over the serving of whiskey from Nancy, who was busy with sewing tiny garments.

Ellie appeared at the door clutching her stomach, and Nancy got up and led her back to her bed.

Daniel went to the door. "Is it time?" he asked.

"Yes, but it will be a good few hours yet. I have a feeling we will go through a great deal of whiskey tonight. Only someone with the soundest of nerves can bear to hear a woman scream hour after hour."

Nancy was right. No more than an hour into Ellie's labor, all but Spode and Ned Johnson had left for home, and Johnson finally bethought him of his own baby and took himself off. John Spode sat belligerently nursing his drink, while the rest of the men, even Nancy's father, paced uneasily about the room. Sometime after midnight Daniel thought he heard a lighter cry, but it could have been Missy, the cat, if she had been locked in the basement. At any rate, Ellie's screams had stopped. An ominous silence fell over the house. Luce paced nervously to the door of the small room and stood staring at it. Nancy almost hit him in the head when she carried out the slop bucket.

"Well?" Luce demanded, running an impatient hand through his long, sandy hair.

"It is a boy. You were not worried, were you? The babe is suckling mightily."

"Yes," Luce gasped, and pushed past her to look on his son.

"I've been meanin' ta speak, Miss Riley." Spode started up from his bench.

"Not now. I still have work to do."

"I will go with you," Daniel offered, throwing her cloak about her shoulders and opening the door for her. He meant to learn all he could about birthing babies. Perhaps Nancy and one of her clients would let him watch sometime.

"Ye're Ellie's master, Riley. I can deal with ye." Spode started anew.

"The girl's nay indentured ta me, if that's wot ye're askin'."

"I know, but an offer was made by yer dotter ta get a husband for Ellie, and I want ta take that offer."

"I see," Riley said sagely, though he had no idea what Nancy had offered.

"Now the babe's born, Ellie can be married," Spode continued.

"'Twould a been a tad more convenient before the babe had come," Riley said.

"I do nay want the child, just Ellie."

"What?" Trueblood and Riley demanded in unison, overturning the wood bench as they jumped up.

"The child's none o' my get. I only want Ellie."

"That's why ye waited?" Riley demanded, his face suffused with anger.

"The babe might o' died. Many do. Or Ellie might o' died, but she did nay die. So I want ta marry her."

"What do you propose to do with the child?" Trueblood roared. "Leave it exposed for the wolves to devour?"

Spode was so alarmed at Trueblood's menacing stance he gave no thought to how articulate the huge man had become.

"No, o' course not. I'm not a heathen," Spode said, then cowered under Trueblood's quelling glare.

"No babe'll come ta any harm in this house," Riley shouted.

"There's many who'd take it and raise it as their own," Spode replied defensively. "Aye, they'd pay ta have a healthy babe, if they'd just lost one."

"You mean to sell the child?" Trueblood was furious by now. Nancy and Daniel came back in to find both Riley and Trueblood advancing on Spode as though they meant to beat him to death.

"Whatever is the matter?" Daniel asked.

Luce appeared in the doorway, carrying the baby, which was wrapped tightly in one of the little blankets Nancy had hemmed. "Ellie fell asleep," he explained. "I did nay want her ta drop him."

To Nancy's surprise he seated himself on the settle by the fire and positioned the sleeping infant in the crook of his arm. Nancy smiled. For some men fathering was an instinct.

"P'haps even Miss Riley would want ta keep the child," Spode desperately offered. "I would nay ask fer any money fer the babe, in that case."

"What are you dithering about, Spode?" Nancy demanded.

"Mr. Spode has offered ta marry Ellie," Riley announced angrily, "if she'll give up her baby, which he proposes ta sell ta a barren woman."

"What?" Nancy shrieked. "Of all the villainous, monstrous suggestions I have ever heard!"

"Well, ye don't expect me ta raise a babe who's not me own, do you?"

"I do not expect you to do anything—" she drew a knife out of her pocket and pointed it suggestively at his chest "—except get out of this inn and never come back."

"It was ye who made the proposition, to get Ellie a husband," he argued, backing toward the door.

"Did it not occur to your pea-sized brain that I was doing it to get a father for the child? Now get out!''

"What's all the noise about? You'll wake him," Luce complained.

"Did ye nay hear what this devil suggested, Luce?" Riley asked.

"Aye, but it makes no matter. Ellie is marryin' me, as soon as she can stand the ride to the church. She loves me.''

"I offered first," Spode challenged.

Luce stared at him, then calmly walked over and handed the baby to Nancy, who dropped the knife.

"I'm marryin' Ellie. It's wot I should ha' done in the first place, for the babe's mine. And I don't want no bride price fer her, neither." He looked earnestly at Nancy. "I've money of me own now and a chanst ta earn more. So you, Mister Look-down-your-nose Spode, can take yerself off.''

Spode glanced desperately from one angry face to another.

"Ye heard him," Riley said. "Ye've had yer marching orders, and don't come back. The very idea…" He continued mumbling after Spode had slithered out the door. "Ye know, I've not held a babe since I held young Nancy. Could I?"

Luce recovered his son and proudly held him out for Riley to cosset. Nancy looked from a stunned Daniel to a grinning Trueblood.

"That has all worked out for the best," Trueblood said, rubbing his hands together.

"We can only hope everyone will be so eager to hold him when he is crying or needs to be changed," Nancy countered.

To her surprise, Luce pulled a sleeping mat into Ellie's room and said he would watch over her and the baby that night. The infant slept there in a cradle Daniel had fashioned during the long evenings of Luce's absence. Nancy watched Trueblood go wearily to bed and her father crawl up to the common sleeping room after only a few celebratory noggins of whiskey.

While Daniel was checking on the stock one last time, Nancy heated her bathwater and carried it into the washing room. She bathed in the large wooden tub where they did the laundry during the winter months. The door had a lock on it, but she did not use it this night, and her instincts served her well.

She had not heard him enter, but Daniel's voice spoke softly in her ear. "If I had had any idea what I was missing..."

"Would you like a bath, too, sir? There is no charge, seeing as how you work here."

"I will follow you, provided you will scrub my back."

"I think we can both fit, if you do not splash about too much."

"Where did you get the soap?" he asked, as he stripped off his clothes.

"I brought it with me from England." She paused to gaze longingly at his lithe form. "I doubt I can ever make anything like it, but I will see what I can concoct. I know a few herbs that do not lose their fragrance or change into something foul when they are boiled."

She had already washed her hair, so he first ducked his head and scrubbed his before sliding into the tub crosslegged with his back to her. He pulled her legs around him possessively and the heat of her crotch against him almost overpowered him. She scrubbed his back slowly, not neglecting that little triangle at the base of his spine that excited him so. Then he turned and demanded the sponge so that he could return the favor. He managed her back easily enough, but her soapy breasts slipping through his hands brought on all of his pent-up desire from the past months.

"I cannot wait until we go upstairs," he whispered desperately.

"That is why I laid the rug on the floor."

He stood up to reveal his arousal, and it caused a quickening of her heartbeat and that wonderfully familiar hunger inside her. They dried each other on the coarse toweling, then sank to the rug in a still-damp embrace, both smelling of English lavender. He laid her down and spread her hair out on the clean rug to dry.

"Is the floor too hard? If you want—"

"No, stay on top. It reminds me of the first time, on that large rock at the ford."

"Mayhap that will excite you, remembering how we were about to die." He began to nuzzle her breasts, teasing the nipples into erect buds.

"I do not need fear to excite me. You do so without even trying. It has been torture to be in the same house with you and not have you." She ran her hands over his shoulder blades and muscled arms, feeling the scar from his shoulder wound, then the one under his collarbone from the deer. She had done an excellent job on his face, for the scar along his jaw was scarcely visible. His taut body bore many other marks, but she did not ask about them.

"I thought I was the only one suffering."

"Why did you not ask me to come to you?"

"I thought you might still be angry."

"I scarcely remember why I was angry," she said softly.

He pulled at her lips with his kisses, increasing the rush of rosy warmth the whole way to her face. "It was that stupid blunder I made when I—"

"Do not remind me, just kiss me." Her legs coiled around him and locked, pulling him down to make contact. He was amazed at the strength in them and pushed himself up to test her. Laughing, she rose with him. "You cannot get away from me," she challenged.

"I do not want to," he said, lowering her to the rug again. He shivered as her feet stroked the backs of his calves. He entered her teasingly slowly this time, inch by inch, until she was shuddering with hunger for him.

"Is this to pay me back for having you wait?" she asked, making an effort to control her muscles.

"I was curious which of us would break first," he panted. "Me, I think." He thrust home, pinning her to the hard floor and wringing a gasp from her. Then he raised himself on his arms and began a side-to-side motion that brought her hands curling up around his neck and reaching into his damp hair.

"Now! You win. Take me now!" she begged.

He laughed and ran his swollen member in and out, bringing her arching up to him. He delighted in the small gasps he wrung from her with each movement—not just that they were gasps of pleasure, but that they were genuine. She was right. She would never lie to him or pretend with him in any way. It was part of her singularity to be completely honest.

The spasm that shook her wrung his seed from him and sent a delicious feeling a lethargy stealing over his muscles. He felt as though he had run many miles and could now rest in her arms. There was a sense of safety and completeness he had never attained before.

When the chill of the room could no longer be ignored, he rose on one elbow to gaze at her in the candlelight. She had been watching him, not asleep as he had thought.

"This rebellion seems likely to cool off," he said, toying with a lock of her hair. "Will you marry me publicly now?"

"Ellie's babe is but a few hours old. Ellie still needs so much help. Unless...unless you would mean to leave me here."

"I want to make a home for you."

"This is a home. We have lived here together as man and wife. Why not continue?"

"You would be safe in Philadelphia," he said urgently.

"No, I would not. Be realistic. The yellow fever will be back again in the summer. If you do not want me nursing the sick, that is the last place you should take me. Besides, now that I have seen everything between here and there I am not sure I would be satisfied to be in Philadelphia.''

''No, not when Ellie's baby is here,'' he said regretfully as he got to his knees.

He picked up his clothes and crept out into the darkened common room, leaving her puzzling over his odd statement. She loved little Gabriel, but she was far from besotted with him. He had a mother and father to dote on him. She would reserve that special kind of love for her own children. If only she could marry Daniel, holding her own baby need be no farther away than nine months. She could not say what held her back. But she had a feeling the rebellion was not over, that there would be fighting and violence in the spring or summer, that people would die. She did not want to be caught pregnant when she might have to flee for her life or defend the inn against soldiers. She must wait until Daniel's business was settled once and for all before she let him get her with child.

Chapter Ten

The talk among the guests at the inn for many nights had been the Democratic Society to be established at Mingo Creek. Since Riley had agreed to go to the meeting, Daniel said he would ride with him.

On the surface Trueblood seemed totally absorbed in rocking the sleeping Gabriel. The look he sent Daniel was a warning to not get too deeply involved, certainly to not become an instigator in the very sort of insurrection they were hoping to prevent. On the other hand, Daniel could not speak against the rebels too definitely or they would cease to trust him. He must only go and report.

All this Daniel read in a look, but the worried glance Nancy bestowed on him meant she also knew the delicate path he trod. She did not approve, but she was worried about him all the same. Perhaps he could make a truce with her, a mutual tolerance for both their vocations. He had to do something.

Nancy and Trueblood both waited up for Daniel and Riley to return. Ellie, Luce and Gabriel were in bed, and the cat had replaced the baby on Trueblood's lap.

"Daniel said you hated cats." Nancy pulled her workbag to her and took out a small piece of knitting.

"People can change."

"Meaning what? That I should give in to Daniel and let him take me back to Philadelphia?"

"No, meaning that you have wrought more change in my so-stubborn brother than anyone else has ever achieved. You have only to persist to get what you want."

"Half the time I do not know what I want, except to be with him. I cannot even stand for him to be away a few hours."

"Do not worry, Nancy dear," Trueblood replied. "Our Daniel can handle things."

"But I have been pushing him, Trueblood."

"What do you mean?"

"I have almost demanded that he make a choice between his work and me. I am afraid that duty will win out."

"You should never mix politics and love, Nancy. They use such different areas of a man's brain. You will leave him unable to think clearly."

"But if I make love to him when we are still disagreeing, will he not charge me with using my body to try to sway him or confuse him?"

"It would not be the first time…"

"What? Not the first time a woman had betrayed him in this manner?"

"I should not speak of it."

"Why does Daniel not trust women?"

"It is not that. He simply does not expect much of them."

"If only this stupid rebellion were over."

"The Revolution lasted eight long years."

"Do you think it will come to that—a break of the western counties from the tidewater region? Will we have to choose sides and fight?"

"If we do, what side will you choose?"

She looked at him. "That is simple. Whatever side Daniel is on."

"Do we know what side that will be?" Trueblood asked.

"Daniel would never betray his country," Nancy said. "Not unless—"

"Not unless a woman seduced him into doing so." Trueblood stared at the fire. "A heavy burden for you, Nancy girl. Not only must you decide your own loyalties, but you must consider what your decision will do to Daniel."

The rumble of Riley's voice outside the door brought an end to their discussion, and Nancy offered the late arrivals tea, which Daniel gratefully accepted, warming his hands around the mug. Riley looked askance at Nancy's offer and poured himself a tankard of whiskey. He wanted to talk, and Trueblood lent him a seemingly interested ear. "I am not sleepy, Daniel," Trueblood said. "I will be up for a few hours."

The inference that he might spend those hours with Nancy was so blatant that Daniel glanced at her for confirmation. She smiled and handed him a candle. She did not even bother going to her own room, but preceded him to the one he shared with Trueblood. A fire had been left burning in the small corner fireplace, so that Daniel was met with warmth rather than the chill he was expecting.

"I suppose you want to know what happened?" he asked as he stripped off his clothes and crawled between the sheets. He watched her appreciatively as she undressed as gracefully as any woman he had ever seen, laying aside her shawl, laced bodice and skirt, then untying her pocket sack and laying it on the chair. A suspicion gnawed at his mind. "You must understand that I cannot stop what I am doing."

Nancy pulled her shift over her head and shook out her hair from its ribbon, then reached between the sheets to remove the warm brick.

"If you are trying to seduce me..." he began.

"Seduce you? I do not think that is possible. Besides, that sort of persuasion should be beneath both of us." She crawled in beside him and rubbed her warm feet over his cold ones, sending a thrill of anticipation up his legs to his groin.

"What do you mean? And stop doing that until you explain yourself."

"I have decided we must separate our political lives from our private ones."

"And how are we to do that? Politics is my whole life."

"I mean that I do not intend to let a mere rebellion come between us. Our love is stronger than all the outrage and angry words on either side. We simply will not speak of it."

"If you think to change my mind—"

Her kiss stopped his protest and he responded, losing himself in the sweetness of her mouth, the lusciousness of her hair as it slipped through his fingers like spun gold.

"I forgot what I was saying," he gasped when he came up for air.

"That I will not change your mind. I do not mean to do so, for you are right. I will stand by you, Daniel."

"Against your own father?"

"Against everyone."

He gave a profound sigh of relief and held her so long he fell asleep. But they had hours yet before anyone came upstairs, and most likely her father would sleep in the kitchen or on the settee, as he often did.

It was then that Nancy realized they were dangerous to each other. Their deep love and need could be used against each other. The knowledge did not frighten her, but it was a danger to guard against their whole future lives. Nothing must separate them, for even as they made each other strong, they made each other weak.

"Riley said Dupree was there," Trueblood mentioned to his yawning brother over their morning coffee.

"Yes, and glaring at me like I was a rattlesnake." Daniel rubbed his hands together, then set them around the warm cup before him. Perhaps Nancy would sew him some mittens, he thought. Even watering the stock made his fingers stiff these cold mornings.

"That must have tested your sangfroid."

"Actually, it took me a bit of time to recognize him, shaven as he was and wearing a pair of breeches and coat rather than those stinking buckskins of his. I did not know him at first. I shall have to keep in mind what a difference such a rig makes. At any rate, it was only when he elbowed Bradford and whispered to him that it hit me we still have Dupree to deal with. I am quite sure he has not been around all winter, for I have asked about him when I have gone into town."

"Really, Norton has not even been worried about you following Dupree. Washington calculates there is no real help forthcoming from France since they have no means of supplying either soldiers or arms to the frontiersman. They have no presence on the Continent. His big fear is that Bradford will make a deal with the British."

"Seems unlikely," Daniel mused.

"If Dupree is working only for France."

Daniel came awake and stared at him. "I know we have considered the possibility before that Dupree may be taking pay from both France and Canada. He might have gone to Canada since he has been missing. Simcoe would not be above lending the same sort of aid the tribes have always gotten from the British. Nice feather in his cap to break off the western half of the country, so long as he does not start a war between England and America in the process."

"And Canada would control the Mississippi. He could make a treaty with the western tribes."

"There are so many ways it can go," Daniel complained, jumping up and pacing to the window. He saw Nancy coming from the stable with a bucket of milk and stirred himself to build up the fire.

Trueblood smiled at his brother's realization of what was really important.

As always, after such a rousing event as the formation of the Mingo Creek Democratic Society, the disconnected communities fell into a few weeks of quiet, until someone should once again call a meeting. So long as their unrest was confined to evenings of drinking and grumbling in inns such as the White Horse, Daniel was content. It meant that the army would find no open revolt when it came.

Missy, the cat, had done an excellent job of ridding the basement of squirrels and wood mice and now lived happily on milk and table scraps. In fact, she was getting positively stout on her diet, and Daniel finally concluded she had come to them pregnant and that there would be no dearth of cats in a few short weeks.

Now Daniel threw himself into plowing and planting, with Riley's encouragement. He wondered why Riley showed such a sudden interest in farming, until he remembered they were planting rye, the source of the makings for next fall's batch of whiskey. They were congratulating themselves on a job well done when news came of the attack on Neville's family as they returned from Pittsburgh. It was a dangerous situation, and they all held their breath for a few days, but no arrests were made. And they hoped the incident would not be blown to its full proportion.

Nancy was particularly upset that women were no longer safe to ride about at night, even if they were the family of the federal tax inspector. Daniel reminded her that it had never been safe for a woman to be abroad at night. She glared at him but said no more. It did not matter that it should be safe, only that it was not, and she could not argue with Daniel's judgment on this. Besides, he looked so pensive afterward, like he expected her to rant at him over the safety of the roads, that she felt sorry for him.

In April a letter from Norton brought the first good news they had had in months. A law had been passed to ease the difficulties of those served with summonses. Previously they had to appear in federal court in Philadelphia. Now they would be able to answer charges locally and be spared the lengthy and expensive trip.

Seated at one of the kitchen tables, Daniel had just finished reading this proudly to Nancy. She looked up from the changing cloths she was folding. "Of course, it would be better if they were not served with summonses at all," she said.

"Not everyone has been clever enough to hide his still from the tax collectors like your father has."

"It is disquieting to think that if even one man informed on him, he could be arrested, too."

"It will give him a chance to see how loyal his friends are," Daniel said.

"You do always look on the bright side," Nancy gibed.

"Your father has been nudging me and pointing out what a comely lass you are," Daniel said with a grin.

"Indeed, and did you disagree with him, to protect your cover?"

"Why no, I admitted I had noticed."

"No doubt you dug your toe in the dirt and did the shy boy bit to perfection."

"I fancy I convinced him my interest in you has heretofore been innocent."

"You do have that knack. And what is your next move? Will you court me like a lovelorn swain, sitting on my porch drinking lemonade and admiring the spring flowers?"

"I take it he thinks you need a bit of softening up. He is going to drop a word in your ear, remind you not to scowl at me so blatantly, perhaps even smile at me once in a while."

"If he knew what you really had been up to he would tar and feather you himself."

"If he knew what a willing lass you are he would drop over with the apoplexy."

Nancy laughed. "I suppose we will have to tell him someday."

"No, I intend to play the innocent to the last. We shall

have a proper wedding as soon as we are free of this back-woods mess.''

''And then what?''

''I have not thought that far ahead,'' Daniel said, reluctant to start another argument and knowing this was dangerous ground.

''That is rather unlike you, Daniel.''

''It must be the flowers,'' he said, gazing out the open door into the yard. ''With all this spring loveliness around it lulls you into believing nothing really bad can happen.''

''I hope that is true.''

''Where has your appetite for adventure gone?''

''I do not know. I can remember thinking how proud I would be to follow an army train and take care of the wounded. Now it seems a totally stupid idea. I want only what I have—you, and enough other things to keep me busy when you cannot.''

He leaned across the table board and kissed her. His eyes fell to the small garments she was folding and he smiled at her sadly.

He wondered if Nancy would be content only with him—if, as he suspected, there were to be no children in their future. He would have to leave her the option of backing out. No one knew of their union except Trueblood. If Daniel could give her no children, and she wanted them more than she wanted him, he would release her.

''What is it, Daniel?'' Nancy asked when he arrived back from Pittsburgh and entered the inn with a look black as thunder.

''Sixty farmers, more or less, have been summoned to Philadelphia for not paying their taxes.'' He kicked at the log in the fireplace, sending an shower of angry sparks up the chimney.

''But that's impossible,'' Nancy said, plopping down on a bench.

"They changed the law. That cannot happen," Trueblood added from his seat at the table.

"Hamilton issued the summonses under the old law."

"That idiot!" Trueblood swore as vehemently as Nancy had ever heard anyone do. "It is almost as though he is trying to provoke a rebellion."

"I am not altogether sure that is not the case." Daniel stalked to the table and sat on the bench. "The tax was his idea. This may be his way of forcing the issue."

"Forcing the rebellion into a reality, you mean?" Nancy asked.

"Something has been set in motion that there is no stopping," Daniel said in defeat. "I do not think I have helped at all. Whatever I did, whatever news I sent back to the president, Hamilton will have used in his own way."

"Damn him!" Trueblood said, smacking his fist into his palm.

Nancy looked at the two brothers lovingly, and knew she could not stand the thought of them blaming themselves for something that they had no power to prevent. "It is a relief, anyway."

"What?" they demanded in unison.

"Knowing we were powerless to stop it. We need never feel that we personally failed. You have both done your duty, and done your best to quiet this thing, but neither side means to let it rest. There are just some men who must make war no matter what the consequences."

"I thought..." Daniel fumbled for words. "I thought you would be angry that I had not done more to stop it. Even in failure you make me feel that I have succeeded."

"You have, both of you. Now it is only a matter of riding out the storm. The farmers will not go to Philadelphia, of course."

"Never," they answered.

Nancy noticed Daniel hardly touched his dinner and only thought he must be distracted by his desire for her. She hurried through her bath and came to him with her hair still damp from washing. He made room for her on the small bed. Trueblood and Luce had gone down to Pittsburgh, and except for Ellie and the baby, and Riley snoring in the kitchen, they were quite alone in the house.

Daniel ran his hot hands over her hips, which seemed to him to be rounder than before. Her breasts were fuller, of that he was certain. Mayhap she was with child already and had not yet told him. That was what he hoped. Then there would be no more delays and they would be together every night and any time of the day they chose. He wondered if a man could ever tire of such a woman and decided it would be impossible. He slid her nightdress over her head. She had left off speaking during their encounters. That, too, was different. Her eyes, with their languorous lids, made her seem intoxicated, half-dazed by the time he thrust himself between her warm thighs.

He held back as long as he could, stroking tentatively, uncertainly, making her mad with the suspense of when he would take her. She kneaded his buttocks in anticipation, and when he thrust deep she clasped him to her and kissed him as flagrantly with her mouth as she yielded to him her innermost place. She arched her back for the spill of his seed, meeting him with an animal hunger. She had been this way ever since Ellie's child had arrived. They were not playing at it, but making love in desperate earnest. Why then was she not carrying his child? Daniel withered at the fear this question let in and came out of her to hug her to him, to arrange her hair on the pillow to dry. She was still gasping, her nipples still erect with latent desire. He suckled at them.

"Oh, Daniel, I want a baby so much."

At the word *baby*, he stopped nuzzling her and pulled her close, resting his chin in her hair.

"Papa does like you, Daniel. He told me so."

"What did he say about me?" Daniel asked, trying to distract Nancy from thoughts of babies.

"That you might make a good husband."

"Might?"

"But I gave it as my opinion that you were too easily led."

"You what?" Daniel pushed himself up on one elbow to regard her.

"He then pointed out that such a man would make an excellent husband, since he would not be forever deciding against my wishes or ordering me about."

"And you had not even considered that, I suppose?" Daniel asked skeptically.

"No, for I countered with how often you would be gone for weeks at a time on the trail, leaving me to fend for myself."

"I bet he saw nothing amiss in that, either, since he did worse to your mother, leaving her for years at a time."

"Best of all possible worlds, according to Papa. I could do as I pleased most of the time and not end up with a baby every year."

Daniel stiffened and stared at her.

"What is it, Daniel? I was only joking. He doesn't realize I would like to have a baby every year, at least for a few years."

"If you want children so desperately, I fear I may disappoint you."

"What are you talking about?" Nancy asked. "We can have our own children when the time comes."

Daniel sat up and turned his face away. "The time, as you call it, has come again and again, without producing any children. It can only mean that I am not capable of it." His voice choked on the words.

"But, Daniel. The only reason I am not pregnant at this very moment is my herbs."

"What?"

"There is a special mixture I use in my tea. It prevents—"

"God's death!" he shouted, thrusting himself from her and nearly falling out of the bed.

"Quiet, Daniel. You will wake young Gabriel."

"All this time I was thinking myself incapable of fathering a child...."

"But I thought you would be glad I had managed so well."

"Managed so well—to kill my children?" He got up and went to stand in naked outrage at the small window.

"How dare you! I have not killed any children."

"You have done the closest thing to it," he snarled over his shoulder.

"So that was your plan—to get me with child so I would have to marry you." She snatched up her shift and pulled it over her head.

"Yes, for lack of any better plan. What was wrong with it?"

"Only that, unlike most women, I have some control over what a man can do to me or not."

"You have all the control. It isn't fair."

"I see my instinct not to tell you was the right one. Trueblood thought you would not understand."

"You discussed this with my brother?" Daniel turned to stare at her in horror.

"Not specifically...but he knew what I took."

"I cannot believe that the two of you conspired to dupe me. I trusted you." He sat down on the wobbly stool and raked his hands through his hair.

"And I loved you. I can see now you will never accept my role as a healer."

"As a murderess!" He threw the accusation at her, then turned his face away.

"I have heard enough. When Trueblood returns you may go away with him. I will not look for you again." Nancy left the room none too quietly, but her father was drunk, as usual, and Nancy supposed that Ellie cared not what they did so long as they did not wake Gabriel.

* * *

Before Nancy had time to regret her harsh words, and certainly before Daniel's anger had a chance to cool, Trueblood had a load of hides and whiskey ready to go to Philadelphia. Daniel left with his brother, despite Trueblood's patent disapproval. He had not even time to get Nancy alone and find out what had gone amiss before he and Daniel were riding down the road to the east.

Luce was pleased to have a chance to spend time with Ellie and the baby, which he pronounced to be growing like a wolf pup. Nancy tried to be pleased for them, but she ached inside for want of Daniel. Had she betrayed him by not telling him what she was doing? It was her body, after all. But it was his, too, she realized, from the moment at the ford when she had first given herself to him. And she had been his in more than name. Now she had driven him away, all because of her fears of what the summer might bring. She would be justly served if peace settled over the valley and left her bereft of Daniel forever.

But before Daniel could have possibly reached Philadelphia her cautious avoidance of pregnancy and marriage was justified. The liberty poles were going up. The tax collectors were making their rounds and being threatened. Writs of arrest were issued, and the men who came to the inn to talk each night were more passionate about their rights, more desperate for conflict than ever. It was like a powder keg. Nancy only hoped Daniel would not be the spark.

Chapter Eleven

It had been blazing hot for a June day. After her bath, the small attic room enveloped Nancy in a warmth that set the fires of her desire burning. She had been standing in her shift looking out the window at the moon, yearning for Daniel and thinking about that night at the crossing, when she thought she heard the familiar thud of pony hooves that had marked the rhythm of their journey here last autumn. She thought she had only wished it, but suddenly there were the pack ponies, coming along the road. She recognized Trueblood, then Daniel, in spite of the darkness, for the bright moon cast shadows of the men and horses on the grass in the yard. They rode around the inn straight for the stable and led the whole train into the corral. She knew they must have been pushing the animals hard to get home, and she hoped it was because of her and not some political emergency. She threw her cloak about her and went to greet them.

"There is stew still hot on the coals and bread just baked today." She thought she could hear Trueblood's stomach growl.

"I'll just get the packs off the ponies," he said. He was quick about his work and left Daniel to water the stock as Nancy tossed down hay from the loft.

After what seemed an eternity, she heard Daniel lead the

ponies back from the spring and let them loose in the stable
to find their feed. He walked to the bottom of the ladder to
wait for her, while she waited at the top. If she went down
to him, they would go inside, she would watch him eat and
there would still be a wall between them. But if he came
up to her she could tell him all. She heard his footfalls on
the ladder and tears sprang to her eyes.

"Nancy." He stood uncertainly in the cramped loft. "I
am sorry I was such a fool. I had forgotten that you are not
like other women. I should have remembered how important it is for you to make things safe, to be sure of everything."

She threw her cloak off and lay down upon it. "I should
have told you what I was doing. It should not have been
just my decision. And I did not kill any babies. How could
I when I want one so much? There is a vast difference
between not conceiving and aborting a child. I could never
do that." She drew her shift off over her head in obvious
invitation.

He staggered to her, the rest of his prepared apology
flitting out of his head. The chinks between the logs had
long since been filled in, but a few bars of moonlight slid
through the ventilation gaps, banding her seductive body as
they had so long ago, nearly a year, since the two of them
had come to this place. These last weeks without her had
made him taut as a bowstring. He knelt and kissed her, then
tore at his clothes like a drowning man weighed down by
something that might prove his doom. When he was free
of them he fell on her as on a safe, dry beach after a fearful
storm. There was no pretense of playfulness this time. He
parted her legs and thrust himself deep in the well of her,
shaking with the effort to hold back, but unleashing himself
at the eager grasp of her hands on his thighs. It was over
in a moment and he kissed her belatedly, promising over
and over never to argue with her again.

He held her then until his own frantic breathing had

stilled to a relaxed sighing. Her hair smelled freshly washed as he stirred it with his face and kissed it.

"It is your choice now," Nancy whispered. "Shall I give up my tea, Daniel?"

He hesitated, desperately turning over in his mind all the possible ramifications. He pushed himself up and looked at her. "Best not, yet. Trouble is brewing. There is no telling when I may be fleeing this country before an angry mob. If I am ever discovered, you will not be safe if you are known to be my wife."

"Oh, I think they would not hold your spying against me. I am too useful to them for my healing skills. Unless...unless you want me to give that up, as well."

"We will say no more about that, for I know you will not give it up, any more than Mara would do so."

Nancy hugged him to her and drank up the kisses he rained upon her lips and neck and breasts. She believed that he meant what he said, but that they would never argue again she considered an impossibility. She simply did not say so.

"Can you wait for your child?" he asked with regret.

"I have waited a year. If nothing happens one way or the other by fall, I will go with you."

"Ellie should be able to manage by then."

"That is no longer a consideration. It was just an excuse. I will go with you because I love you and for no other reason."

"I believe you. I suppose we should go in."

"No," she said desperately. "Papa is asleep already and Trueblood cannot have eaten all the food in the house yet."

Daniel chuckled. "Very well. In a little while I shall be able to make love to you properly."

"Let us never be angry again, never waste another night apart."

"I promise never to be such a fool again."

He lay down beside her and fell silent.

"What are you thinking about, Daniel?"

"Politics. Forgive me?"

"I cannot help myself, either."

"I suppose it is true, what Norton told me—that the Washington Democratic Society condemned President Washington's neutrality in the war between France and England?" He twisted a strand of her hair around one finger.

"Yes, the idiots. According to Papa that was incited by Bradford and some of his cronies who have been speaking at the local societies. The fools feed on each other."

"Dupree's idea, no doubt. There I was, just telling Norton that these Democratic Societies that have been springing up are a lot of talkers who will never do anything, and he let me have it between the eyes with that news."

"Oh, Daniel." She turned to him and laid a hand on his chest. "Was it very bad for you?"

"It did not lend me any credit and gave him an excuse to berate me for leaving my post."

"That was my fault. I sent you away. Will he dismiss you?"

"Do not look so hopeful. Fortunately, I said it to Norton, not to President Washington. Norton nearly laughed his head off, but no, he will not let me go. He needs me too much. He asked after you." Daniel pulled her close to him and rested his chin on top of her head.

"That was sweet of him. What are you going to do now?"

"Build that brick smokehouse you wanted. A log one is all very well, but impossible to secure against animals."

She laughed. "I mean about the insurrection."

"Oh, that. Only my job. I will report through Trueblood, but I will stay and take care of my own." Daniel stroked her back and left his hand resting on her hip. "Should things get really hot, I want you to take Ellie and the baby to the little cabin by the still."

"But what if this is not cleared up by winter? We will not be able to build a fire there without someone discovering us."

"Hence the new smokehouse. Where I will place it, the smoke drifting down the valley night and day, smoking venison, will assure that no one will notice the smoke from your fire."

"Daniel, that is brilliant." She craned her head back to gaze at him. "Why did I not think of that?"

"I am sure you would have, eventually."

"It will be a lot of work, burning the limestone, then digging the clay, baking the bricks...."

"Most of which also requires making a lot of smoke. So you will be safe at any time should the rebellion heat up. And it is something to do while we wait."

"You mean you will be too tired to pace?"

"Yes, I now see what you were about, keeping me forever busy. Hard work keeps me from worrying so much."

"About things over which you have no control."

"Then that was always your plan?"

"Yes, but sometimes it made you too tired to be interested in me, I think."

"No, I was always ready for you."

He kissed her hungrily, invading her eager mouth with a promise of more to come. This time he stretched out the experience, toying with her with his tongue and fingers until she begged him to come inside her. Even there he could pace himself, pushing her beyond all patience and endurance until she gripped him with her internal muscles, urging him on with a hot tightness that made him moan. He gave up to her then and surged against her like the tide, with powerful thrusts that finally satisfied the weeks of hunger and made her sigh with contentment as the last shuddering spasm released her.

The next day a more relaxed Daniel gathered from Riley and Luce an appraisal of the dangers they were facing. The excuse of not being able to get a load of whiskey safely away without arousing the suspicions of the tax collectors should serve to keep him and Trueblood lingering for a few weeks.

After listening to one evening's talk, Daniel could see what a pass local feeling had come to and was convinced the White Horse had become a hotbed of rebellion. Both the lower rooms had been filled, with several dozen angry farmers in attendance. After they had ridden home to their families and the others had gone to bed, Daniel helped Nancy gather up the used mugs and firkins.

"Is this true—that your father has joined the local militia?"

"Yes, they are always in need of men, and with his army experience…"

"But does he not see that he might be called upon to fire on some of the men who drink here and speak so openly of rebellion?"

Nancy hesitated in her washing up. "I think he is assuming the militia will go over to the rebels' side."

"Indeed! Things are come to a pretty pass, that an insurrection should be so organized, almost like a military campaign."

"But not a surprise when one thinks about it. Many of the men are veterans, if not of the Revolution, then of some other war. It is in their blood to enjoy the fighting."

"Surely no one enjoys it."

"Perhaps you do not. And perhaps they do not always like the consequences, but I have listened to them talk. They are looking forward to the uprising, to doing great deeds."

"And do you try to discourage them?"

"As much as I can. I treat them like children, but they do not pay much attention to me."

"That is good, in a way."

"Bradford came once."

"At the instigation of Dupree, no doubt. What was his purpose?"

"To see if Papa was trustworthy, I think. Dupree was not with him."

"Did he ask about me and Trueblood?"

"Only about you, but Papa vouched for you. When he said you buy illegal whiskey from him, Bradford seemed satisfied."

"Good. Was he suspicious of you at all?"

"He noticed me, if that is what you mean," she said with a toss of her head.

"I am sure they all notice you," Daniel agreed, coming up behind her and rubbing against her hips. "And I cannot like my wife serving liquor to such an untrustworthy bunch."

"They are not so frightening now that I know them. I assure you I could stop any of them with no more than a word."

"And have you had occasion to stop them from doing anything?"

"Once or twice. After all, word has got around that we have quarreled and you no longer lay claim to my affections."

"I suppose my coming back will start the rumor mills going again."

"People must have something to talk of. Even this rebellion grows thin after a time."

"So Bradford does not suspect you of being more than a serving wench?"

"I am skillful enough to keep any man from suspecting that I am taking in every word that is said, but even Ellie could fool a man such as Bradford. He is one of those men so caught up in his own self-importance, it never occurs to him that a woman might be intelligent or even dangerous."

"A tragic mistake for any man." Daniel wrapped his arms around her.

"And one you did not make. You are an unusual man, Daniel." Nancy's eyes glowed with admiration.

"A spy, and that is what I am, is not a great deal dif-

ferent from a traitor, at least in the eyes of these people.''
He paced to the fireplace and raked the embers together
before he turned to regard her. ''If I were discovered they
would hang me from the top of one of those liberty poles,
like they used to hang the British tax collectors before the
Revolution. That is what I find so ironic. We are repeating
the same mob violence that started that war, the tarring and
feathering, burning in effigy. How can it end but in another
war? People expect it by now.''

''There is a world of difference in my eyes,'' she said,
coming to stand by him. ''You are not a traitor just because
you are on the other side, now. You are doing your job the
best you can to hold the country together. And they are
adults. They know the risk they run.''

''You do not know what it means to me to hear you say
that.'' He took her by the shoulders and gazed into her eyes.
''But then, you are English. Your loyalties are not strong.''

''I beg to differ. I have a great liking for this new country. I think I was meant for it. But I would take my life
here, with all its hardships, and not whine about a tax. I
would merely avoid it.''

''If only there were more like you. And if you were
served with a summons to answer for all this illegal whiskey your Papa makes?''

''Why, I suppose I would have to appear in court and
pay my fine.''

''And what if the court was in Philadelphia?''

''I would not like that.''

''And so I told Norton. Hamilton could have arranged it
otherwise, but his pride is at stake. He promised that the
whiskey excise would pay the war debts.''

''I see. Now he has to make it work, and he will not be
overly sympathetic to anyone who stands in his way.''

''He wants to make an example of those evading it, and
he may think justice would be lenient here.''

''Yes,'' she agreed. ''Even those who can afford to

maintain a staunch federal front are somewhat sympathetic to their neighbors.''

"Or afraid of them?'' He drew her into a protective embrace.

"That is the worst of it, the violence between neighbors. Where will it end?''

"I do not know, but be ready to fly at a moment's notice,'' he warned.

Worry disappeared from Nancy's brow and she smiled. "Why Daniel, how exciting!''

"You would think so.'' He knelt and ran a hand up under her skirt and petticoats to grasp a bare buttock.

"Again, Daniel? You are insatiable.''

"So are you. I do wonder if, at my advanced age, I am equal to the task to keeping you satisfied.''

"You are, but where shall we go? Trueblood is in your room.''

"Your papa must be sound asleep in the common room by now. I will come to you. Does your door still squeak?''

"No, I worked some tallow into the hinges.''

"Always prepared is my Nancy.'' He kissed her lightly, then went to shut up the inn for the night.

Trueblood smiled contentedly at both of them as they shared a late Sunday breakfast. Others in the household had already eaten and were nowhere about.

"Where do you go with all this food you are making?'' Trueblood asked, eyeing the saddle baskets Nancy was packing.

"Yes,'' Daniel agreed. "You have enough there to keep even my brother for six or seven hours.''

"The militia are drilling at Mingo Creek today. The women usually make a meal for them afterward.''

"And might there be dancing and frolicking later?'' Trueblood asked.

"If there is enough whiskey.'' Nancy grinned impishly.

"Which most assuredly there will be," Daniel said. "May we come?"

"Being veterans of the Revolution, you will be most welcome. Papa says we will be impressed with how he has whipped the men into shape. I know he is eager for you to see his troop."

"Is that where he went off to at the crack of dawn?" Trueblood asked.

"Yes, it is the only pastime that will get him up so early. Luce and Ellie have already packed up Gabe and started on the way."

"I may as well see what the opposition looks like," Daniel decided, finishing his tea. "Do you realize, Miss Riley, what would happen to you if those people ever found out you were hand in glove with a spy?"

"Hand in glove is not how I would describe your relationship," Trueblood said.

"I do not think they would do anything to me," Nancy replied calmly as Daniel cuffed Trueblood. "I would merely lie."

"What?" Daniel asked.

"I am sure I would be quite convincing. I would weep over how you had turned my head with false promises, when all the while you were only here to gather information for the government. No, I would be quite safe if you were found out, but you would be in the gravest danger of sporting a coat of tar and feathers, sir."

"I see my fears for your safety are quite unfounded, then."

"Yes. As always, you underestimate me," she said as she hefted the heavy baskets. Daniel took them from her and thrust them at his chuckling brother with the warning, "Do not eat it on the way."

They dismounted and tethered their horses to a rope stretched between two shade trees.

"A motley band if ever I saw one," Daniel said, glanc-

ing at the fifty-odd men forming up on the field. Trueblood
grunted.

"Ah, but they have been impressed with the importance
of going into battle sober, at least," Nancy said as Daniel
lifted her down, restraining himself—admirably, she
thought—from fondling her. "You should have heard some
of Papa's lectures. And any man caught with a dirty rifle
is so derided he cannot show his face again for a week.
You will see."

"A liberty pole?" Trueblood asked. "Even here where
the militia drills?"

"Makes one wonder what exactly they are drilling for,"
Daniel replied.

He turned his attention back to the men dressed in
fringed hunting frocks and leggings, or rough coats and
knee breeches. There was nothing uniform about them as
they formed an uneven line to listen to their captain's lecture on disrespect and disobedience. It was a stern warning
and was received with mock solemnity.

"Very well, Sergeant. Start the drill."

"Yes, sir, Captain, sir," Riley said, trying to instill respect by example. He boomed out orders as he marched
the small band about the field to make them sweat a little.
It was a hot day, and it could not have been very comfortable tramping about in the sun with their rifles on their
shoulders and their haversacks slapping their thighs. When
Riley thought they had had enough, he called a halt and
looked back to see that half the troop had missed the last
order and were in column rather than line. Riley did a dou-
ble-take at the L-shaped formation this presented. The captain covered his eyes and strolled away, shaking his head.

Nancy giggled, and Daniel chuckled as well. He ventured
to put his arm about her waist. She wondered if this was
to demonstrate how hand in glove he was with Nancy Riley
or simply because he wanted his hand there. She rather
thought he was publicly staking his claim to her, since she
had mentioned the interest of others after his abrupt depar-

ture. If she repulsed him, other men would know she was fair game. If she did not, they would suppose Daniel's attentions were again welcome and that she was off-limits. As much as she resented the notion of belonging to someone, she did not move away from him but regarded him with a tolerant smile, since she wanted his hand about her waist as well. So long as Daniel knew he did not own her, she did not care what the rest of them thought.

The men were now formed in line and beginning to fire their weapons with a scattering of pops.

"I want ta hear all the shots together this time," Riley chided, "as though ye were firing one big rifle."

"Then why don't you give us one big—"

"Fire!"

The firing was becoming more focused, in spite of occasional grimaces and remarks from the men. The captain conferred with Riley, who formed them up in a double column to practice shooting, the two who had just fired trotting to the back of the column and reloading on the march, until their turn came again. This was quite impressive when they fired in unison, but a pair misfiring brought a derisive laugh from the crowd of old men, women and children who had gathered to watch. The troops ran through the column again, frantically reloading as they marched. Evidently the same two men had not shaken enough powder into the pan to get a spark through the touchhole, and misfired once more. The crowd laughed.

"They shall pay for keeping dirty rifles," Nancy warned.

Daniel smiled sympathetically. With luck they had only a fouled touchhole and would be able to fire the rammed ball out.

When all the troops had fired thrice in this manner, they performed some further drills under Riley's bulldog glare and deafening orders. He'd finally sent them marching back toward the crowd in preparation to dismissing them, when the captain, who was following behind and remonstrating with Riley about the lack of respect, said quite calmly,

"And, Sergeant, what are you going to do about that pole?"

"What pole?" Riley asked, as the powder horns of the double column of men started to click against the liberty pole that had sprung up in their path since the previous week.

Riley quick-marched to catch up, bawling an order to spread ranks and avert a minor catastrophe.

Nancy was by now in hopeless giggles. Daniel sought to maintain more sobriety, but found it difficult. Trueblood could keep up his stoic, impassive facade only by biting his lip. Nancy leaned against Daniel for support as her father made the men form up into line for a final dressing down before they were dismissed to their dinners and their whiskey.

"What did ye think, Nancy dear?" Riley asked as he came over to them, wiping the sweat from his brow.

"Much improved, Papa," Nancy said, handing him a tumbler of liquid she had poured from a jug.

"Very impressive!" Daniel said.

"Augh, what have ye given me?" Riley coughed and sputtered.

"Water, and you need it."

"Not when I was expecting a drink o' pure heaven. Did ye not bring any whiskey, Nancy girl?"

"Of course, I did. It is right here."

"Never give a man water when he's been about the devil's own business," he said, emptying the tankard and filling it from the other jug.

"I suppose I need not ask what kind of marksmen they are?" Daniel commented.

"Better than any. They have been used to killing deer and firing at will. The question is, will there be any holding them back if there's a real fight?"

"Yes, a stray shot could turn a mere confrontation into a battle."

"Ye were in the army, wasn't ye?"

"Yes, I saw a bit of fighting during the Revolution."

"I'll wager ye did."

"They are as good as any troops we had then and far better provisioned. Let us hope it does not come to an armed conflict."

"Ye were not always one for caution, Daniel boy." Riley clapped him on the back paternally.

"What I heard in Philadelphia has me worried. The government will not be able to afford to let this rebellion, if that's what it is, succeed."

"Need the money that bad, do they?"

"It is no longer a matter of money. It is now a matter of authority and national pride."

"What are you worryin' over, Daniel boy? These are the militia. They'll be keepin' order in these parts." Riley sent him a challenging look.

"I hope so," Daniel said, wondering if his warning had been too blatant. Nancy had by this time spread a blanket in the shade and unpacked their dinner. Luce and Ellie joined them with little Gabriel. Nancy handed Daniel some bread and a tankard after she served her father, who sank tiredly to the ground. Daniel tasted the liquid and found only water. Either she guessed that he wanted to stay sober or she was reminding him what a fool he had made of himself the one time he had gotten drunk. He would never let that happen again. As many nights as he had with Nancy, he coveted the mislaid memory of that one missing night and had spent a deal of leisure on the road to Philadelphia trying to call it back. That was a new experience for him, actually wanting to remember the past. But then, his life was so much better now than it had ever been. It only meant he had more to lose, he reminded himself grimly.

There was much joking and boasting, and both Daniel and Trueblood were persuaded to take part in marksmanship competitions. After winning his accolades and watching Nancy smile fondly on him, Daniel toyed for a moment with the notion of writing Norton that he was finished. To the rest of the world his life would seem quite normal—a trader who had taken a fancy to a frontier girl and decided to settle down and raise a family.

Some of the women had laid out blankets with wares upon them, treating the gathering in the manner of a market day. Luce and Ellie produced a quantity of homemade baskets, shirts and moccasins that Daniel had seen them working on the previous evening. Nancy smiled proudly on their enterprise, as she fed to the loose dogs the few scraps that remained of their meal, before dusting off her hands and looking with satisfaction at Daniel. He took her arm to stroll with her among the wares and bought her a set of pewter buttons he thought particularly fine for having been made locally.

Trueblood purchased some homemade knives with horn handles for trade in Philadelphia. "You are not coming with me on the next trip, are you?" he asked his brother.

Daniel was jolted from his pleasant reverie of watching a couple of children play tag and desperately searched for some excuse to keep him with Nancy.

"You do remember Norton's orders, don't you?" Trueblood reminded him. "You are to stay and keep track of events here and I am to carry news. If there is anything urgent while I am gone you may post it."

"I do not like to do that."

"Then ride post yourself. You could make the trip faster than the mail carrier, anyway."

"I will stay," Daniel agreed with feigned reluctance, his gaze now traveling to Nancy, who was dickering for some homemade beads.

"Good," Trueblood said, slapping him on the back. "I'll make up a load of whiskey this afternoon. I want to leave at dusk and travel during the night."

"Were my forged receipts no good, then?"

"I do not want to have to test them in this vicinity."

Nancy came over to them. "Are we ready to leave? I

shall need some help persuading Papa to come away before he sets a really bad example for his men."

"I will persuade him," Trueblood said. "I need him to help me make up the pack train."

Nancy looked desperately at Daniel, and Trueblood chuckled. "I am taking Luce with me this time."

Nancy came and took Daniel's arm possessively. There had been one or two local maidens eyeing him, and she thought it was as well for her to warn them that he was already taken. It worked both ways, this ownership.

Trueblood returned in mid-July, in what for him was record time, since he'd left the middle of June. He brought little in the way of trade goods back with him, though Luce had purchased a good deal and insisted on paying for the use of the ponies. After Luce had taken Ellie to the stable to help unpack their wares, the three conspirators talked as Trueblood polished off the remains of dinner.

"The U.S. marshal served his summonses today, not without incident, I might add," Daniel reported. "He took Inspector Neville with him and there was a confrontation at the Miller farm. There is violent talk, not just here, but by report at every inn and tavern in the area."

"We could have done without that!" Trueblood said between large bites of venison steak.

"Why did you come in such haste? What has Norton to say?"

"That it is a damned bad business, Daniel. About the beginning of the month Washington asked the local senator to negotiate the selling of some of the president's lands in this area."

"He is writing the district off, then," Daniel concluded. "I had hoped he would retire to Mount Vernon when Congress adjourned, and would lose interest in these affairs."

"He did go home, but wrenched his back so badly on one of his horses he can barely walk. He is in no very good humor."

"He will not be well pleased to get my next report then."

"Shall I go back immediately?" Trueblood asked, reaching for the skillet of rhubarb cobbler, which was a favorite of his since Nancy had contrived a way to sweeten it with maple sugar. He looked to her for a knife, but she merely handed him a large wooden spoon.

"No, not until we see what the next few days bring," Daniel said. "Anything else to report?"

"Washington is also ranting about the Democratic Societies. Norton thinks he may use this rebellion as an excuse to wipe them out or outlaw them."

"But you assured Norton there is nothing to fear from France, even though the French started these damned societies."

"Yes, but as British seizure of shipping has almost put us in a state of war with that country, Washington fears the rebels may try to make a deal."

"With Canada?" Nancy asked.

"Canada is not England," Daniel said. "They don't much like General Wayne's expedition to put down the Indian unrest on the frontier."

"I don't like it much myself," Trueblood mumbled between mouthfuls. "For the Canadians will not be above supplying the Indians with weapons, as they have in the past, or turning discontented half-breeds like myself against Americans."

"Are you discontented?" Nancy asked, as she amusedly watched him demolish the rhubarb dish.

"I mean that I can see their view. There are many men who like the savage way of life better than the civilized one. And they are not all half-breeds. Many are white."

"None of them seem very civilized to me at the moment."

"Yes, we may end up with war on two fronts, but not by contrivance, I think," Daniel said. "Canada will not do anything openly. They do follow orders when they get them. But if both pots boil over at the same time..."

"War is war whether it is an accident or not," Trueblood said, draining the mug of tea Nancy had made him. "What message shall I carry? It may not be too late to stop the army coming."

Nancy watched Daniel. Those blue eyes regarded her with sorrow, for he knew he could not let her sway him. She knew it too, but she would not, even if it had been possible. There was more at stake than this stupid rebellion. What Daniel thought of himself was more important to her than any trouble the army might cause.

She reached across the table to take his hand and put a stop to his soul searching. "You must do what is right for the country," she said, "and forget we have a personal stake in it."

"In case I have not time to write it out, tell Norton that if the Federal army is disbanded without making its presence felt, the rebellious part of the populace, possibly including the local militia, will resume a position of belligerence."

"And," Nancy added, "this will become a lawless country, where anyone who does obey or uphold the law will not be safe."

"That is why they must come," Daniel finished. "There is no other way now, except by a show of force."

"Let us hope it is only a show," Trueblood said. "In the meantime, I am famished and wasting away to nothing. Is there aught else to eat?"

Nancy groaned.

"Just joking, Nancy dear."

It was not long past daybreak when a rider raced up to the inn. Nancy was up and sweeping the floor. Daniel was starting a fire for her and Trueblood was encouraging him to hurry, since he really had awakened famished.

"There's men wounded, Miss Riley. My brother's one o' them. Can you come?"

Nancy turned to Daniel with pleading eyes.

"I will saddle the horses," he said, "while you get your medicines."

"I am coming, too," Trueblood said as he stuffed a loaf of bread into a sack.

As they rode, the frightened boy poured out a garbled story of the attack on Inspector Neville's house. The lad had not been there himself, so it was difficult to tell if the force that laid siege to Bower Hill consisted of a dozen, fifty or several hundred men.

When they arrived at the cabin where one of the wounded lay, Trueblood whispered to Daniel, "I will stay with Nancy, where I can be of some use. If you ride about, inquiring whether the other wounded have been treated and where they lie, it will give you an excuse to find out what really happened."

"Good idea. Do not leave her for any reason."

By the time Nancy had settled her first patient comfortably, Daniel returned to carry her off to another household. "This man's wound is not life threatening," Nancy reported as Daniel helped her mount. "What about the one we are going to now?"

"A flesh wound, but Oliver Miller has been killed by Inspector Neville," Daniel reported.

"It has begun, then," Trueblood said.

Daniel mounted. "Yes, word has gone out for the militia to muster at Couch's Fort. Nancy, I want to ask you not to go anywhere alone."

She looked at him and nodded, since it was a request, not an order. She was relieved that he had accepted her role as a healer, though he plainly did not like it. She would do what she could to keep worry from him. If only she could hope for the same consideration from him.

* * *

Riley never came home that night, and Daniel was gone at first light. Around midmorning Trueblood escorted Nancy to check on her two patients and dress their wounds again. They returned to find a hot stew and biscuits waiting for them, prepared by a rather nervous Ellie. Luce had cleaned and loaded every gun he could find in case he should have to defend the place. He had also provisioned the still house so that the women and baby could retreat to it at a moment's notice. Nancy thought it was sweet of him. No one had any idea where Riley was.

Daniel rode up to the inn about dusk and ran in to grab the heel of a loaf of bread and a drink of water. He ordered Luce to saddle him a fresh horse and refused any of Nancy's stew.

"What news?" Trueblood asked without getting up.

"The militia is going to arrest Marshall Lenox if they can find him and force Neville to resign as an inspector of revenue."

"You must be joking." Trueblood stared at his brother. "They have no authority in the matter. If they have a duty it is to protect public officials, not harass them."

"You do not have to tell me that! Nancy, where is your father?"

"I do not know." She wiped her already dry hands on a piece of toweling. "He has not been here since sometime yesterday."

"Probably in the thick of it, then," Daniel decided. "I'll see what I can do."

"Daniel, be careful," Nancy pleaded, then added in a stern voice, "that is an order."

Daniel saluted her with a laugh and ran out to mount the fresh horse Luce had saddled for him.

"Why is he so happy, Trueblood?" She stood staring out the window after her husband. "This is a terrible mess. Anything could happen."

"Because he is finally doing something, Nancy dear. Ever eager for action is our Daniel."

"Would he ever be content with a quiet life?"

"He never has until now."

"But this winter he seemed to take a deal of joy in making things. Are you telling me he could not long be content unless he was in some kind of danger?"

"I do not honestly know. I cannot promise that he will settle down to family life. I wish he would." Trueblood pushed himself away from the table and came to stand behind her.

"It might only have been a passing phase for him," she said unhappily.

"And if it was?" Trueblood asked, testing her.

Nancy took a deep breath and pulled herself erect. "Then I shall have to adapt, as I always have. If Daniel wants that kind of life, I will want it, too."

Trueblood put his arm around her. "Little sister, you are a wonder."

When Daniel got close to Bower Hill, he heard the unmistakable sounds of drumming and shouted orders. Riley was drilling the troops in full view of the house. Daniel left his horse with those being held by a couple of boys, to search out the officer in charge. As he did so, he saw an unarmed man approaching the house under a flag of truce. That was a good sign.

"Are you in command of this rabble?" Daniel's quasimilitary demand almost made the officer he finally located snap to attention.

"Major McFarlane. What do ye want?"

"You're not the regular brigade commander," Daniel accused.

"Colonel John Hamilton refused to command. So did Benjamin Parkinson."

"I am glad to hear someone has some sense. Why did you agree?"

"Impulse, I suppose. The chance to command again."

"Take my advice. Once they have done with the parade, say your piece and depart."

"Flee from a handful o' soldiers?"

"Troops from the fort?" Daniel asked, nodding toward the house.

"Yes. I don't know how Neville got them here in time, but he cannot hide behind them. They should have no stake in this matter."

"The militia is sadly misusing its authority. No doubt there are women and children in there, as well, frightened out of their wits."

"All the more reason for Neville to concede to our demands."

They were both staring as the man with the white flag returned from the house.

"They say Neville isn't there," he reported.

"Did they let you search?" McFarlane asked.

"No. Would he run off and leave the women?"

"I don't know. Go back and demand that a committee of half a dozen be allowed to search for papers. That will tell us if Neville is there or not."

"What if they refuse?" Daniel asked as the man strode toward the main house again like some reluctant medieval herald.

"They can't hope to hold out against us."

"But even a dozen regulars can cause a lot of damage before they are forced to surrender. Think, man! Whoever is in command in there dare not lose face by submitting without a struggle. Blood will be spilled today."

"Who the devil are you, anyway? You've no business here."

"Oh, yes, I have," Daniel said proudly. "I'm Sergeant Riley's son-in-law, and my wife gave me orders not to come back without her papa. Now finish this business up peaceful-like or you'll have Nancy Whiskey to deal with."

"If ye've done with yer advice, move on before I have ye arrested."

Daniel turned on his heel and made as if to walk toward the horses. Instead he worked his way around the circle of men, looking for Riley. He saw the women and children being escorted from the house, and soon after that the pop of musket fire began on both sides.

"Get yer head down, ye young fool," Riley shouted from a stand of trees.

Daniel loped across the open space and threw himself down beside Riley. "May I ask what you think you are doing besides worrying Nancy to death?"

"I very nearly had this command. If that piker Mc-Farlane had nay taken it, I believe they would've offered it ta me."

"What a place to glorify yourself, laying siege to a handful of soldiers in a farmhouse."

"We let the women go."

"Do you think that will stand you in good stead with the law when it comes time to pay for this foolishness?"

"Those summonses Lenox and Neville delivered were illegal. Besides, there's too many of us now. They can nay arrest us all."

"They can and will."

"Who? Now that they know the militia has taken up the cause they can nay even form a posse. No one would be that stupid."

"If we are talking of stupid—"

"Get down!" Riley pushed Daniel's face into the grass as a shot whistled past. "If it comes ta worryin' Nancy, she will nay be pleased if I have ta carry ye home with a bullet through yer head. Now make off, lad, if ye've no taste fer a bit o' action. Ye're just in the way."

"I will not, until I carry you with me."

"Do ye think ye can, lad?" Riley challenged.

"No, I suppose not. Not with your men glaring at me."

"Well then, help us out if that pistol o' yers is loaded."

"Help you to your destruction? You must be mad."

"'Tis naught but a bit o' frolic. Nothin' will come of it, mark my words."

"Nothing, indeed," Daniel said as he drew his pistol and hit Riley on the side of the head with it. To his amazement the blow did not knock the Irishman out, but only made him chuckle wickedly as he threw an uppercut to Daniel's ribs. Daniel feigned unconsciousness and caught Riley in the stomach with his boot when he ventured too close. They grappled then and rolled down the slope of the hill, out of range of the bullets from the house and away from the pall of powder smoke that was shrouding the other men.

"Ye've no right ta interfere!"

"I am your son-in-law. That gives me every right to try to save your stinking hide."

"Wot?"

"I am married to your daughter, but she will not leave you until she is reasonably sure you can take care of yourself. At this rate, I will never have my wife to myself, for you threw yourself into this nonsense like a stupid boy."

"Ye married my dotter without my permission?"

"I did not need your permission."

Suddenly a cry went up from the soldiers.

"God save us. McFarlane is hit. I'll take command now—"

The Irishman's joy was cut short by a blow from a convenient rock. Daniel collected their pistols and rolled Riley up onto his shoulder to make his way to the horses, no easy task with a man who weighed half again as much as himself.

"Where am I hit?" Riley demanded, half rising from the small bed in the storeroom and feeling his head.

"You are not wounded, Papa," Nancy said, "and you cannot possibly feel much worse than when recovering from a bout of drinking."

"If ye've any mercy at all in ye, girl, ye'll bring me a drop o' whiskey 'afore I expire."

"Just a small one," she said, pouring some into a mug. "Considering what you normally imbibe, this may revive you better than coffee."

"Now I remember!" He succeeded in sitting up this time and finding the lump on his head. "Tallent was there and gave me a damned bad time. Is it true?"

"What?"

"Ye've wed him without my consent?"

"It is true, Papa, and do not be blaming Daniel, since it was all my idea."

"Marryin' the lad or sendin' him ta interfere?"

"Both. How could you join the rebels, Papa? You are no better than a criminal."

"And ye're a disobedient daughter." He pointed an accusing finger at her.

"How so? You never forbade me to marry Daniel."

"I never expected ye ta throw yerself away on a young upstart like Tallent."

"You rather expected me to remain a serving wench for the rest of my life?"

"I did nay think you would desert me in my old age."

"But I have not. Daniel has been most patient about me staying with you this past year. Once Ellie can manage the inn with Luce to help her, then I will go with Daniel, wherever that may be. But I will visit you."

"'Tis nay fair!"

"Neither was leaving me with Aunt and Uncle until you needed me, so do not be trying to make me feel guilty. Now eat your breakfast."

"I'll nay eat it."

"Suit yourself, but I have work to do."

"I'm the one who should be angry," he accused as she left the room.

"I am not angry with you, Papa, just very disappointed."

Riley pushed the trencher away, heaved himself out of bed and poured a longer draught of whiskey into his mug. He limped into the kitchen in his nightgown, to find Daniel writing at one of the tables as he rocked little Gabe's cradle with his foot. It was an incongruous sight even to a man who was having trouble focusing.

"I might ha' known ye'd still be hangin' about."

"You will lower your voice unless you want this babe splitting your already aching head with a scream." Daniel's pen moved relentlessly over the paper, as if he were a military commander writing orders with most of his attention, while he spared a little for the interruptions of a subaltern.

Riley slumped onto the opposite bench as Daniel finished with a flourish and shook sand over his papers. "What did you hit me with, anyway?" the Irishman demanded.

"A large rock," Daniel said proudly. "You became straightway very reasonable."

"I imagine I might. Wot 'twas the upshot o' the affair?"

"McFarlane's dead. They burned Bower Hill to the ground."

"I thought I saw him fall. I might've been in command."

"What would you have done?"

"Charged the house."

"Then there would have been more than a dozen wounded. At least I have prevented a bloodbath."

"Interfering young… Here I was teaching ye everything I know about the making o' fine whiskey and ye stab me in the back."

"I may have saved your life."

"I mean ye've stolen away my Nancy."

"Oh, no." Daniel looked vaguely into the fire and smiled foolishly. "It is she who has stolen me."

Chapter Twelve

They managed to dissuade Riley from joining the muster at Braddock's Field by threatening to tie him to the bed and take away his whiskey. He finally conceded that his head ached much too badly for him to be marching about in the hot sun. Besides, troops trained by him would give a good account of themselves whether he was there or not.

When a rider thundered up to the house, they all assumed Nancy was being called to attend yesterday's wounded, but the man was frantic about his wife in labor. Daniel glanced from Trueblood to Riley, silently assigning his brother the task of keeping an eye on the Irishman. Daniel went to the stable to saddle the horses himself. As they rode down the hill toward the ferry he puzzled over why Nancy would be called to Pittsburgh, which had doctors, but he supposed these might all be busy with wounded from yesterday's engagement.

They left the ferry and rode through the streets, noticing knots of people here and there discussing the events. After examining the woman, Nancy discovered her to be not so very far along. "It is her first, so I shall be fixed here at least six hours, Daniel. If you want to go play with the bad boys you may do so, but please try not to get dirty."

He gave her a crooked smile and a wink. "You will be safe enough here. Just stay inside."

* * *

Darkness had fallen by the time they rode back up the southern bank toward the inn. The birthing had been successful, but Nancy was tired.

"What is the climate in the town?" she asked, stifling a yawn.

"Not exactly prorebel. They fear, just as we do, what punishment will be visited on all the western settlers if this is perceived as a general uprising."

"There cannot be more than a few hundred whiskey rebels, now that I think of it."

"Unfortunately, there are only a dozen or so men with the courage to speak out against them."

"I know," Nancy said. "Everyone else is afraid of being burned out of their homes if they say anything. I must confess I would feel some qualms myself about taking a stand against them. It would be easy for them to burn the stable again, and I am sure they could find the still if they looked for it."

"The inn is made of stone."

"Not the roof. We could be completely wiped out, Ellie and Lucius with us, if..."

"If anyone ever found out my real occupation."

"Oh, I am not worried about that. I would be just as shocked at how I had been taken in by you as the rest of them."

"I have no doubt you could carry that pose off, too. You are wasted keeping an inn."

"At least this game is worth playing. I could never be a politician's wife, like Elise, pretending to be polite to people only for what I could get out of them. Now a spy's wife, that I could fancy."

"You will never play such a dangerous role."

"Worried about my safety or the fact that I might upstage you?"

"About you, of course. You already outplay me."

Daniel was silent for a moment, wondering if she was going to ask about their future. If she did, he had no idea what to tell her except that they would be together. If the role of a merchant's wife bored her, then he did not know what to do, but thrust her into anything more dangerous he would not. She ran enough risk being familiar with him as it was.

Nancy was discoursing about the birthing, and Daniel was nodding tiredly himself, when a huge weight fell on him. He vaguely heard Nancy scream as the crack on his head sent him spinning into unconsciousness.

"Don't you dare!" Nancy commanded, drawing the pistol from her pocket.

"Is that thing loaded?" a rough voice demanded.

"Of course. If you try to scalp him, one of you will die."

The ragged man holding a tomahawk and standing over Daniel's still form weighed her words.

"We'll leave him, then. He's probably dead anyway. It's ye we want."

"What?"

"I've a wounded man—my brother. He needs nursing."

"Then why did you not come to the inn like everyone else and say so?"

"We're nay welcome."

"Where, at the White Horse?"

"Anywhere!"

"You are the white savages, the ones who attacked us," Nancy guessed, then wished she had said nothing.

"How'd she know—" the second man began.

"Never mind!" the first commanded. "We'll not stand here talking all night. Gimme the pistol and we'll leave yer man in the road."

"Not good enough. That one must ride ahead of us and no doubling back. You will ride beside me. Leave Daniel's horse for him."

"I give the orders."

"Not until I have discharged my pistol, and I am not at all sure which one of you I dislike more. We are wasting time, are we not?"

"Keil, ride ahead. Let her keep ye in sight. Satisfied?" the rough voice asked as the party of three started down the road.

"And who are you?"

"Ramp."

"Is that your first name or your last?"

"Ramp will do. Ye're the one they call Nancy Whiskey. Ye heal everything from a fever ta a leg boil with a bit o' your magic brew."

"Hardly. I only give whiskey for pain. It has very limited medicinal properties."

"You talk like some goddamned queen."

"I am a midwife. One must know something to be able to do that."

"And I've taken more lives than ye've ever saved. Let's nay forget that."

"Including Cullen! And now, perhaps, Daniel."

"Ye killed four o' my men."

"What did Dupree pay you to kill us?"

"Not enough. Ye ast too many questions."

"And why were we to be killed?"

"Ye were not. Ye were part o' my payment."

"Then you do not mean to let me go, even if I cure your man."

"Why should I? Ye're mine already."

"Dupree had no right to barter away the lives of three men and my freedom."

"Right has naught ta do with anythin' out here. A man takes wot he wants."

"But what he wants may not be what he gets."

"Wot do you mean?"

"I have a reputation for being very shrewish. I do not think you would enjoy having me about as much as you may think."

"Are you threatenin' me?"

"Merely a warning."

"The gun."

"Not for another mile or two."

They rode southeast down the hill, picked up Braddock's Road and traversed the Youghiogheny where she, Daniel and Trueblood had once forded it. Eventually they struck off onto a deer track, and Nancy feared for a time that they would carry her back to Forbes's Road and the scene of the original attack. But they pushed on toward Chestnut Ridge without coming to any more signs of civilization. So she did not have to look upon the limestone rocks where she had first lain with Daniel, but she saw many other rocks like them. They were carrying her farther and farther from the man she cared about most, and he might be dying at this moment. But to try to escape and get back to him would mean they would surely kill him. She must take the chance that he could recover from the blow, or that someone would find him. As for her, she was lost. Try as she might she could not store all the trail signs in her head. She was breaking twigs at every opportunity, but even if she got away she would have no idea how to get back. And Trueblood could never track them. If Daniel were dead, then she would never be found. But if he were dead, she did not care very much if she were found or not.

"Daniel, can you hear me?"

"Trueblood," he said thickly. "What happened?"

"That is what I was going to ask you. Riley gave me the slip yesterday and I headed into Pittsburgh to tell you. You were lying on the road in a pool of blood and Nancy was nowhere in sight. What happened to her?"

"I do not know. Someone hit me." Daniel plunged from the bed and staggered with dizziness.

"Who?"

"I never saw him. I just heard her scream. Oh, God. I must find her." Shakily he poured water into a basin and plunged his head into it, coming up blinking and groaning.

"All in good time. Drink this. It will help clear your head."

"Is it day yet?"

"Nearly so. We will look for her then."

"But the news. Someone must carry it to Philadelphia. You will have to go," Daniel decided as he bent to pull on his boots, groaning again with the effort. He removed the packet from his left boot and handed it to his brother. "Whatever you do, do not mail it. Now, can you take me back to where we were attacked?"

"I think so."

"Trueblood, if there was ever a time to be precise about direction, this is it."

As it turned out, they had no trouble finding the exact spot of the attack, for there was a quantity of blood there from Daniel's scalp wound.

"Which way?" Trueblood asked after Daniel had walked up and down the road in both directions several times.

"That way, I think, to the south. If I am wrong and they have carried her into the town again, I will never pick up their trail, anyway."

"Let us go, then."

"I meant what I said. Carry my packet to Philadelphia," Daniel said as he mounted with a grunt. "I will find Nancy."

"Very well. I will see that it gets to Philadelphia."

"Promise?"

"I promise."

Daniel left him in the road, wondering if Trueblood would break his word and try to follow him. But he had promised. Daniel followed three sets of tracks that he saw intermittently heading southeast on Braddock's Road. They were the freshest sign, but that meant nothing. Anyone might be going in that direction, especially with the recent traffic in and out of Pittsburgh. Even where the three horses left the road and took a deer track there was no logical reason to assume he was on Nancy's trail, except for the occasional broken twig. Not likely there would be so many of them by accident. There was something else, some inexplicable gut feeling that he was drawing closer to her. There was another broken twig at head height. Not done by a horse or deer and therefore not an accident. In the dark Nancy had been leaving signs even Trueblood would be able to follow.

She uncovered the wound and managed not to recoil at the stench from the gangrene. The man shuddered at her touch. She got out the flask of whiskey she carried and gave him a drink of it mixed with water. It could not hurt him now. She set about cleaning the leg wound, all the time knowing it was hopeless. If they had come for her when it happened she might even have saved the leg. It was broken badly, the bone protruding through the skin as the muscles had contracted and forced it out. Had the men come even a week ago, she could have amputated and saved his life. But the red streaks running up the veins told the tale. There was no saving this man or herself. All she could do was go through the motions to try to buy some time. What for? Even if Daniel had survived he would be in no fit state to come after her for days. And she did not have days. If she guessed aright, the man would not last through the night. She cleaned the wound anyway and poulticed it. It was still terribly hot but did not smell as much. Then she set about washing the body, as she thought of the man. She had helped lay out the dead before, but never this prematurely. She would not make him endure the agony of having the bone set. There was no point.

"When will he be better?"

"I am not a miracle worker. You have let it fester too long. Why did you not come for me before?"

"Are ye telling me ye'd have come?"

"I have never turned down anyone before."

"Just cure him or ye'll be sorry."

* * *

Sometime in the night the man breathed his last. She did not move to cover him, but wondered how long she could pretend to wipe the brow of a dead man.

"How is he?" Ramp demanded.

She knew she could not lie any longer, not even to this savage. "He is no longer in pain."

"Wot?"

"He is dead."

"Ye were supposed ta cure him, not kill him."

"He would have died if I were here or no."

Ramp grabbed her and threw her across the small cabin. He touched his brother and bowed his head for a moment before he rose and stalked toward her. "Take off yer clothes!"

"Before his burial? How can you enjoy yourself with your brother lying newly dead?"

"We'll bury him at daybreak. Then ye're mine."

He left her, and she heard him giving orders to Keil to dig the grave. Not much time. And even if she got away, her chances of escaping them altogether were slim. Nancy slipped to the low door and peeked out around the deerhide. Certainly she could not take her horse. Her mare was still saddled, but tied on the other side of the clearing. Ramp was helping to dig, and the sound of their scratching might give her some cover. Apparently there were only the two of them left. She slipped along the side of the small cabin and into the woods, forcing herself to go as slowly and soundlessly as she could until she thought she was out of earshot. Then she began a panicked flight, slipping over rocks and slicing her shins on brambles. At one point she lunged through a thicket with such force she nearly went crashing over a precipice into the river. If she had she would have been killed by the rocks, not the water that swirled at the bottom.

If she panicked again she would never find her way home. The river was the key. She had only to follow it downstream and she would find her way back. She remembered that it crossed Braddock's Road somewhere. If they were east of that she need follow it only as far as the road. If they were west of it there was still the river, which eventually led to the crossing. But she must get away from the bank, where it was rocky and the going was rough. She had only to keep it within earshot.

There was shouting behind her now. She stopped planning and ran, in spite of her exhaustion. If she heard them closing on her she would drop and hide. Until then she stumbled in a headlong flight that, for all her fear, was as exhilarating as the first night she had made love to Daniel. When it came to thriving on danger she was as bad as he was.

There was one behind her running and one on horseback on the woods side of her, driving her toward the river. She knew this instinctively, but there was nothing she could think to do about it. If they pushed her as far as the rocky banks she would have to slow down to avoid falling, and then they would have her. Never! She would throw herself in the river first and let it take her. She could swim a little, if it came to that.

Suddenly, while they were still out of sight and calling to each other, she made a sharp left turn toward the sound of rushing water. There was always the chance that they would run past her. But even if she doubled back, they were expert trackers. She knew she could not evade them long. Did it matter so much? If Daniel was dead she hardly cared what happened to her, except that no other man would have her.

She stopped short at the edge of the river on a small plateau of limestone long abandoned by the grinding waters. There was a steep, rocky face upstream, a muddy beach below and a raging torrent before her. She had a disgust of being taken on the run, tomahawked or shot in the back. She turned and faced her fate, drawing the knife from her pocket. With luck she might be able to carry one or both of her pursuers into the rocky river course with her.

Ramp stopped at sight of her, as did his companion. Nancy was incensed that Keil had been riding her mare full tilt over treacherous rocks. Ramp chuckled. "What the hell do ye mean to do with that?"

"Stop you."

"Aren't ye goin' ta plead, ta beg me not ta come any closer?"

"No," she said, raising her chin and standing as straight as one of her father's soldiers on parade. "As you are not very intelligent, I expect you to come. I am ready for you."

Ramp hesitated and glanced at his companion, who seemed as mystified as Ramp. Keil slid off the horse, and at a nod from Ramp, they both ran toward Nancy. A rifle shot redirected Keil's forward plunge and carried him into the river. Ramp knocked her down and got her knife, then turned to look into Daniel's blazing eyes.

"I thought ye was dead," Ramp said.

"Nancy, are you hurt?" Daniel demanded as he drew his own knife.

"No," she said, trying to edge away from Ramp. He made a grab for her, but Daniel leaped between them. The men were locked then, hand to arm, as each strove to hold the opponent's knife hand, while trying to free his own to get in a cut. Nancy bethought her of the rifle. She grabbed the shot pouch and powder horn Daniel had dropped by the gun and reloaded it as swiftly as the best of her father's troops. She then tried to aim, but the flurry of straining bodies made it uncertain that she could hit Ramp rather than Daniel. When she finally had a clear shot, she hesitated. Having talked to the man, having known him as a person, albeit a barbaric one, she found that she could not kill him. She was setting up to wound him when Daniel got the upper hand by dint of knocking Ramp against a boulder and dazing him. Ramp spun and Daniel landed on him, raised the knife and—

"Do not kill him!" Nancy commanded.

"What?" Daniel gasped, his other hand choking a gurgle from Ramp's throat.

"Let him go."

"Do you not realize he must have killed Cullen, would have killed me? God only knows what he would have done to you!"

"I know. You have beaten him. That is enough. Either let him go or take him back to stand trial."

Daniel's face was contorted with rage now. He dragged Ramp to his feet and pointed him toward the river. "I can arrange justice a little quicker than that. You have your choice. The blade or the rapids." Ramp turned his head slowly and smiled at Nancy, then leaped.

She rested the rifle butt on the ground and sank to her knees with exhaustion. Daniel snatched her up by the shoulders. "Did he have you?" he demanded.

"No," she said, in confusion at his rage. She had thought he was going to embrace her and was unprepared for his anger. "Daniel, what is wrong with you?" She trembled at his glaring eyes and the covetous look he cast over her body. Before she could protest, he kissed her savagely, bruising her lips and making her struggle to be free of him. She felt hot and hungry in the deepest part of herself, but it was not desire this time. It was exhaustion from her mad flight. How could the two reactions feel so close to each other? she wondered, with her healer's intellect. She would need to turn to that other, saner self if Daniel had become some sort of monster. The spasms deep inside her were still causing her to struggle with him and grasp his shirt when he broke contact and pushed her away.

She was gasping for breath and still shivering with contractions as she knelt before his rage, trying to gain control of herself. She felt strangely abandoned, as though she were trying to give birth alone to a child that had died inside her. Then her leg muscles went limp from the running, the fear and Daniel's assault. She could not stand. He picked her up and carried her to the horses. She stood clinging to her own mare's saddle while he got his rifle.

"You told me the truth?" Daniel demanded on his return. "He didn't have you?"

"Of course I told the truth. Why would I lie to you?"

Daniel picked her up and threw her roughly up onto her horse, then mounted and led the way out of the rocks to a deer track. For many hours she could do no more than cling to her mare. Gradually the feeling returned to her legs and reasoning took possession of her mind again, squeezing out shock, fear and hurt.

"Daniel, you are acting strangely," Nancy said as she guided her horse after him.

"Why did you make me let him go?" he asked through gritted teeth.

"I could not bear to watch you kill someone. You are very frightening when you are in a murderous rage."

"A very pat answer, madam."

"What is the matter with you, Daniel?"

"Why would you take a liking to that savage?"

"I do not like him. I fear him and hate him, but..."

"But what?"

"I also feel sorry for him. Perhaps, under other circumstances..."

"Do not waste your pity," Daniel said over his shoulder. "He lives this kind of life because he likes it."

"He has also just lost his brother."

"I wager that meant no more to him than it would to a dog. These savages—I cannot call them men—have no feelings."

"Perhaps not. But that is no excuse to lower yourself to their level. You could have taken him prisoner, brought him to justice. Instead you acted like some wolf claiming his mate."

"You are mine," Daniel growled.

"I am not. I am my own person. I love you, but you do not own me."

"Now that you are my wife I own you and every stitch of clothes on you."

"I am not really your wife yet, and you had better stop talking such nonsense if you expect me ever to marry you." Her horse had been following so closely that it almost ran into Daniel's when he reined in abruptly.

"You foolish girl. You cannot know the law. When I said you were my wife and you said I was your husband we were as legally married as if the Archbishop of Canterbury had performed the rite himself."

"You cannot be serious! There were no witnesses, no banns or license."

"There need be none, only that the two parties agree that they are married. Do you mean to lie and say it did not happen?"

"I made that vow because I loved you even then. I had no idea I was being deceived. You tricked me!"

"If I might remind you, *madam,* making love naked on those rocks while we were about to be tomahawked was your idea, not mine." He urged his horse on, guiding them through the trees.

"You were angry then, too."

"Because I knew I had ruined you, but I want you so much I keep on doing it," he said in despair.

"But I am the same woman I was then."

"No, you are entirely different. There is no shyness about you anymore. You like to make love. You like it too much."

"How is it possible to like it too much? You said yourself it should be pleasant for women."

"Women are not supposed to enjoy it that much. They are merely supposed to—to tolerate it."

"What the hell is that supposed to mean?" she demanded.

"That you are not a proper lady."

"And you are a total idiot if you think women would

endure childbirth if they only tolerated what came before. You are just a man. You know nothing at all about it.''

"I have had many women," he boasted.

"Or they have had you and you were too stupid to realize it.''

Daniel swore and opened his mouth to blast her when she continued, "That is another thing. Why is it proper for you to have had many women when you are so upset at the possibility that I might have had another man?''

"It is not the same thing." He rode to get ahead of her, but she doggedly kept up with him.

"It is exactly the same thing.''

"I do not want to talk about it," he finished lamely.

"What if I had said yes?''

"I do not want to talk about it," he shouted over his shoulder.

"What if I had told you Ramp had gotten me? What would you have done then?''

"You have said enough, Wife, and because of you I have neglected my duty. The whole country may rise up in arms because I have had to come chasing after you.''

"That is absurd. You cannot do anything to stop the rebellion. The most you can do is keep Washington appraised of what is going on. And do not try to turn the discussion to politics. We were talking about us.''

"I said I do not want to talk about it." Daniel rode off from her and she had to knee her horse with her aching legs to keep up with him. She hated this arguing on horseback.

"Is that why you kissed me so possessively, because you were afraid he had had me?" Nancy asked Daniel as she got her second wind. She was no longer blazingly angry, but she was not going to let him get away with such high-handed tactics even if he was her husband. "Surely you know I would kill myself rather than let him take me.''

"Yet you did save his life," Daniel reminded her.

"If he had raped me I would have killed myself.''

"Yes, the knife in your pocket," Daniel said.

"No, I would have thrown myself in the river."

"Knowing you, I am sure you can swim like a fish," he shouted angrily.

"But I cannot," she said, her voice breaking a little at being so unjustly accused.

He was silent, remembering one of the few times he had seen her afraid—at the crossing of the Susquehanna.

"Daniel, I was trying to save you from being a murderer."

"Too late for that." The bitterness rang in his voice.

"Now there is one thing I must know."

"What?" he shouted.

"If I had answered yes, what would you have done?"

He was silent for a long time, wondering what he should answer, but under her persistent attack his anger was giving way to childish irritation, and he knew it. "Nothing."

"Nothing? You mean not marry me?"

"No, I love you. I want marriage with you more than anything."

"Then what was the point of the question?" she reasoned.

"I had to know if you..."

"What?" she asked.

"If you thought him better than me." Daniel had blurted the truth out with a rush, remembering that frankness often appeased Nancy.

"That's hardly likely, seeing as he has not washed in— Daniel! It was not Ramp you were afraid of."

"I do not know what you mean."

"You were afraid of me, my passionate nature, that I would like him."

"No! That is not it," he retorted.

"I think if you examine your conscience you will discover that is exactly it. You have no need to be threatened by my liking for lovemaking. Do you imagine I would let anyone have me? If you cannot trust me to be faithful to you, we had best give up any thoughts of a real marriage, a public marriage. You would spend all your time being jealous, and I would worry that every man I spoke to would be attacked by you.''

Daniel rode on, responding to any other sallies from Nancy with a refusal to discuss it. Here he was, arguing with her, when he should only be glad to have her back in one piece. What demon had caused him to act so irrationally? He had been coming to think that he could settle down to a quiet life, but now he doubted it. Perhaps he would always need war and killing, some danger just to know he still was alive. Perhaps she was right. He was not fit to love a woman because he could not bear to lose her. How could he expect Nancy to share such an existence? It would be better if they both lied and said they were not married.

At least there were no children to consider. This was the most bitter thought of all.

''What was that?'' Nancy interrupted her tirade to ask.

''Keep quiet,'' Daniel whispered desperately as he checked the priming of his rifle. He had been a fool not to have done so before, since Nancy had been in a desperate state when she had loaded it. That is what came of falling in love. You made the most stupid mistakes. He slid off his horse and handed her the reins.

''Be careful,'' she whispered.

He slipped noiselessly into the woods, not knowing if he was leaving her in danger or not. He glanced back a last time at her, but she sat as still as stone. The crackling brush was not anywhere near the trail. Suddenly a mounted Trueblood floundered into view, and Daniel cursed vehemently.

''I thought I ordered you to leave for Philadelphia,'' he shouted through the woods at him.

''I could not just leave, not knowing if either of you would survive.''

''So what were you doing?''

"Following you."

"I do wish, brother dear, you would stick with tasks at which you have some chance of succeeding. If we had not heard you crashing about you would have overshot us and been lost in these woods forever."

"I am not that bad."

"Yes, you are. And you disobeyed orders." Daniel turned to shake a finger at him and found himself eye-to-eye with Trueblood's horse instead, the beast merely looking disdainfully down at him.

"We are not in the army now. Besides, I could hear Nancy ranting at you from half a mile away. What have you done to her?"

"I do not need your help and I do not need your interference in my affairs," Daniel said as he stomped off in the direction of the trail.

They both spun at the sound of a snapped stick. "Do not shoot me," Nancy said, leading Daniel's horse up to them. "It is getting dark. I think we should make camp."

"You and your camping!" Daniel grumbled. "If you think I am going to listen to the two of you hammer away at me for an entire night, you are much mistaken. Besides, we are no more than ten miles from the inn."

"How can that be," Trueblood demanded, "unless I have been riding in circles?"

Daniel leered at him and mounted his horse.

Daniel and Nancy continued to argue sporadically the entire way back to the White Horse. Daniel had a raging headache, but Nancy's tongue showed no signs of fatigue, and as her accusations became more lucid, Daniel's mind slid further into a quandary. For all he denied it, she spoke the truth. Other women had taken advantage of him, tricked him. Nancy was the only one who told him the truth, and the truth was very brutal. The very thing that made her such a wonderful lover made him afraid that he could not hold her, that he was not man enough for her. If she were as insatiable as she seemed, then her appetite would far outrun his ability to fill it. She was scarcely twenty-four, and he was thirty-three, an old man. At least he felt old at the moment, with her tongue flaying him alive and Trueblood occasionally agreeing with her.

Chapter Thirteen

Thus it was that, as they approached the inn, whatever altercation that was causing the shouting and the swinging lanterns came to Daniel as a welcome relief from Nancy's recriminations.

Riley was on the doorstep, talking to the gang of men gathered in the yard.

"Not more fighting," Nancy said wearily as they rode into the midst of the party.

"That's Tallent! Seize him. He's a spy."

Daniel was pulled off his horse and held by two men, while a half-dozen others grumbled and threatened Trueblood, but made no move to try to dislodge him, perhaps out of fear that he might fall on them and do them an injury.

Trueblood dismounted with his usual lack of emotion. Nancy looked to him for guidance, but he was staring at the mob, perhaps calculating his chances of freeing Daniel.

"Do not be so absurd," she chided as she slid off her mare unassisted. "You are like a bunch of children, taking fright at the least hint of rumor. Now let Daniel go. He has been rescuing me from the white savages again."

Nancy saw Dupree's face in the crowd, though it was hard to recognize him in a coat and breeches rather than his greasy buckskins. It was like seeing a wolf in ball dress.

Always those dark eyes slid back and forth under half-closed lids, calculating, assessing. If he had duped Bradford, he could certainly convince the rest of them.

"Daniel Tallent's been informin' on our activities," Ned Johnson accused.

"Nonsense. As you all talk openly of rebellion day and night, I should not wonder that the whole world knew of your activities." Nancy swaggered toward Daniel's horse, trying not to glance at his rifle in its sling.

"Let him go," Riley demanded. "Daniel's no more a spy than—why, than Dupree here."

"He's a spy and ye've been harborin' him at yer inn," Spode shouted.

"Hasn't Tallent bought untaxed whiskey from me time and agin?"

"That means nothing," Hiram Johnson said.

"Hang him!" Dupree's unmistakable voice came from the midst of the crowd.

"I know naught about that," Riley conceded, "but whatever else he is, he is my Nancy's husband and I will nay see him hung."

"Too late," Dupree returned. "He's condemned himself with his own hand."

"What's that?" Riley demanded.

"A letter we took off the mail rider headed fer Philadelphia," the younger Johnson said.

"Well, I can nay read it," Riley said impatiently, pushing the much-creased paper from him.

They thrust it at Nancy. "But this is signed 'Talon,'" she said. "What has this to do with Daniel?"

"It has to be him," Ned Johnson said. "Besides, I have a receipt from him and the writin's the same."

"That is impossible," she protested. "You have made a mistake."

"It is him or his brother," Dupree insisted. "They are both *espions,* I say."

"I wrote it," Daniel said quite clearly.

"That's enough fer me," Spode said bitterly. "Let's hang him." There was a general shout of approval.

"No!" Nancy pulled the rifle from Daniel's horse and pointed it at one of the men holding him.

"Now put that down, Nancy, or ye'll hurt someone," the younger Johnson said.

"Most assuredly you, Ned Johnson, if you do not listen to me. Ramp, the white savage who captured me, admitted that Dupree paid him to attack us at the ford. They were instructed to kill us. They did kill Cullen. Dupree is already guilty of murder. He is using all of you to finish the job."

"Trueblood knows nothing about this, neither does Nancy nor Riley," Daniel stated. "This was all my own game. I only regret that Trueblood has been wrongly accused and that I have deceived Nancy."

"Daniel!" she gasped in genuine shock, that he would give up his pretense so easily. Then she realized that if she revealed why Dupree wanted them dead she would not be helping Daniel. He was sacrificing himself to protect her and Trueblood.

"I did it for the money, Nancy," Daniel said, so desperately that if she had not known better she would have believed him.

"Then you hang for your greed," Dupree shouted.

"I said let him go," Riley demanded. "He could nay have done ye any harm."

"Let him ride away now!" Nancy threatened, taking careful aim at Dupree.

"Now ye don't know what ye might do with that gun, Nancy," Ned said, inching toward her with a placating motion.

"Of course I do. I will hit at least two of you the way you are bunched together."

This statement caused an immediate easing of the crowd away from the target area and made Dupree start to sweat.

"Ye can nay do it," Hiram said. "Ye've always been a healer."

"He is right, you know, Nancy," Daniel agreed. "If you did shoot someone, you would only have to patch him up again."

"Damn you, Daniel! I am trying to save your life."

He shook his head and she wavered. As much as she hated Dupree and disliked the rest of them, she found that she could not shoot, knowing that she might hit someone other than the cowardly Dupree, who was inching behind Ned.

But there was a rifle shot—from the other side of the clearing, an impossible distance. Two men went down, careening into the men holding Daniel. He leaped to Nancy's side and relieved her of the gun.

"But I did not shoot," she said in amazement as she watched Dupree clutch his arm and Johnson's blood gush redly from a wound high on his chest. She knelt by Ned to stanch the flow of blood and help it clot. Dupree would survive. Ned Johnson might not. She knew this instantly and felt a measure of sorrow in it. Dupree had got the glancing shot and the ball was now lodged—who knew how deep—in Ned. It would be a long night.

"I know you did not," Daniel said. "It came from the woods."

"Who was it then?" she asked, pulling another wad of linen out of her pocket to make a larger pad for the wound, then instructing a man to raise Johnson while she tied the bandage in place.

"Never mind that. Will he live?"

"Yes, of course," she said automatically, in case Johnson should still be conscious. "Daniel, I do not understand."

After a scrutiny of the edge of the forest, Daniel said, "It must be Ramp."

"He meant to kill you!"

"Perhaps. There only remains to be decided if these men will let me go or try their luck against possibly two rifles, both of them crack shots. And unlike Nancy, I will have no scruples about stopping any of you."

"Will ye swear on yer honor that ye will leave this country never ta return?" Hiram Johnson demanded from his kneeling position by his brother.

"And give up this spying?" another voice demanded.

"*Non! Non!* You cannot just let him go," Dupree insisted, as someone else bound up his arm.

Daniel leveled the gun at Dupree's head. "I may be a spy, but at least I am in the pay of our own country, unlike Dupree here, who is working to start a war so that the French can take advantage of it. I would not be surprised if he is being paid by the Canadians, as well."

Dupree struggled to his feet and began to sidle away. "Do not listen to him. He is a traitor."

"I am an American and I am doing my duty."

"Let's have Dupree back and question him," someone shouted.

Dupree tried to get away, but two men held him between them.

"I'll ask again, Tallent," the older Johnson said, "will ye agree ta leave the western counties?"

"I'll swear, if you give me your word as gentlemen that no harm will come to my wife, Trueblood or Riley for my villainy."

"We give no assurances ta a spy," Spode grumbled.

"Then I suppose I will have to kill one of you—Dupree I think, though I had rather it were Bradford, but he has not the courage to show his face."

"He could not come," Dupree said, looking nervously at Daniel's rifle.

"But sent his agent in his place."

"I do not work for Bradford."

"No. I wonder who all you do work for. It used to be

Genet, but France has suffered another change of government. Genet and his men are out of favor. Your only choice now is to cast your lot with Bradford and hope the rebellion succeeds.''

''If I support the noble cause of these patriots it is fellow feeling.''

''And Bradford will be governor of the western counties, or king? No need to ask who will be his second-in-command. Beware kings, gentlemen,'' Daniel raised his voice to say. ''We have all worn that yoke before.''

''Traître!'' Dupree shouted. ''I will kill you myself.'' He drew a knife and lunged, but two of the men restrained him.

''It was me you were after all along, wasn't it?'' Daniel asked. ''You were not really trying to recruit Riley for the rebels. You were watching me. And the attack at the ford—it was me you wanted to kill. But you would have had three others murdered and scalped to cover your crime.''

Dupree glowered at him.

''Tell them!'' Daniel shouted, taking careful aim at Dupree's head.

''Your death was ordered. You are a spy.''

''By whom?''

Dupree locked his lips and stared at the gun.

''No matter. I am sure there are any number of people who would have paid to see me dead. Gentleman, I ask again. Do I have you word not to let Dupree tempt you to murder these innocents, no matter what else he may tempt you to do?''

''No harm will come ta them,'' Hiram Johnson rose to say. ''Is it agreed?''

There was a general murmur of assent to Johnson's promise, though Spode held his silence for once.

''Nancy is safe with us,'' another agreed.

''A wise choice, gentlemen, since Nancy is Ned's best

chance of recovery.'' Daniel turned to look down at his wife. "I am sorry, Nancy. Can you forgive me?"

"I—I'll...think about it.'' What she wanted to do was to run to Daniel and throw herself in his arms to ask forgiveness for all the pain she had caused him these past two days, but she must not get in the way of his rifle. And she must pretend to be as shocked by his villainy as everyone else. Daniel had bought this protection for them dearly and she must not throw it away.

"I will send to you when I can. I will have your answer by whether you come or no. Trueblood, take care of her.'' He mounted and rode off. Nancy did not even watch him go, but began ordering the men how best to move Johnson into the storeroom, where he could most easily be attended.

"Dupree," Hiram ordered. "Ye must leave, too.''

"*Mon Dieu!* I am your comrade-in-arms. And I am wounded.''

"No more. We don't trust ye. We want rid of all spies.''

"Yes, 'tis our affair," Riley said. "Take yerself off and don't show your face 'round here agin.''

Nancy sat on the back steps watching the fireflies dreamily. She had not slept the night before, after she had extracted the ball from Johnson's chest, nor this day, when his numerous family came to sit with him. They had been more a hindrance than a help, especially his wife with her fretful baby. Nancy almost forcibly sent her home with Trueblood, stating quite truthfully that Ned needed to sleep and could not with an infant crying in his ear all night. In spite of his fever, there had been no recurrence of the bleeding, and so long as she could keep infection at bay Nancy rather thought Ned would survive. There was a measure of contentment in the knowledge that she had made a difference by being here. Of course, if she and Daniel had not been, Ned might never have gotten shot.

She emptied her mind to gaze at the fireflies, winking on

and off. They always seemed to be moving away. Eyes played such tricks in the twilight. The sky was still a delicious pink in the west and the shadows were creeping through the woods, shrouding them in deepest green. The darker it got the louder the crickets chirruped. A cool wave of moist air was creeping up from the creek bottom. Nancy thought back over the other evenings Daniel had been here with her as she paused in her work to capture the last dregs of the day for her memories. They had been short evenings, but satisfying, with him on the steps beside her, furtively holding her hand and waiting tensely for the darkness that meant he could claim her for his wife once again. That her father had defended Daniel made her very proud of Patrick Riley, in spite of his many flaws.

All things considered, she had much to be thankful for. They were all still alive, for one thing, and Daniel had promised to send for her. But it still hurt to be parted. She could remember these evenings, but they would always be tinged with sadness, since she was now alone.

Trueblood came down the steps and handed her a mug of tea—Oswego, she thought, as she took a long drink and sighed.

"Why do you not go to bed and let me watch your patient? I promise to call you should he take a turn for the worse."

"What would I do without you, Trueblood? You are my trusted right hand as well as Daniel's. I do wish you were with him, though. I place no reliance of him keeping himself safe."

"I imagine Daniel would not be so pleased to have me with him. After all, I did disobey orders."

"What do you mean?" she asked vaguely.

"He told me to carry his report to Philadelphia. Instead I followed him, or tried to."

"Since he has been married to me I am sure he is getting used to being disobeyed." Some puzzle worried at the back of her mind, but she was so tired she almost could not verbalize it. "Daniel's report. But Dupree had it. How did...?"

"I mailed it."

Nancy was silent for many heartbeats until she could grasp the magnitude of this admission.

"Trueblood, really! You mailed it?" she demanded in astonishment. "Does that not seem a rather negligent way to handle Daniel's secret papers?"

"Shush, Nancy dear. We have to be careful now, with Johnson in the house."

"But really, that seems so irresponsible." Nancy sat up straight, suddenly fully awake and alert.

"I—I care more about him than this business. How could I go off to Philadelphia, with him following you in a half-crazed condition?"

"Sorry. I should not condemn you. You are a true friend to me. But surely Daniel warned you not to mail anything."

"Of course he did."

"He knew they were going to try to stop the post rider."

"Unfortunately, he omitted to tell me that part."

Nancy covered her eyes, and Trueblood thought for a moment she was crying. Then her rich laughter overcame her and she shook her head at his look of concern.

"Are you bound by some sort of oath to follow Daniel?"

"No."

"Why then do you do it?"

"If you are asking why I follow him into such danger, I would answer because someone must."

"To pick up the pieces, so to speak?"

"A somewhat accurate description of his usual state at the end of such an adventure."

"I am glad you are always there."

"Truth to tell, though I have failed him miserably in this case, he would usually not survive without me."

"Though he would gamely try, whereas you could manage quite easily without Daniel...so long as there are no woods involved.''

"Ah, but would it be at all interesting?''

Nancy laughed tiredly. "Where do you suppose he is by now?''

"Well on his way to Philadelphia. He will be back.''

"I hope he has the good sense to stay away. Surely he knows we will come to him when this is all over.''

"You mean when the army comes.''

"That does seem inevitable now. I was right when I sensed that I could be used against him. It never occurred to me that Papa would blurt out that we are married, as though being his son-in-law was some sort of protection.''

"Perhaps he was merely determined to go down with Daniel, if it came to a fight.''

"Papa may drink too much, but next to you and Daniel, he is the most courageous man I have ever known.''

"Yes, there is nothing wrong with his courage, but it may take more than that to bring us all out of this adventure safely.''

"Adventure? It is a mess.''

"What is the matter, Nancy Whiskey? Have you lost your taste for adventuring?''

"Yes, now that I am a danger to others. And we still do not know if Ramp meant to kill Daniel or no. He is still out there somewhere.''

"Give Daniel some credit. He used to slip in and out of New York when it was occupied by the British. Very cool, is our Daniel.''

"Yes, I keep forgetting that. If only we could get some word of him, but neither of us dare write to him if the mail is not safe, nor even to Norton or Mrs. Cook.''

"And Daniel can certainly not communicate with us. I think we must trust him to think of something.''

"I am too weary to do anything else.''

Trueblood helped her to her feet and she started to laugh again.

"You mailed it!"

"I am never going to live that down, am I?"

The days came and went, Ned grew well enough to be moved in a well-padded wagon to his own house and Nancy went back to her routine of gardening and putting up foods for the winter. Braids of onions adorned the cooler corners of the kitchen, strings of dried pumpkin rounds hung near the ceiling and potatoes were laid out on the cool dry earth of the cellar.

The inn became rather quiet, since the group that had habitually gathered there were giving it a wide berth. For her part Nancy could be quite content with just their immediate household, but she worried how her papa would take being ostracized.

To her surprise he spent more evenings sober than not, playing with young Gabriel on the floor in front of the hearth or holding him on his lap on the settle, telling him stories of all his battles. They all listened raptly to these, even the infant Gabriel, and Nancy thought it would be the closest thing to having a family if only Daniel were here. Her papa did go into Pittsburgh once a week for supplies and news. He reported much terrorizing of tax collectors by insurgents. He actually went to the Parkinson's Ferry meeting to see if they really meant to elect Bradford governor. Trueblood accompanied Riley. Nancy had just begun to hope that her papa had been weaned away from the rebels when the militia was called to a muster at Braddock's Field. Once again Trueblood went with him. Though left with instructions to abandon the inn if there should be trouble, Nancy and Luce merely kept a close watch on the road.

"They're coming, Miss Nancy," Luce reported from his seat at the window.

''Papa and Trueblood?'' Nancy asked, wiping the flour off her hands.

''Hundreds of men. They must be coming up the road from the ferry.''

''If there had been shooting in Pittsburgh, would we have heard it here?''

''Never—too far away. P'haps we should go to the still house?''

''Take Ellie and the baby there. I'll shut myself up here.''

''No,'' Ellie said, ''we'll stay with ye.'' She picked Gabriel up from his cradle.

''Then take Gabriel to the cellar. We'll keep the doors barred unless we see Trueblood or Papa.''

But the backwoodsmen, and also the women who trooped by, did not seem to be desperate fugitives from some attack, nor a victorious mob. They carried no spoils of war, no plate, spoons or casks. They seemed one and all to be exceedingly drunk, well fed and in good spirits. Nancy could not make it out at all. But she did not unbar the doors all the same.

''There they are—Papa and Trueblood,'' she said to Luce. ''And they look—they look exceedingly drunk, too.''

''I'll open the door ta them.''

''No. They are going around back. Meet them at the back door. I will keep watch.''

The constant stream of foot traffic kept going along the road, some of them singing tavern songs, and none of them seeming to notice much the defection of two of their number.

''Nancy girl, ye've missed a time.''

''Papa, you are drunk.''

''No, just a bit on the go. Could I turn it down, I ask ye, when they was giving it away fer free?''

Nancy gaped and turned her gaze to Trueblood, who belched and flopped down on one of the benches with a groan. "I have eaten until I can hold no more, and you may guess what a prodigious amount that is."

"Eaten? What happened then? Not a battle?"

"More like a fair. The merchants and good people of Pittsburgh, when it appeared attack was inevitable, agreed to exile from the city those among them who had been named as informers. As a show of good faith they also cooked all their hams and chickens and threw up table boards on trestles in the streets. They baked and glazed and mashed and buttered. The militia and backwoods rabble have been vanquished by their stomachs and appeased with all the whiskey they can hold."

Nancy sat down across from Trueblood, shaking her head in disbelief. "Does that ploy have the ring of Daniel about it?"

"Well, I did not actually see him, but it is just the sort of scheme he might suggest to diffuse a situation."

Nancy frowned.

"What is the matter? If Daniel was the instigator he saved the city from being sacked."

"Yes, but it means he is here still or here again. It means he is in danger."

"You worry too much. After today I think we can count on this whole rebellion fizzling out."

"I wish you may be right."

Two days after the march on Pittsburgh and the subsequent rout of the backwoodsmen, there was a scurrilous-looking newcomer sitting alone at a table. Nancy hoped he would not demand lodging as well as dinner, since she was quite sure his buckskins were infested with fleas. He growled through his beard for whiskey and a meal, and she thought the voice familiar. The pinch she received when she delivered to him a tankard of plain water was definitely Daniel's. She watched in fascination as he wolfed down the stew she provided and wiped his trencher with a biscuit, which he then devoured. He belched loudly, wiped his mouth on his sleeve and threw a coin on the table. Then he shouldered his pack and left.

She shook her head for the benefit of the other customers, who chuckled and stared after the trapper. Even for this rough country, he was uncommonly filthy.

Nancy knew Daniel could not go to the stable, since Luce was still out there tending to the stock, so she took up a bucket to get some water.

"Daniel?" she whispered as she ducked her head to enter the springhouse.

"You did not give me away."

"I did not know it was you until I heard your voice. You stink."

"Too much to kiss me?"

"No, not too much for that."

Nancy found his mouth in the midst of the whiskers and let her tongue linger there while Daniel explored her body with his hands.

"I rather like that beard. Do you think you might keep it?"

"I'll think about it," he said as he pushed her back to look into her eyes. "That's what you said when I left. You said you would think about forgiving me."

"For being a spy? But that is your job."

"Not for being a spy. Do not be so provoking. Do you forgive me for trying to treat you like a piece of property, then being too pigheaded to admit I was wrong?"

"I would forgive you anything."

"I miss you so much I ache all the time. And it is not just physical. The thought that I might have lost you through my own stupidity..."

"I was playacting, you fool. I knew we would be together again."

"It certainly felt to me like a real parting."

"Only because we are all very good at this game—you,

Trueblood and me. But you have broken your word. You came back."

"Not as Daniel Tallent."

"Will you break your other promise?"

"What was that?"

"To give up being a spy?"

"That is all over now that I am found out."

"You could take up a new identity, keep playing the game."

"But you do not want that, do you?"

"Not if we are to have a family."

"Is that a condition of you coming with me?"

"No. I will go with you anywhere. But I do not want to bring children into such a dangerous world."

"I do not blame you for that. But I do not know when I can make a safe world for you and our children."

She began to tug at his greasy shirt, wanting to wash him in the spring, to feel his body next to hers.

"I cannot stay. I only came to warn you. The deadline for dispersal is the first of September. After that Washington will send the army."

"But that is only two weeks. These men talk and talk. They do not actually do anything very quickly except run into trouble."

"To tell you the truth, the gathering of the armies has been set in motion. Washington neither expects nor would heed assurances that the insurgents had dispersed."

"That is what you expected."

"Your father's name is on the list of those to be arrested."

Nancy's breath hissed as though she had been wounded. "So even if he had a change of heart, they would never believe him?"

"Not likely. He must flee, either to Canada or down the river. Will he need money?"

"I will give him some of Uncle's."

"When I come again, I will claim you as my wife."

"Now that I have accepted you unconditionally, do you take me on my own terms?"

"If you mean have I accepted your propensity for falling into adventures, far from it. But I suspect we will always argue about that."

"Most married people do argue, but that need not keep us from enjoying each other when we are in accord."

"My thinking exactly."

"I mean, do you accept my vocation?"

"Your midwifery? I—"

"Someone is coming," Nancy whispered.

Daniel thrust her aside, to have room to grapple with an assailant in the small space.

"Trueblood!"

"Daniel, you stink!"

"So happy to see you, also. You knew me?"

"A man knows his own brother. What is amiss?"

"The army is on its way. They will be here no later than the end of October."

"Because of you or in spite of you?"

"I find myself very ineffectual in this case. I did manage to give them a more accurate picture of the situation than they have had either from their suspicions or from the delegation. I have orders to join them at Carlisle and appraise them of the local terrain."

"And try what you can do to blunt their enthusiasm for law and order?"

"So!" Riley's gruff voice caught them all unawares and made Trueblood hit his head in the confined space and curse.

"Riley!" Daniel whispered. "Get in here and do not shout. I have come to try to help you."

"I knew that was ye under all that filth. Ye stink, and that comes from a man whose standards are nay high."

Nancy giggled.

"So I have been told," Daniel said, with a glowering look at his wife.

"Papa, Daniel came all this way to warn you. You must flee before the army gets here."

"You had better take this seriously, and do not be dragging Nancy off with you," Daniel warned.

"I suppose 'is the last I'll see of any of ye, then," Riley said, taking Nancy's hand.

"I will endeavor to work for pardon for all those accused, except Bradford. But that is not to be thought of until the commotion dies down."

"You can visit us when the danger is past," Nancy said.

"How'd I find ye, Nancy girl?"

"I will see that Ellie always knows where we are."

Riley embraced his daughter. "I meant it fer the best. I'd no more have brought ye into a rebellion than a war, but these things happen. I'd best go pack and be off before the list is made public. God only knows wot will happen then."

"Papa, wait." Nancy tore a strip off her petticoat and handed it to him.

"What is this—for luck?"

"No, a fresh start. Uncle gave me a small fortune in gold and silver coins. I sewed them into little sections in my best petticoat."

"Ye're a clever girl, Nancy dearie," Riley said, as he dangled the strip and judged its worth by the weight. "But I can nay take it. Yer uncle would have apoplexy if he knew ye gave it me."

"I want you to have it. I will never use it for passage back to England and it will keep us from worrying about you so much."

Riley kissed her on both cheeks. "She's a quick one and a comely lass," he said to Daniel. "She inherited both from her mama. I hope ye know ye're lucky ta get her."

"Very lucky."

"Come, Riley," Trueblood commanded. "I will saddle your horse for you while you pack."

"What is it to be?" Daniel asked. "Canada or New Orleans?"

"Ah, winter's comin' on. Bad road to start for Canada this time o' year. Besides, I might run inter that fella Dupree."

"You know he was a spy, then?"

"I know naught of spying. Besides, I do nay mind a spy or two. Isn't my only dotter married ta one? The thing is, I still owe Dupree a pile o' money from cards. So I guess 'twill be New Orleans. This is it, Nancy darlin'. Give me one last kiss."

She complied and looked inclined to cry.

"Listen to me, Nancy girl. Ye've nothing ta fear from these Whiskey Boys, but when the army comes keep yer pistol by ye. Ye never can tell what sort o' scum will surface in an army."

"But Papa, Daniel is in the army."

"He is, is he? Well, I suppose this lad is nay so bad, but if I was ye I would nay have him till he bathed."

Daniel and Nancy went to help Trueblood get horses ready, two of Daniel's best.

"I will ride downriver with him," Trueblood volunteered. "If there is no boat willing to take him to New Orleans, I will ride the first day's journey with him. He should be safe enough so long as he stays on this side."

"Do not get lost yourself," Daniel chided warmly, with a hand on his brother's shoulder.

After they had seen the party off, Nancy looked longingly toward the loft.

"I think you should listen to your father and not have me without a bath."

"I have never heeded him before."

She preceded him up the ladder and got down a bundle

of blankets she had tied to the ceiling, out of the way of mice. Daniel helped her make up a bed in the hay, chuckling to himself.

"What is so humorous, sir? If you make fun of my desperation for your body again we are likely to fall out."

"It is only that, as always, you think of every eventuality."

"I see nothing wrong with being prepared, for the best that can happen as well as the worst." She stripped off her clothes and crawled between the blankets. "Actually, I think it is those buckskins that smell so bad, not you."

"I bought these from your friend, Ramp."

"What? He is not my friend. He abducted me."

"Do not worry. I did not kill him. He is an interesting fellow. I found it politic to change clothes with him, as I was a fugitive. It is a good disguise. I think I will use it again."

Nancy let this pass because she truly did not want to argue with him about the future, and whether she could tolerate him continuing his clandestine work. All she wanted was to love him. "He was not trying to kill you then?"

Daniel slid in beside her and rubbed her arms and back to warm her. Her flesh felt hot against him after so many weeks without her. "I am not sure," he said sleepily, "what he originally intended by following us. To steal you back again, I suppose. But something about seeing me outnumbered and about to be strung up brought out his feelings for the underdog."

"So he helped you?"

"Well, he said he and I are now even."

"Did you explain that we are married and that he must leave me alone?"

"Yes, he has agreed not to abduct you again, but only after I told him how lethal you can be and how you trapped me into marriage."

"Daniel!"

"Once he realized what a near miss he had had he vowed never to cross your path again."

"So we will never know…"

"I asked him about Dupree. He said the Frenchman paid to have me killed. I was right. They would not have hurt you."

"That is a matter of opinion. But actually, we have a great deal to thank Ramp for. Without the threat of imminent death, I wonder if you would ever have got round to offering for me."

"Of course I would have. It simply would not have been so precipitous."

"I regret nothing that has happened to us. Though I am growing rather weary of discussing your business affairs." She ran her hand down to lightly stroke his aroused member, while he ducked under the blanket to tease at her breasts with his so-talented tongue.

"Daniel…"

"Mmm?"

"Without you here I have left off putting herbs in my tea."

"You mean tonight we could make a child?" His whisper vibrated with excitement, not dread. "Do you want me to stop?" he asked in despair.

"No, I want a child. Ironic that nothing much happened around here the whole time I held off from you.…"

"Held off? If that is what you call reserve—"

"I mean the whole time I avoided getting with child. Now that I feel safe with the idea, things look to be getting very violent."

"And why do you suddenly feel safe with the idea?"

"I am going to trust you to keep both the babe and me safe."

"Nancy Whiskey, who has never trusted anyone before, is going to trust me? I am honored." He spread her legs and wrapped them around his waist as he prepared to tease her in his usual fashion. She arched against him, impaling herself on his shaft and making him chuckle. "So impatient! What are you going to do when I am too old for this sort of thing?"

"We will never be too old for this!" She gasped as he thrust her down onto the blanket and began his assault. She could tell he was holding his own desperate needs in check to bring her to the fullest possible enjoyment of him. The final swelling drew a gasp of delight from her. It had never been so satisfying before. He had wiped away all her uncertainties with his love. He lay on top of her, sweating and paralyzed with fatigue. She pulled the blanket over his shoulders when she realized he had fallen asleep inside her.

Chapter Fourteen

Rumors flew up and down the country after Daniel left. There was word of the shooting of an innocent boy near Carlisle. Nancy could not discount it. Her father had told her tales of what a conquering army could be like. "Mind ye, Nancy, ye've little to fear from the folk around here, but watch out fer the soldiers. Don't trust a one o' them." And that was how the troops under Washington's command were marching into western Pennsylvania—not as peace-keepers coming to put down an uprising, if they should find one, but as conquerors of a populace in rebellion. There were rumors of appropriation of food and horses, or out-right theft.

The rumors of rape Nancy's logical mind discounted, as she stroked her still-flat stomach with pleasure. She was sure she was carrying Daniel's child now, and that would be to the good if any soldier should try to take her against her will. She thought about what she would do in that case, since saving the life of her child meant saving her own life. Ordinarily she would fight such a man to the death, but not anymore. She could see how a family, even one you still carried inside, made you vulnerable, changed your actions. If she were to kill a soldier she would probably be hanged.

So she would not kill him, but she would make him pay, she thought, as she tucked her knife in her pocket.

She ordered Luce and Trueblood to make tight the shelter at the still and to supply the small cabin with provisions and firewood for some weeks. Luce had orders to take Ellie and Gabriel there at the slightest rumor of the soldiers' approach. Nancy and Trueblood would hold the inn, unless that seemed dangerous. They could always fade into the woods if need be.

"Nancy, what are you doing?" Trueblood asked near the end of one long day of preparations. "I worked hard on that sign."

"I'm only painting out the word *inn*. Can you paint *tavern* in there again?"

"After all your insistence that this is not a common tavern, but an inn?"

"But the soldiers are coming. I do not want any of them sleeping here."

"I do not think this will stop them," he said, but obligingly took the cup of paint from her and smoothed over her work. "We could just take this down and make it into a private residence."

"Turn away our regular customers? In one respect I would like that very much, especially Spode. I do not know why I let him start coming back."

"As I recall it was to demonstrate how happily married Luce and Ellie are, and what a fool he was not to want Gabriel."

"Yes, that must have been it, but I do wonder if trying to teach Spode a lesson is not a waste of time. At any rate, they do bring us a deal of information that is useful to Daniel—especially Spode, who seems to hear everything. Otherwise, you would have to go drinking elsewhere to find out what is going on."

"Oh, I think we can rely on the *Gazette* to supply us with the news."

"Days late. No, our customers got us into this mess. I intend to make as much use of them as I can." She left Trueblood to his task and went inside to lay the table for dinner.

In spite of her many arguments with Ned Johnson, and perhaps because Nancy had saved his life, it was he who rode up with his horse in a sweat to warn of the approach of the soldiers. Nancy ordered Luce to carry Ellie and Gabe to the still and not leave them until morning. A troop of men came down the road looking wet, chilled and not very dangerous at all. The sergeant in charge, Stark by name, called a halt at the inn, and Nancy was so caught up in serving the forty or so men whiskey and stew, and Trueblood was so busy feeding and watering their pack animals, she did not have time to be afraid of them. She thought perhaps she had overreacted, as she collected halfpennies.

But they showed no sign of going off to Pittsburgh as she had hoped.

"We want accommodations," Stark said, sneezing and burying his wizened face in a large handkerchief.

"This is a tavern, not an inn for overnight guests, nor a hospital." She stared at several men shivering in front of the fire. "If you have men with the flux you should take them to Pittsburgh."

"I can see with my own eyes ye have rooms above."

"For the family. There are too many of you."

"Some can sleep in the stable."

"I will not have them setting that on fire, trying to keep warm. They can sleep down here on the floor, but they have to get out from underfoot when it is time for me to make breakfast. Then I suppose you will be off to Pittsburgh."

"We're to billet ourselves wherever we can on the main

roads. I've sent a man across on the ferry ta tell them our position.''

"How long do you mean to stay, then?"

"I don't know. Till the rebellion is put down.''

"There is no rebellion.''

"We'll find one.''

"Or provoke one.''

"I'm follerin' orders. I could take what we need and not pay fer it.''

Though the sergeant was shorter than Nancy by an inch or two, he confronted her tenaciously. Much as she would have liked to send him packing, the way the soldiers were staring at them made her hesitate. If she won the argument she would undermine the man's authority. Then he would either let the soldiers carry off anything they liked, or he would not be able to prevent them.

"In that case you would have to cook it yourselves. I shall need more provisions from Pittsburgh. I was not expecting to feed this many mouths for days at a time.''

"I'll send fer flour next time I send my messenger in, but they are not likely to have any meat. The provisioning of this expedition has been poor.''

"Is that not always the case? Trueblood can find fresh meat besides what we have smoked.''

"How would ye know about provisioning? Ye're just a lass.''

"My father was a soldier.''

"Ah, ye're used ta army ways then. I fought in the Revolution myself. If it wasn't for the Oneidas we would have starved to death at Valley Forge. All because Washington would nay let us forage.''

"That is because he did not want the population turned against you. And you had best keep his reasoning in mind in these parts.'' Nancy stopped herself from telling him her papa had fought on the other side. "I spent the better part of my youth expecting to be following an army train, but it is more work than even I thought.''

"But ye will do it?'' Stark half asked, half threatened.

"I will need some of your fellows to fetch and carry water and wood, since it looks like Trueblood will have to spend all his time hunting.''

"Fair enough, but I'll expect somethin' off the bill in that case.''

"You are a shrewd man,'' Nancy said, hands on her hips. "I think we can deal together.''

Before the soldiers came Nancy had spent half her day cooking one thing or another. Now she cooked constantly and had to set Luce to watch over what was on the hearth so that a soldier did not wander in and abscond with it, half-done. What a worthless lot. She got no work out of them unless the sergeant berated them, and she really wondered how much control such an old man had over them. The rumors of mutiny, should the army turn back without seeing action, now seemed vivid to her. It would be so easy for this group of men to get out of control.

Of course, with Luce watching the kitchen and making furtive trips to check on Ellie and Gabriel, and with Trueblood hunting and trying to keep up with the stable chores, the burden of the work fell on her. When the sergeant suggested she do their laundry she sent him a dour look. "The laundry kettle is in the yard. They can make a fire and start it boiling. I will give them soap, but I cannot be two places at once. I really think you should find them some employment, or at least drill them to keep them out of trouble. My papa would have had them marching and drilling half the day.''

"There's nothin' ta do but wait fer orders. I would sooner be in town myself, but I expect they're afraid ta quarter all the troops in Pittsburgh.''

"So they have farmed them out to keep them from getting drunk and burning the city. Fine, but find them some-thing to do.''

"Like wot?''

"Have them dig another privy. They will fill ours in a week at this rate. There is lumber for building it behind the stable.''

The sergeant looked mulish. "That's not a proper use o' federal troops.''

Nancy suspected he did not think he could get them to do it. "Tell them any man who works on it will get a free noggin of whiskey each night.''

"I'll...consider it.''

After they had served up the meal a few hours later True-blood whispered to Nancy, "I heard some of them talking. They must think I have no English. Several are prisoners released from the Philadelphia jails.''

"A fine irony, men who deserve to be jailed coming to arrest...''

"Our fellows are rebels, at least some of them.''

"Oh, I know they brought this on themselves, that they were unwise, but I cannot help sympathizing with them.''

"Speaking of them, here come the Johnsons now,'' Trueblood whispered.

"That is a surprise. I did not think they would come nigh the place with the soldiers here.''

"Perhaps they have come to check on you.''

"Take that risk for me?'' Nancy asked. "Let us make them welcome, then. If they left now they would look sus-picious.'' She beckoned the Johnsons to sit at the cooking table, since there were soldiers sprawled everywhere else.

Trueblood poured them each a mug of whiskey as they seated themselves on the bench.

"How long do they mean ta stay?'' Ned whispered.

"They do not know, but they are billeted here for the duration,'' Nancy answered.

"And who might ye lads be?" The sergeant wandered over with his mug. "Some o' the Whiskey Rebels?"

"If they were, they would hardly be likely to stop in for an evening of cards, now would they?" Nancy chided.

"We're regular customers here, farmers if ye must know."

"And have ye got a still?" Stark, a little bombastic from drink, demanded.

"Not anymore," Nancy answered. "The rebels burned it."

The Johnsons stared at her, for they did operate a small still, but as her answer was as ambiguous as the sergeant's question, it could have applied to her as easily as them, so they let it pass.

"Ye should be glad ta see us here ta keep order, then."

"We'd just as soon take care of our own problems," Hiram said.

"Did ye go ta those meetings they've been holdin'?"

"Aye, ta hear what they'd to say."

"And did ye agree with them?"

"I agreed it's an unjust tax," the older Johnson replied. "A man should have a right ta say what he thinks in a free country."

"That's right," Ned agreed. "We've a right ta free speech, ta assemble and ta petition the government...and ta not have our houses invaded," he said, staring around him and drawing guffaws from half-a-dozen men lounging close to the fire.

"You haven't a right ta commit treason and open rebellion," the sergeant replied.

"It's nay like that," Ned retorted, but his brother laid a restraining hand on his shoulder.

"We—they just wanted ta be heard."

"Ye taunted the government 'cause ye thought it was far away, that it couldn't touch ye. Well, it's here now." The small, grizzled sergeant almost swaggered.

"If a man has the money ta pay the tax he gets his still burnt," Hiram said. "If he doesn't he's accused o' being a rebel. There's not much ta choose between the two. He's ruined either way."

"He is right," Nancy agreed, feeling herself allied with the Johnsons, in spite of their past differences. "Honest folk are caught in the middle."

"If ye all had paid the tax, this never would've happened."

"We'd have—most folk would've paid, if they'd had any money," Ned said.

"Ye sell yer whiskey. Ye must get money fer that."

"Trade goods," Ned scoffed, then saw Jackson, the provisioner, break off talking to the soldiers and walk toward them.

"Ye must be able to sell it," Stark insisted. "The army pays money fer it."

"Only ta the big producers like Neville and ta—" He broke off before he named Jackson as well. "They're the ones who get the army contracts. O' course, Neville can pay the tax."

"He's right, ye know," Jackson said unexpectedly. "Up until now people haven't been able ta afford ta buy goods from me fer the same reason they can't pay the tax—no hard currency in the area. And it is an unjust tax." The provisioner held out his tumbler and Trueblood filled it. Jackson downed it in one draught and rubbed his stomach as though the liquid had burned a hole through it.

"They can nay defy the federal government and expect ta get away with it," Stark growled. "First 'twould be the whiskey tax, then all taxes."

"We could live with a fair tax—a land tax," Ned returned. "Let those rich seaboard landowners pay some tax on the thousands o' acres they have tied up, or maybe think about selling land ta those who deserve it."

"Most likely they would only raise the rents, eh Nancy?" Jackson asked.

"No doubt." But Nancy did doubt that the farmers would be content with a land tax. It would not solve the problem of how to pay it. Ned was most likely quoting some of the rhetoric he had heard at the meetings.

The soldiers were following the argument with lazy interest, ready for a brawl if one seemed likely, but too full of stew and biscuit to initiate one. Nancy had a sense of how hard they would be to handle if they all decided to attack these few men. They would be like a pack of dogs egging each other on, each one gaining bravado from the others. That was how this whole rebellion had gotten started. The loudest rebels had aroused even sensible men to anger and convinced them they could defy the laws and make a difference. Now they were beginning to realize they could not get away with it.

An oath from the sergeant brought her attention back to the matter at hand. "Just or not, the rebels have no right ta defy the government."

"It doesn't pay ta ship grain east over the mountains, or even flour," Jackson said. "The only way these men can make a profit off their grain is ta make it into whiskey and trade it ta me for goods. I send it east by wagon or on Tallent's pack train." He nodded toward Trueblood, who had been pretending to ignore the squabble. "He sells it and brings back trade goods fer me."

"If ye had paid us money instead o' goods fer our whiskey, we..." Ned paused at the withering glare his brother sent him. "People could have paid the tax."

"I didn't have any money ta pay you with, not till the army came," said Jackson, as he jingled his money pouch.

"So if someone brought ye whiskey now, ye could pay hard cash fer it?" Ned asked.

"Now I could."

"So now farmers could afford ta pay the tax," Hiram said, shaking his head.

"But only because the army came," Jackson said. "They had ta send an army ta make it possible for farmers ta do what they could nay do before the army came."

"But that's stupid." Ned hit the table with his fist.

"We are talking about the federal government," Hiram said with resignation.

Nancy laughed. "So the army will remedy the situation one way or the other. This is such a male solution to a problem. Does no one see that there is a net loss involved? The government will have to think of another tax to pay for the army that is supposed to collect this tax."

"Exactly," said Jackson with a chuckle.

Nancy wondered if he would have been talking so freely if he were not half-drunk himself.

"Oh, Trueblood," he said. "I assume you're in charge o' the pack train now that Daniel is gone. The *Gazette* publisher wants ta know when he can expect another load o' paper."

"Best send one of your wagons. Luce and I must help Nancy," Trueblood said with a grunt.

"I'll send a load o' pelts, rather than have a load o' whiskey confiscated illegally. Though the wagon will probably shake apart on the road."

Trueblood nodded and accompanied Jackson to the stable. Nancy could imagine him elaborating on the events in something more like his normal style of speech. She wondered when it would all fall apart and they might have to flee.

It was a bone-chilling cold that set in with freezing rain the next evening. A protective Luce was with his family at the still, which he reported was fairly cozy. Nancy missed Ellie and Gabriel, but would not endanger them with a visit. The soldiers were playing with the cards and dice Nancy had supplied. It was a little like trying to keep a large group of very big, dangerous children amused. She was getting to know them, but there were some she simply could not like, such as Private Lowe, who sneaked about and stole food and cutlery.

The sergeant's daily messenger came back that evening with orders, and Stark caused a deal of grumbling by marshaling the men and marching them off. Nancy hoped she had seen the back of them for the last time, but decided not to send Luce for Ellie and the baby yet.

Nancy and Trueblood were up late keeping the fire and wondering why they had not heard from Daniel yet. She had the most awful fear that something had happened to him, that all she would have of him was the baby she now carried.

It was far past midnight by the time they had talked through all the possible reasons the soldiers had left so precipitously and in such foul weather.

Without warning the door was thrown open. "We've arrested some o' the rebels. Where's Patrick Riley?" Sergeant Stark demanded.

"He's not here," Nancy said, surprised into telling the sergeant the truth.

"I know you're not Riley," he shouted, pointing at Trueblood, "but what about that young fella who works here?"

"That's Lucius."

"Look upstairs," the sergeant told a pair of soldiers. "He might be Riley himself."

Trueblood warned Nancy with his eyes not to object to this intrusion.

"Riley is my papa and is somewhere near fifty years old. Luce is just a boy."

The soldiers thumped back down to report, "No one here."

"I might ha' known this was a nest o' rebels after the

conversations we've heard here. We have to arrest Riley. Where is he?''

"I do not know," Nancy said in obvious distress.

"Or ye do know and ye're not saying."

"I do not know and I have no idea if I will ever see him again." Nancy buried her face in her hands, and Trueblood watched this sudden display of sensibility with mute attention.

The implication that it was the army's fault Nancy would never see her father again was not lost on the sergeant, not after Trueblood's accusing look, and the man might have been taken in by Nancy if Lowe had not whispered, "After havin' us here fer weeks and not breaking down, she can't be weepin' fer her pa now."

"I thought you had gone, that it was all over. Now I find I have to feed you again. Anyone would weep at the prospect," Nancy sobbed.

"I suggest ye get on with heatin' us some soup and save yer weepin' fer later. We're perishin' wi' the cold."

"And how many prisoners are there to feed?" Nancy demanded tearfully.

"The prisoners don't need ta be fed. We'll be haulin' them ta Pittsburgh in the mornin'."

"That's inhuman."

"Those are our orders. They're not ta be given any comfort."

As Trueblood built up the fire, Nancy cut potatoes and carrots, along with some cooked venison, to make up a quick soup. "They are punishing them already, Trueblood," she whispered. "The stable will be freezing tonight."

"I will take something out later for the guards. Perhaps they will let them have some."

"There are some blankets in the loft and plenty of hay."

"I will see to it."

* * *

With his men fed and warm and stretched out around the fire, the sergeant was feeling full of himself again. He stopped Trueblood at the door and demanded what was in the steaming pot.

"I assume you did not leave the prisoners unguarded. Are your own men to have nothing, either?"

"Take it out then, but be quick about it."

Nancy waited impatiently and began to peel more potatoes for the breakfast that she would no doubt be expected to produce in the morning. When Trueblood returned he sat on the bench by her.

"Who is it?" she whispered.

"The Johnson brothers, Spode and another man I do not know. They must have roused them from their beds and not permitted them to dress. They are barely covered. They begged me to help them."

Nancy was about to explode in a fierce whisper when Trueblood flicked his eyes toward the sergeant. She gained control of her temper before she spoke, continuing her task. "I suppose they would not let you get the prisoners either food or blankets."

"No, and I did not like the way those privates were eyeing your milk cow. One of them made an observation about how good a beefsteak would taste."

"Let me guess. Private Lowe."

"Yes, I was thinking of moving Charlotte down to the still house in a roundabout way. It will give me a chance to warn Luce to keep clear of the inn."

"Good idea, Trueblood. They can keep her in the shed where the firewood is."

"Are you sure you will be all right here? I may be gone an hour or more."

"I will be fine. They are three parts asleep already."

Trueblood's departure, with the excuse of watering the cow, roused the sergeant enough to demand another round of whiskey, since they would be leaving for Pittsburgh at an early hour with the prisoners. Nancy brewed up a whiskey punch with sugar, the last of her lemons, an inordinate amount of ginger and another herb.

"That smells tempting. What is it?"

"A punch. I thought, seeing as how you are leaving, I would show you there are no hard feelings."

"That's well done of ye. This will set us on the road with a will."

The brew was passed around and Nancy met no resistance when she left to carry tankards to the guards by the stable entrance. She would have liked to reassure the wretches within that help was forthcoming, but she dared not tarry.

She returned to the house and went upstairs to gather her papa's and Daniel's discarded clothes into a bundle. By the time she came down the ginger, lemon and sugar had driven the alcohol through their systems so fast the soldiers were all snoring. She made her way to the stable and found the same satisfying situation.

"Nancy, they've fallen asleep. If ye could just untie us, we could get away," Ned said.

"She'd best not," advised his brother. "She could get in trouble."

"Didn't you stick by me when Daniel turned out to be a government spy? Of course I came to set you free." She produced the knife from her pocket and cut their bonds, trying not to notice their state of undress. "Put these clothes on while I saddle some of our ponies."

Ned dressed quickly and came to help her. "How will we get them back ta ye?"

"Go to Brownsville and leave them there. If need be you can go downriver from there. You will need some money," she said, giving him a pouch of coins.

"Why are ye doing this?"

"Because what they are doing is wrong. There have been mistakes made on both sides, but to drag men out with the

purpose of degrading them, perhaps letting the weather kil
them, is less than human. I will never forgive Presiden
Washington for this, never. May he never know anothe
moment's peace or comfort himself.''

"Ye'er a rebel at heart, Nancy Whiskey. Mayhap y
should come with us," Ned suggested.

"No, I must make sure the soldiers leave here in th
morning without finding Luce's family.''

"They're hiding at the still, aren't they?" Spode asked

"Yes," Nancy said.

"I must thank you—" Spode started to say.

"We are neighbors, after all.''

"Goodbye, Nancy," Hiram said, taking the reins of the
pony she was holding.

"Keep safe," Ned added as he mounted his own pony.

"Yes, Godspeed, Ned. I know we have had our differences, but I will not tolerate barbarism from anyone. Papa
went downriver to New Orleans. If this does not settle
down soon you might have to do the same. I imagine they
will leave a military presence behind, but I should not think
they would bother searching for you very long.''

"The best o' luck ta ye, too, Nancy," Hiram said.

She was waving goodbye to them when Trueblood
walked back by a circuitous route from the still. The first
streaks of gray were appearing over the horizon, and the
soldiers continued to snore incongruously.

"Don't condemn me, Trueblood. I had to do it.''

"Actually, I had some such idea myself, but how did
you get the guards to sleep through it?''

She told him her recipe as they walked back to the inn.
He chuckled quietly and began to build up the fire in preparation for the bread dough she had set to raising.

This was well on the way to baking and the day was
upon them when the soldiers woke up groaning. One by
one they made for the privies and came back in, looking
bleak and empty, to be handed weak tea and warm bread.

The sergeant was gone longer than most and came back n to sit hunched over the table. "My head feels like it's about ta explode."

"Have some tea," Nancy advised.

"What was in that drink ye made last night?"

"Whiskey, sugar, lemon and spice. It's a very popular punch hereabouts."

"It tasted right enough, but who would want the mornin' after?"

"It's my papa's recipe."

"For what, murdering customers?"

"Well, I thought it tasted—"

Someone collided with the outside door, then tore at the catch and finally got it open.

"The prisoners are gone!" Lowe yelled.

"Gone? That's not possible, the way they were trussed up," Stark said, wincing as he lurched to his feet.

"The ropes were cut. One of them must of had a knife. Could have cut our throats in our sleep...." Lowe fingered his throat fearfully.

"Sleep? Sleeping, was ye? When ye were set to guard those prisoners?" Stark pummeled Lowe ineffectually. "On yer head it will be if they get away. Up—up all of ye and start searching." The sergeant kicked and prodded the few remaining sleepers awake and shouted out the door to the others not to mess up the tracks.

"Do you think they will find the still?" Nancy asked Trueblood when the room had cleared.

"Not likely, past all those bramble thickets. Once they see the pony tracks go down the road I imagine they will confiscate the rest of the horses and ride after them."

"Well, we could not prevent it, after all, but we have perhaps cheated the army out of a bit of deliberate cruelty. Why would they give such orders, to demean men in such a petty way?"

"It is part of war to demoralize the enemy. Usually that

takes the avenue of raping women in front of their father and husbands..." Trueblood paused.

"I know. Since they did not think they could get away with that, they did the worst they could to the men short of killing them. I cannot like the army—any army—after this. No matter who is in command, no matter what the cause, there will be atrocities and injustices."

"Daniel is in the army."

"I know. If he insists on staying in it, then he will not find me waiting for him."

"Do not say such a thing. You are distraught."

"I am seeing the world a bit more clearly now. It is not all adventure and bravado. I was ready for that, ready even for hardship and gallant wounds. What I was not prepared for was meanness and bullying, cowardice masquerading as courage, brutality with a uniform. If Daniel means to stay in the army, then I will have nothing to do with him."

"These watermelon soldiers are not typical of what a real army is like."

"What? A nobler cause would ennoble them? I do not think so, Trueblood. You would always have the most of them joining up for the worst of reasons. Unless they are taken into the army against their will they are suspect."

"How are they unlike the rebel militia with their marching and drilling?"

"They are not ours," Nancy said with a shuddering breath. "I find I have chosen a side, Trueblood, and it is not the same one Daniel is on."

"Nancy!"

She turned from him and shed real tears this time. Trueblood knew enough about women to know when to let them alone. He went outside to see if there were any horses left, just as the sergeant came back and dismounted, along with the guards of the night before and several others.

"Where is she?"

"Who?" Trueblood asked stupidly.

"They have got clean away and it's all her fault, her and that whiskey punch o' hers."

"It befuddles a man's brain so he can't help but fall asleep," Lowe agreed.

"She'll answer for this," Stark warned.

Trueblood followed the two inside to find Nancy petulantly sweeping the floor.

"This is all yer fault," Stark accused.

"My fault? I never asked to have you here, dirtying up my inn and eating all my food."

"You made us drunk."

"I did not. It was you who demanded another round of whiskey. If your men are going to drink themselves into a stupor and fall asleep that is not my fault. They are just trying to throw the blame on someone else." She put the broom down and went back to the cooking table to knead the remainder of her dough.

Since this was exactly the case, the sergeant sputtered incoherently and might have been cowed enough by Nancy to depart empty-handed for Pittsburgh, if Lowe had not spoken. "We have ta arrest someone. She's the one they call Nancy Whiskey. We could take her fer questioning." The whisper was followed by a leer that brought Trueblood to stand beside her.

Nancy restrained him with a motion. "Have you a warrant for my arrest?"

Stark eyed her resentfully. "No, but I think I can stretch my authority ta hold ye until I get instructions."

"And give yourself an excuse to stay here and eat your heads off another day," Nancy said.

"We must report ta the fort today with our prisoners. We've no more time ta waste at this inn."

"Tavern. Then I suggest you start looking for them."

The door was thrown open again, and an officer, booted and spurred, appeared silhouetted in the shaft of cold sun spilling in the opening. "What the devil's going on here?" he demanded in a clipped seaboard accent.

"We're arrestin' this woman," Lowe said, causing Stark to growl at him.

"On what charge?" the captain asked, striding into the room with an arrogant step as he kicked the door shut.

"Suspicion o' aiding the rebels...sir."

"Have you a warrant?"

"No," the sergeant said, gaping at this intrusion. "I've no warrant, but I think it my duty ta take up any suspicious person who might be used as a witness against the rebels."

"In other words you are acting on your own initiative," the captain snapped in a stiff voice.

The sudden lessening of tension in Trueblood's body made Nancy stare at the tall man in the plumed hat and cutaway blue uniform who smacked his gloves down on the table. He looked nothing like the skin-clad trapper of a few weeks ago and very little like Daniel, the merchant, but it was Daniel beneath the elegant mustache. Perhaps he had left that for her when he shaved his beard.

"My orders, sir, are ta arrest suspected rebels and witnesses. This woman has contrived the escape o' four o' them."

"Can you prove that, Sergeant?"

"The provin' or not provin' can come later. I'm taking her in fer questionin'."

"You seem to be taking a lot on yourself, Sergeant. I really begin to doubt if you have any orders, verbal or otherwise. It appears you may be acting independently to deliberately harass the populace. President Washington would never tolerate that before and he will not wink at it now, if it comes to his attention."

"This woman poisoned us."

"That hardly seems likely, seeing that you are standing here talking to me."

"We nearly died," Lowe agreed.

"Nonsense. You cannot blame me because you let your men all get drunk," Nancy said.

"And let your prisoners escape," said Trueblood.

"This is not looking good for you, Sergeant. Who is your commanding officer?"

"Let's not get excited, now. I arrested the men on me list, all but one—" he threw an accusing look at Nancy "—and would ha' been on the road ta Pittsburgh by now had she not interfered. I'm just doing my dooty."

"I suggest you be on your way then and face up to your superiors like a man instead of trying to hide behind a woman's skirts."

"She may know where they're hiding."

"I do not," Nancy maintained. Having told them to go to Brownsville and wait did not mean they had listened to her. Most likely they had not.

"We'll see wot she has to say for herself after a couple o' days in the stockade."

"You cannot arrest this woman, Sergeant."

"And why not...sir?"

"Because, Sergeant—and soon to be Private—I am arresting her. This is an order from Secretary of State Hamilton. You are dismissed." Daniel flashed the paper at him.

"But, sir—"

"Are you deaf? I thought I made it clear that these are my prisoners, both of them."

"Yes, sir, just leaving, sir." The sergeant and his cohorts scurried out the door, but stood conferring outside so that Daniel was forced to keep up the pretense.

"I am here to arrest both of you. You are to be brought directly before Mr. Hamilton. In courtesy to the lady I will allow you to collect your things, if you give me your word you will not try to escape." With this Daniel handed Nancy a letter, which she unfolded and read.

Daniel observed the sergeant staring in the window and wondered how the man would interpret the knit brow with which Nancy scrutinized the papers. Daniel hoped they could not hear her whispered reply.

"Really, Daniel, these are merely your orders. How did you know the sergeant could not read?"

"I didn't. I got lucky. I expect you will not get back here anytime soon, so leave a note for Ellie. I take it she can read?"

"Yes, I have taught her." Nancy sat to write a brief, reassuring letter to Ellie, along with a few instructions on keeping up the inn and her assurance that she had the utmost confidence in her and Luce.

Trueblood went upstairs for their packs, but returned in such a few minutes that Daniel chuckled under his breath. "Always prepared for a march," he whispered appreciatively as he put Nancy's cloak around her shoulders and leered at her. She looked trustingly up at him. He had saved her again. He had a way of doing that at the last possible moment, when all her resources were down to nothing. If not for him being in the army they would make a good team. She did not know how or when she would get a chance to tell him her decision, but she thought the moment would come all too soon.

Outside, the soldiers turned away. "We was that close ta havin' her," Lowe said. "No need to ask whose bed she'll spend the night in."

"You're right there," Stark agreed. "She won't be locked up in any stockade. She's far too pretty."

The flush that rose to Nancy's cheeks made Daniel realize she had overheard the exchange, as well. "Sergeant!" he bellowed, so abruptly that Nancy jumped, too. "What are all these horses doing tied here?"

"We was using them ta hunt down the rebels."

"You rented them?"

"No, as it was an emergency…"

"If you have any thought of making off with this lady's property just because she is being arrested you had best rid yourself of it. If so much as a spoon is missing from this inn I will see that you personally answer for it. Now let me see the back of you and these scoundrels and be quick about it.''

Stark formed up his men into two untidy lines then and started them down the road to the ferry. Luce appeared from the back of the inn.

''They've made a right mess o' the place,'' he said to Nancy.

''Sorry, Luce, to leave you with such a lot of work, but we have to go to Pittsburgh.''

''And we may not get back again soon,'' Daniel added. ''You can keep the rest of these pack ponies for your own use.''

''Yes, you are in charge now, you and Ellie,'' Nancy said with a warm smile.

''We'll do a good job, keepin' the place fer ye, don't ye worry.''

''I know you will. Say goodbye to Ellie and Gabriel.''

Daniel boosted Nancy up onto her mare as Trueblood tied their baggage onto a pony, and she looked back at the White Horse as on a home one was leaving for a long time. She had learned some valuable lessons here. The most important was that no matter how strong, how prepared she was, it sometimes was not enough. You did need someone to share the burden. Yet she was about to give that someone up.

''Well, Daniel, why did the soldiers not think it strange that you have come on such a mission unescorted?'' Trueblood asked.

''It is only by the merest chance that I am here. Actually, I just came to see how you were.''

''What?'' Nancy demanded. ''I thought you had come to rescue us. Do you mean I was within a minute of being arrested and hauled off to the stockade and you knew nothing about it?''

"Now, Nancy. I would have managed to get you away from them on the way to Pittsburgh. Besides, it is just the sort of adventure you have been craving."

"But I do not, not anymore. I am heartily tired of adventuring."

"I am sorry, Nancy. I did not know there were troops quartered on this side of the river until today. Also, I miscalculated. I never thought the army could behave so badly."

"I am sorry, too. I was wrong about myself."

"You wrong?" Daniel joked. "I cannot credit it."

"I thought I would be content to follow an army train and care for the wounded. I expected to be on their side, but I cannot condone the high-handed way they behave to civilians."

"What did you expect soldiers to be like?"

"I do not know, but I did not expect the scum of the earth."

"They are like any other group of men, some good, some bad."

"No, they are a pack of dogs with authority, licensed to harry those weaker than themselves."

"They face court-martial, possibly hanging, if they commit any serious crime."

"After the damage is done."

"And did they hurt you?"

"No, but they worried me."

"And just what did you do to them? What was the poison the sergeant was talking about?"

"I gave them the whiskey they demanded, and they did not pay for all of that," she retorted, beginning to sound even to herself like an angry fishwife.

"What else? Nancy, what did you do?" Daniel taunted.

"She merely flavored their drink with some cowslip and Jamaican ginger," Trueblood supplied.

"And what effect would that have?" Daniel asked, trying to remember if he had heard of the combination before.

"It made them sleep," Trueblood replied, "and made sure they were cleaner on the inside than they have ever been on the outside."

Daniel rode in silence for a few steps before he burst out laughing.

"They had it coming," Nancy said resentfully.

"But you cannot just go drugging soldiers and hope to get away with it."

"What does Washington mean by releasing prisoners from jail to put in the army? They are very much worse than any of the men around here."

"You will always have some in the army who abuse their power."

"It would be bad enough if it were an invading army, but to have our own army stealing and—"

"You forget, it is an invading army. There was talk of secession."

"By a few. For that we are all to be punished."

"I thought you were on my side."

"As my husband, yes, but since you are a soldier I cannot like you at all right now. And you have arrested me."

"That was a joke."

"It is not a joking matter. After all my training and preparations I have failed."

"What are you talking about?"

"I have failed to cope with them. I cannot stay married to you if you mean to be a soldier."

"But I would never ask you to follow an army train."

"No, you would ask me to sit at home and wait for news of your death. I cannot, I will not do that, either. You will have to chose between me and your profession."

"Would you give up being a midwife for me?"

"I could not, not if I were needed."

"So I am the only one who must make a sacrifice?"

"What I do is useful."

"And what I do is necessary."

Daniel was silent for the rest of the journey. Nancy had not meant to argue with him, but the sergeant had made her feel powerless and she had resented it. Being rescued at the eleventh hour by Daniel was better than being in the stockade, but she wished she had been able to manage the soldiers better herself. Now Daniel was angry, and he had a right to be. She had pledged him her loyalty and she was recanting.

After taking the ferry across the river they did not ride to the main encampment, nor to the fort in Pittsburgh, but to a respectable inn near the center of the town.

Nancy knew she had acted imprudently, but she could not lie to Daniel. Trueblood ducked into his own room, and Nancy half-expected Daniel to stay in hers, but after lighting the lamp for her he opened the door to the hallway.

"What will happen now?" she asked.

"Before month's end, the army will conduct the prisoners to Philadelphia to await trial."

"But Daniel, have you any idea of the condition of these people?"

"Some. That is why I intend to ride with the army. Being on Norton's staff, under Washington, I hope I might exert a moderating influence."

"At least threaten to report on anyone who abuses his power."

"No, I shall bring formal charges against him. Now I have told you what I mean to do. What do you mean to do?"

"I will go, too."

Daniel relaxed with a sigh of relief and was about to take Nancy in his arms when she continued, "They will be needing care. There is sure to be sickness among them after the mischief of last night, and I doubt the army will nurse them."

"I doubt they will let you do so, either."

"But you might be able to persuade them to let me help."

"Help some of the men who almost hanged me?"

"Oh, I had forgotten about that." She sat down on the high bed and stared at him, in his glittering uniform. "I am so confused."

"Perhaps I will leave you alone tonight to sort out your loyalties," Daniel said stiffly as he turned to go.

"If this is meant to punish me, it will not work. You know you want me just as badly as I want you."

He spun around at that, his composure destroyed, and was within a breath of sweeping her into his arms and the bed when some niggling memory stopped him. Perhaps it was time it ended. Women always betrayed him in the end, no matter how much he loved them. Nancy was doing it more honestly and openly than any of them, but it was a betrayal. He turned away again and went downstairs to drink in the common room.

She threw off her clothes and slid into bed in her shift. The bed was cold and she thought of all the nights she had crawled into Daniel's warm bed or he into hers, of all the nights in the stable loft, and of that first night at the crossing. Did they mean nothing now?

She had been so certain of Daniel, of her enduring love for him, but these last few weeks without him had distanced them. He was one of the enemy now. He wore the same uniform, though his was new and clean. He acted different in that uniform than when he dressed as a merchant, certainly far different from the filthy trapper he had impersonated. What other roles had he played, did he still play? And would this go on forever?

All questions and no answers. Perhaps Daniel's work was too much a part of him for him to ever be content with a quiet life. Yet he had been happy, building the springhouse and the smokehouse, helping to take care of little

Gabriel. That was the real Daniel. And the real Nancy was not an English lady, or a tavern wench, she was not even the shrew who'd distressed Daniel tonight. That had been because of the injustices of the army, some of the army. What some of the army did was not Daniel's fault. Had he not said he would work for better treatment for the prisoners, that he would try to get them pardoned?

She was certainly not the naive girl who had landed on these shores and set out for the frontier, thinking war would be an adventure. If she had to define herself it would be as a healer. That was where she felt the most competent. That was the one aspect of her life that Daniel most disapproved of, probably more so than her dislike of his soldiering.

But she would not lie to him. She knew she could not give up midwifery, so she should not demand he give up his work, either. She was his wife, and she was also tied to him by a bond stronger than any vow. She was carrying his child. This was no time to be having second thoughts.

Yet to go with him only because of the baby would be a terrible mistake. What had changed between them that made her so upset with him? It suddenly occurred to her that the being growing within her was changing everything. She had seen it in other women and had not suspected she could be affected by it—feelings of isolation, anger; the urge to make a cozy nest and stay there; frustration that it was not possible now. And she was blaming Daniel for her strange mix of feelings when it was not his fault.

If she had listened to the girl-child in her she would have fled back to the White Horse to await the birth of her baby, and she would have looked back on this night with the deepest regret a woman can have about anything. But the healer had awakened and saved her. That part of her knew she had been pushed too far, but that she had not been defeated. When she rested she would be her old self again, or at least she would remember to remind herself that she might act a little out of character for some months because of the baby. But someday when they were old she and Daniel would look back on this night and laugh about it.

The next day Daniel shuffled his feet outside her door and approached it for the third time, then turned away and paced to the end of the hall. Trueblood threw his door open, knocked on Nancy's door, then disappeared back into his own room, leaving his hapless brother standing open-mouthed in the hall.

"Daniel, what is the matter?" Nancy asked when she came out. "You look so surprised."

"I didn't know...I didn't know if you would be here or not."

"Silly, where else would I be?"

"But last night—"

"Last night I was still getting over being forced to feed and clean for forty-three men whom I'd come to detest. I see now that not all of the army are like that, just as not all the rebels are good. What I want to think about now is us. The rebellion is over, or nearly so, I think?"

"Yes, all but the legalities. Then you will come with me?"

"Yes, without condition."

He hugged her to him with more tenderness than passion, with more relief than joy.

She ran her hands though his hair, wanting him as badly as she had ever wanted him, then got control of herself and brushed his hair back to its original tidiness. He seemed to remember where they were and took her into the room, closing the door with a sigh.

She looked at his polished boots, the tight-fitting buff breeches and the blue coat with buff facings and gold buttons. His tan face sat handsomely in the folds of the white stock and he smiled.

"To think I ever doubted you," he said.

She thought about telling him he had good reason, but

that was not what he needed to hear today. "What do you think I should do today?" she asked. "I am not used to being without employment."

He cleared his throat and stepped back to regard her. "Do you still have that cream-colored silk dress?"

"Yes, I kept that one as you liked it so much."

"Then I think we should get married—really married."

"We do not need a church wedding to prove our love."

"Actually, I was wondering if you would not like to be married over the drum."

"Why Daniel, how romantic."

At Ellie's insistence Luce had run the dangers of being arrested and brought her into the town to say goodbye to Nancy. They were in time to stand with Trueblood as witnesses to the brief ceremony, which was capped by a shout of joy from the troops who were assembled, and the firing of many rifles into the air.

An odd wedding, Nancy thought, for a Whiskey Rebel, but she had gained a degree of tolerance with her realization that she had moods and vicissitudes like anyone else. She was not a constant, and she felt a deal of relief to realize no one expected her to be perfect all the time. She decided to judge each man on his own merits, not by the uniform or the actions he committed when part of a gang.

The celebration later was attended by officers, though Daniel had supplied whiskey for the common soldiers. Ellie and Luce left first, since they wanted to get back across the river before dark. Gabriel was already asleep. Nancy gave her assurances to visit them the next year, and Daniel did not contradict her.

When it was time to take their leave of Daniel's fellow officers he did not, to her surprise, escort her to the inn, but to one of the officers' tents in the fort. It contained a smoldering brazier, a campaign bed, a camp chair and, magically, her baggage.

"Well, Captain Tallent, I would have thought an officer of your status would have been bivouacked in a house in town," Nancy said, as she tested the sturdiness of the bed by bouncing on it.

"Oh, I could have, right enough," Daniel said, watching her breasts bounce. "In fact, I had to borrow the tent, along with the uniform. But you see," he said, beginning to strip off his coat and shirt, "I remembered your predilection for discomfort and inconvenience."

"And how much I wanted to camp in a tent," she said, watching his body with fascination as he sat on a stool to pull off his boots. She picked up one booted foot and straddled his leg to tug at the wet leather, and he gasped.

"What is it?" she asked, looking around at him. "Have I hurt you?"

"No, I just remembered that missing night when I got drunk."

"It has taken you long enough," she said, pulling off the other boot.

"I just fell asleep, didn't I? I'm so glad I didn't miss anything."

"So am I," she replied.

"Now let me undress you, lest anyone who might be peeking think you an easy mark." He took his time over this, baring her breasts first and watching them tighten in the cold air.

"Do you think there might be someone watching?" she asked, looking suspiciously around the tent in the dim lantern light. Daniel did not know whether her nipples had hardened from that thought, the cold or the feel of his wet tongue running over them.

"Probably not. They are fairly well disciplined for an army. At least this lot is." He untied her skirt and let it drop to the ground, and then her petticoats. He pulled her shift off her shoulders and let it fall in folds at her feet. "No, there cannot be anyone watching unless he be a mute.

No one could look at you naked without a gasp of pleasure.''

She stretched her arms over her head as a sudden recoil of anticipation arched her back, and hugged him around the neck. Daniel kissed his way down to her stomach and knelt, pausing to glance up at her with those blue eyes of his. His hands rested possessively on her rounded hips.

''Yes, we are three now!'' she said as he laid his head against her stomach and clasped her to him. She loved the way he worshipped her, his hair feathering across her belly. She ran her hands through it. ''But that is not why I married you.''

''You did not have to tell me that. You alone among women would be completely competent to raise a child by yourself.''

''No, Daniel. I find I do not go on very well by myself at all. Without you, nothing matters. There is no joy in life.''

''There were times when I did not think you even needed me.''

''I need you more than life itself. Say we will always be together.''

''Yes, always, no matter where we are.''

''Is it possible to make love on such a bed? I think it might collapse under us.''

''All part of the adventure, Nancy dear.'' He conducted her to it as though he were leading her into a dance, then laid her down upon it and shed his breeches with a barely suppressed urgency. Instantly she hooked her legs around him. ''Not so fast. If there is anyone watching, they will think you too eager.''

''I do not care what anyone else thinks of me, so long as you do not think me shamelessly forward.''

''I find I like you hot and ready.'' He toyed with her as always, deriving pleasure from teasing her and putting off his ultimate pinnacle of wanting her until she was almost insane with desire. Then he stroked in and out with those powerful thrusts that jolted her beyond pleasure and pain into some euphoric dream. What could possibly go wrong now? They would be together always somewhere, even if that place was a tent, a hovel or a naked campfire.

Epilogue

The freezing rain had resolved itself into snow, which coated the treacherous mud so that the prisoners slipped and stumbled instead of merely slogging along.

On top of her horse and wrapped in a wool cloak, Nancy frowned at the soldiers who rode impassively on either side of the rebels. Some of them were not cruel. One or two had even given up their mounts to the frailest of the prisoners. Daniel would not let Nancy do so, even though Trueblood had. Daniel had allowed her to bandage their sore feet and barter blankets for them. But he had to keep up some pretense of being an army officer.

A few days short of Philadelphia, Trueblood had parted from them to go home to Champfreys in Maryland. "Well, Daniel," he had said as he embraced his brother.

"Mind you do not get lost," Daniel had replied at parting.

"Mind you find your way home again yourself," Trueblood had returned. "Make him bring you, little sister. Mother will want to meet you."

Nancy had promised, but was afraid to broach the subject with Daniel. He had enough trouble keeping his temper as it was. She suspected his irritation was not with her taking such care of the prisoners, as this did not raise objections

from his superiors. She thought it had to do with his home
and family. But she had promised not to nag him about
that.

She was just trying to picture Mara and Constance when
Daniel rode up beside her. "Three more days to Philadelphia. I will leave you with Mrs. Cook while I do what I
can to intercede for these fellows. Let us hope President
Washington is more willing to listen to reason than Hamilton."

"I see that he must make examples of them." Nancy
pulled her horse off the trail to regard the ragtag line of
men who passed. Had it not been for Daniel, her own father
would have been among them.

"Perhaps once that is done he will relent." Daniel took
his hat off, beat the snow loose, then put the bicorne back
on.

"There must be an end to it eventually, Daniel. I have
been so looking forward to it being over, I have not even
bothered to think of what will happen next. Another adventure, I suppose."

"With you several months pregnant? Not likely. We will
winter in Philadelphia, where I am sure Mrs. Cook will
cosset you and fill your head with all sorts of motherly
advice."

"She is a comfortable sort of mother. I missed all that.
Aunt Jane was close, but it was not the same."

"Then, before that wretched plague strikes again..."

"What?" She looked at him with joy, blinking her eyes
to get rid of the snowflakes settling on her lashes.

"I thought you might like to visit your aunt and uncle."

"Oh, no, to be tossing about the ocean heavy with child
is not my idea of—unless, of course..."

"Unless what?"

"Unless you have taken another assignment. Then I will
go with you. But if you are merely looking for a safe place

for me, then I would as soon go back to the White Horse as anywhere.''

"No, for I will not soon be welcome in that region again.''

"Simply serving in the army, or even working for the government in the open, is too easy for you, is it not?''

"I get impatient with the waiting. I always have.''

"If you need to keep busy you could go into the diplomatic corps,'' she prompted.

"Too frustrating. Besides, there would be no near death scrapes, no adventure at all.''

"I have decided that since I cannot give up nursing, though I know you disapprove of it, I will never ask you to give up your work. So I suppose it will be the army, after all. How ironic that I should end up exactly where I dreamed I would be, following an army train.''

"What makes you think I disapprove of your nursing?''

"Everything. Do you now pretend you enjoy being awakened in the middle of the night to saddle the horses and escort me to some primitive farmhouse where the servants have not the sense to keep the fire going?''

"Actually, I did enjoy those adventures, because it was something we did together. What terrifies me is your experimentation with herbs.''

"What? My tea again?''

"No. When Trueblood was seven and Constance was just an infant, Mara was testing the strength of some new herb—I do not even remember which one—and she fell into a profound sleep. I did not know what to do. Father was drunk, but he would have been no help, anyway. Nancy, she stopped breathing at one point.''

"What did you do?''

"I got her on her feet and made her walk—dragged her around the kitchen. I kept her awake, or as close as I could. I was afraid that if I let her lie down and sleep as she begged to do she would never wake up.''

"Oh, Daniel, you saved her life. But I would never tamper with anything like that. I am a novice and I do not even use herbs in the strength they are recommended. Certainly I have no ambition to discover new ones. I have enough to do as it is."

"Then my worry was groundless."

"You have faced so much, Daniel," she replied. "Tell me this one thing and I will never raise the subject again. What was there between you and your father that you cannot confront?"

Daniel looked away, and she feared for a moment that he would answer her coldly or ride off in anger. That is what the old Daniel would have done. Instead he pulled off his glove and reached for her hand. She did likewise and held his strong, cold fingers in her warm, soft ones, watching the snowflakes settle on the union. His brows were furrowed over those intense blue eyes. "He accused me of coveting Mara—not just coveting…"

"But that is absurd. You love Mara like the mother you never had. I have a feeling you knew no love or tenderness before she came into your life."

"Rather than have him make the same accusation to her, I left."

"How unfair. You were innocent."

"But running away may have looked like an admission of guilt to him."

"Weak men like your father always feel threatened, especially by a son as formidable as you. If it had not been Mara, he would have devised in the animal part of his mind some other lie to drive you away from his den."

"You speak of him as though he was a wolf or some such creature."

"All that is still a part of us, more than we like to acknowledge. The veneer of civilization wears very thin, especially where survival is in doubt."

"Even for you?"

"Especially for me. I had not thought myself so much a she-wolf. But I have chosen the most cunning and resourceful of mates. If I could not have had you, Daniel, I would have hunted alone."

"And will the she-wolf finally bear her not-so-cunning mate more than one pup if he agrees to settle down?"

"The she-wolf will follow her mate anywhere, even if the trail does not lead to Champfreys. You do not have to face that particular pain. I would not ask it of you."

"I find the prospect not so daunting with you at my side. We will go to Champfreys."

"And then?"

"And then I plan on embarking on the most frustrating, difficult, dangerous and probably thankless task that has ever been set for a man."

"Why Daniel, you are exciting me. What is it?"

"I plan to become...a farmer."

"Daniel! How shocking! But I expect President Washington will sympathize with you."

"Oh, yes, in fact, it is upon his suggestion."

"Of course, it will not be all that difficult without the inn to run as well."

"Oh, no, Nancy. Not an inn, too. I want no one to have a chance to pinch your bottom except me."

"Then you will have to keep me busy, sir."

"I intend to."

He leaned over and kissed her, then looked around to see if anyone was watching.

"The army train has passed us by, Daniel. I expect we should catch up with them if we do not want to camp by an open fire."

"An open fire, a bed of oak leaves and you. Perhaps just this one last time."

* * * * *

HARLEQUIN WOMEN KNOW ROMANCE WHEN THEY SEE IT.

And they'll see it on **ROMANCE CLASSICS**, the new 24-hour TV channel devoted to romantic movies and original programs like the special **Harlequin® Showcase of Authors & Stories.**

The **Harlequin® Showcase of Authors & Stories** introduces you to many of your favorite romance authors in a program developed exclusively for Harlequin® readers.

Watch for the **Harlequin® Showcase of Authors & Stories** series beginning in the summer of 1997.

ROMANCE CLASSICS

If you're not receiving ROMANCE CLASSICS, call your local cable operator or satellite provider and ask for it today!

Escape to the network of your dreams.

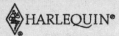 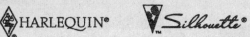

Let's Celebrate!

LOVE & LAUGHTER™

invites you to
the party of the season!

Grab your popcorn and be prepared to laugh as we celebrate with **LOVE & LAUGHTER**.

Harlequin's newest series is going Hollywood!

Let us make you laugh with three months of terrific books, authors and romance, plus a chance to win a FREE 15-copy video collection of the best romantic comedies ever made.

For more details look in the back pages of any Love & Laughter title, from July to September, at your favorite retail outlet.

Don't forget the popcorn!

Available wherever
Harlequin books are sold.

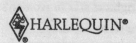

◆ HARLEQUIN®

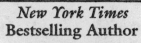

HARLEQUIN AND SILHOUETTE
ARE PLEASED TO PRESENT

Born in the USA

Love, marriage—and the pursuit of family!

Check your retail shelves for these upcoming titles:

July 1997
Last Chance Cafe by Curtiss Ann Matlock
The most determined bachelor in Oklahoma is in trouble! A
lovely widow with three daughters has moved next door—and
the girls want a dad! But he wants to know if their mom needs
a husband....

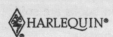

August 1997
Thorne's Wife by Joan Hohl
Pennsylvania. It was only to be a marriage of convenience—
until they fell in love! Now, three years later, tragedy
threatens to separate them forever and Valerie wants only to
be in the strength of her husband's arms. For she has some
very special news for the expectant father...

September 1997
Desperate Measures by Paula Detmer Riggs
New Mexico judge Amanda Wainwright's daughter has been
kidnapped, and the price of her freedom is a verdict in
favor of a notorious crime boss. So enters ex-FBI agent
Devlin Buchanan—ruthless, unstoppable—and soon there is
no risk he will not take for her.

◆HARLEQUIN®   ▼*Silhouette*®

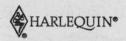

Not The Same Old Story!

Exciting, emotionally
intense romance
stories that take readers
around the world.

Vibrant stories of
captivating women
and irresistible men
experiencing the magic
of falling in love!

Bold and adventurous—
Temptation is strong women,
bad boys, great sex!

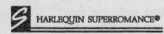

Provocative, passionate,
contemporary stories that
celebrate life and love.

Romantic adventure
where anything is
possible and where
dreams come true.

Heart-stopping, suspenseful
adventures that combine the
best of romance and mystery.

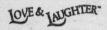

Entertaining and fun, humorous
and romantic—stories that
capture the lighter side of love.